P9-DKF-785

Praise for the work of

LOUIS L'AMOUR

MAY THERE BE A ROAD

"These are professionally written stories . . . gems."
—*Publishers Weekly*

OFF THE MANGROVE COAST

"L'Amour was a man who lived life to the fullest.
Fortunately for the rest of us, he remembered the
details and possessed the talent to bring those
experiences to life on paper." —*Booklist*

BEYOND THE GREAT SNOW MOUNTAINS

"L'Amour's brassy women and dusty men keep the
action of these cinematic stories hot. . . . These
adventure tales offer their share of the high
drama L'Amour is famous for." —*Publishers Weekly*

MONUMENT ROCK

"[A] compelling blend of explosive action, period
detail, humor and insights about human nature."
—*USA Today*

END OF THE DRIVE

"Awesome immediacy, biting as creosote slapped on a
fence post." —*Kirkus Reviews*

BANTAM BOOKS BY LOUIS L'AMOUR
Ask your bookseller for the books you have missed

MAY THERE BE
A ROAD

Louis L'Amour

BANTAM BOOKS

NEW YORK TORONTO LONDON SYDNEY AUCKLAND

MAY THERE BE A ROAD
A Bantam Book

PUBLISHING HISTORY
Bantam hardcover edition / May 2001
Bantam paperback edition / May 2002

ISBN 0-553-58399-9

Published simultaneously in the United States and Canada

PRINTED IN THE UNITED STATES OF AMERICA
OPM   10   9   8   7   6   5   4   3   2   1

CONTENTS

MAY THERE BE
A ROAD

A FRIEND
OF A HERO

The gravel road forked unexpectedly and Neil Shannon slowed his convertible. On each side orange groves blocked his view, although to the right a steep hillside of dun-colored rock rose above the treetops. On that same side was a double gate in a graying split-rail fence.

He was about fifty miles northwest of Los Angeles, lost in a maze of orchards and small farms that was split by abrupt ridges and arroyos.

Neil Shannon got out of the car and walked to the gate. He was about to push it open when a stocky, hard-faced man stepped from the shrubbery. "Hold it, bud . . . what do you want?"

"I'm looking for the Shaw place. I thought someone might tell me where it was."

"The Shaw place? What do you want to go there for?"

Shannon was irritated. "All I asked was the directions. If you tell me I'll be on my way."

The man jerked his head to indicate direction. "Right down the fork, but if you're looking for Johnny, he ain't home."

"No? So where could I find him?"

The man paused. "Down at Laurel Lawn, in town. He's been dead for three days."

Shannon shook out a cigarette. "You don't seem upset over losing a neighbor, Mr. Bowen."

"Where'd you get that name?" The man stared suspiciously at Shannon.

"It's on your mailbox, in case you've forgotten. Are you Steve Bowen?"

"I'm Jock Perult. The Bowen boys ain't around. As for Shaw, his place is just down the road there."

"Thanks." Shannon opened the door of his car. "Tell me, Jock, do you always carry a pistol when you're loafing around home?"

"It's for snakes, if it's any of your business." He tugged his shirttail down over the butt of a small pistol.

Shannon grinned at him and put the car in gear. Scarcely three hundred yards further along the gravel road on the same side was the Shaw place. Marjorie Shaw saw him drive through the gate and came out to meet him.

The man who followed her from the door had a grizzle of gray beard over a hard chin and a short-stemmed pipe in his teeth. He looked at Shannon with obvious displeasure.

There were formalities to be taken care of. She read the contract standing by the car and looked at his private investigator's license. Finally she raised the subject of money.

"Let's not worry about that right now," he told her. "Johnny Shaw was a friend of mine, I'll do what I can for a couple of days and we'll see where we are. I'm warning you, though, on paper his death looks like an accident. I'm not sure there is much I can do."

"Come in, and I'll fix you a drink."

As he turned to follow he caught a tiny flash of sunlight from the brush-covered hillside across the way. Then he glimpsed the figure of a man, almost concealed. A man interested enough in what was going on to watch through binoculars.

Shannon glanced at the older man. "You're Keller? How about it? Did Johnny have any enemies?"

"Ain't none of my affair and I don't aim to make it so," Keller replied brusquely. "I'm quitting this job. Going to Fresno. Always did figure to go to Fresno."

Marjorie Shaw was Johnny's sister, and though Shannon had never met her, he and John Shaw had been friends since the days before he had joined the police force. They had first met on a windy hillside in Korea. Now John was dead, his car crushed in a nearby ravine, and his sister thought that he had been intentionally killed.

The inside of the house was dim and cool. Shannon sat on the plaid sofa and listened to the girl moving about the kitchen. The door to the Frigidaire opened and closed; there was the sound of a spoon in a glass pitcher.

"After you called"—he spoke to her through the

doorway—"I checked the report on the wreck. There was no indication of anything wrong. The insurance investigator agreed with the report. Clark, who investigated for the sheriff's office, said it was clearly an accident. Driving too fast or a drink too many."

She came in carrying a pitcher of iced tea and two glasses. "I didn't ask you out here, Mr. Shannon, to tell me what I've already heard. However, Johnny did not drink. Furthermore, he was extremely cautious. He had never had an accident of any kind, and he had been driving over that road two or three times a day for four years. I want it looked into. For my peace of mind, if nothing else. That's why I called you. Johnny always said you were the smartest detective on the Los Angeles police force."

"We'll see. . . . I'm not with the police force any longer."

After the iced tea Marjorie Shaw drove Shannon out to the site of the wreck. They cut across the property on a dirt track and headed to where the county road came over the mountain from town. Emerging from Shaw's orange groves, they cut along the base of the hill. Although the car threw up a large cloud of dust, the track was well graded, and in the places where water drained, culverts had been installed. Obviously, Johnny Shaw had worked hard on his place and had accomplished a lot.

Marjorie pointed off to one side. "Johnny was going to dam that canyon and make a private lake," she explained. "Then, he intended to plant trees around it."

The canyon was rock-walled but not too deep. Dumped in the bottom were several junked cars.

"Did he intend to take those out?"

"Johnny was furious about them. He insisted the Bowens take them out, and they said that if he cared so much he could take them out himself."

She paused. "This could be important, Mr. Shannon. . . . He tried to take it up with the county but the sheriffs and commissioners are all friends of the Bowens. I was with him when he went to the courthouse. They all got in a big fight and Johnny told that county commissioner that he would go to the DA if that was what it took and they got real quiet. After that we left. I was angry for Johnny and I didn't think about it much, but that's why I called you . . . it wasn't two weeks later that Johnny died."

"He mentioned the DA?" Shannon asked.

"Yes, why would he do that? Over junked cars, it doesn't make sense!"

"Unless he knew about something else and was making a threat."

"That's what I thought, but what could it be?"

"Well, if it has something to do with his death it's something that either someone in county government or the Bowen brothers don't want known."

The Bowen brothers . . . Shannon thought . . . and their buddy Perult who carried a gun inside his shirt.

. . .

They turned out onto the county road and within minutes were at the curve where Johnny had run off the cliff. She stopped the car and he got out. The afternoon shadows were long, but down below he could see the twisted mass of metal that had been Johnny's car.

"I'd like to go down and look around. I'll only be a few minutes."

At the edge of the road, starting down, he paused briefly. There was broken glass on the shoulder. Bits of headlight glass. He picked up several fragments, and the ridges and diffusers in them were not identical. Pocketing several, he climbed and slid down the cliff.

Examining the wreck, he could see why Johnny had been killed. The car had hit several times on the way down. The destruction was so complete that the sheriffs had had to use a torch to cut the body out. Surprisingly enough, one headlight was intact. Two pieces of the glass he had picked up conformed with the headlight pattern. The others did not.

The police and ambulance crew had left a lot of tracks, but there was another set that stood off to the side, and they turned off down the canyon. In two places other tracks were superimposed upon them.

Curious, he followed the tracks down the canyon where they met with the tracks of someone who had waited there.

He was back beside Johnny's car when there was a sharp tug at his hat and an ugly *whap* as something struck the frame and whined angrily away. Shannon dropped and rolled to the protection of some rocks. In the distant hills there was the vague echo of a gunshot.

It could have been a spent bullet . . . from someone hunting or shooting targets in the hills. Yet he knew it was nothing of the sort. That bullet had been fired by a man who meant to kill or, at least, warn. If he tried to get back up to the road, he might be shot.

He glanced up. Marjorie Shaw stood at the cliff's edge, looking down. "Get into the car," he called, just loud enough for her to hear, "and drive to the filling station on the highway. Wait there for me, in plain sight, with people around."

She looked pale and frightened when he got there a half hour later. His suit was stained with red clay and he showed her his hat.

"I called the sheriff," she said.

They heard the siren, and Deputy Sheriff Clark drew up. It was he whom Shannon had talked to about the accident.

He chuckled. "You city cops!" he scoffed. "That shot was probably fired by a late hunter, maybe a mile off. Now don't come down here trying to stir up trouble when there's no cause for it. Why would anyone try to kill someone investigating an accident?"

"What do you know about the Bowen outfit?"

Clark was bored. "Now look. Don't you go bothering people up here. The Bowens have got them a nice little place. They pay their taxes and mind their own business. Furthermore, the Bowens are rugged boys and want to be left alone."

"Didn't Johnny Shaw complain about them once?"

Clark was annoyed. "Suppose he did? Shaw was some kind of a hero in the Korean War and he came out here thinking he was really going to do big things. He may have been quite a man in the war, but he sure didn't stack up against Steven Bowen."

"What's that? They had a fight?"

"I guess so, seein' that Johnny Shaw got himself whipped pretty bad. I think Steve got the idea that Shaw was throwing his weight around over those junk cars, comin' on high and mighty because he had a medal or two. They went at it out back of the hardware store in Santa Paula. I offered to take Shaw's complaint afterwards but I guess he was too proud."

Marjorie turned abruptly and got into her car, eyes blazing. Shannon put a hand on the door, then glanced back at Clark. "Tell me something, Clark. Just where do you stand?"

Clark was beside their car in an instant. "I'll tell you where I stand. I stand with the citizens of this community. I don't want any would-be hero barging in here stirring up trouble. And that goes double for private cops. The Bowens have lived here a long time and had no trouble until Shaw came in here. Now, I've heard all about these scrap cars and who wants who to tow them out of there. But I looked into it and there is nothing to prove that they ever belonged to Steve Bowen or anyone else on his place. If you ask me, that and this *investigation* of the car accident are just examples of city folks getting wild ideas and watching too much of those television shows."

Three days of hard work came to nothing. Shaw had no enemies, his trouble with the Bowens was not considered serious, at least not killing serious, and as the Bowens had defeated Shaw all down the line, why should they wish to kill him? Of course there was that mention of the DA, but no one seemed to know what it meant.

The fragment of headlight glass he checked against the *Guide Lamp Bulletin,* then sent it to the police lab for verification. The lens, he discovered, was most commonly used on newer Chrysler sedans but was a replacement for other models as well. He filed the information for future reference.

His next step was to talk with other farmers in the area. He drove about, asked many questions, got interesting answers.

The Bowens had two large barns on their place, which was only forty acres. They had two cows and one horse, and carried little hay. Their crops, if stored unsold, would have taken no more than a corner of the barn . . . so why two large barns?

Market prices for the products they raised did not account for the obvious prosperity of the brothers. All three drove fast cars, as did Jock Perult. At nearby bars they were known as good spenders. Some of the closest neighbors complained of the noise of compressors from the Bowen place and of their revving up unmuffled engines late at night, but these questions were soon answered—the Bowens built cars that they raced themselves at the track in Saugus and around the state at other dirt-track and figure-eight events.

At the county courthouse he researched the Bowen property, how long they had owned it and how much they had paid. While he was looking through the registrar's records a young man peered into the file room several times and had a whispered conversation with the clerk. The man had the look of someone who worked in the building, and Neil Shannon took a quick tour through the hallways on his way out. He spotted the young man sitting at a desk typing in the office of a particular county commissioner . . . a county commissioner who happened to be a neighbor of the Bowens.

Late at night—he was taking no chances with stray bullets this time—Shannon took a bucket of plaster back over to the crash site. While he was waiting for his casts to dry, he walked along the moonlit wash and into the canyon that Johnny had wanted to dam. The old rusted cars lay stark in the moonlight, and he used a pencil flash to examine them. One was a Studebaker and the other, not so old as he'd imagined, was a Chevrolet. Neither had engines; he searched hard for the Vehicle Identification Numbers on the body and could not find one on either car . . . they had been carefully removed. He pulled parts, the few that were left, off the Chevy and examined them carefully. They should have had a secondary date code on them, but every plate had been removed, the rivets meticulously drilled out.

. . .

He met Marjorie Shaw for a drink in Santa Paula. "Little enough," he replied to her question. "Steve Bowen is a good dancer and a good spender, left school in the seventh grade, wasn't a good student, likes to drink but can handle his liquor. Likes to gamble and he drives in amateur races a little. Not sports cars . . . the rough stuff."

"So you think I'm mistaken?"

He hesitated. "No . . . I don't. Not anymore. I think your brother discovered something very wrong with the Bowens or their place. I think he was killed to keep him from causing trouble. Now that I know about the racing it fits too well; who better to force someone off a mountain road than a man who drives in demolition derbies!"

"Johnny once told me that the less I knew the better. That knowing about what went on out here could be dangerous."

"He was right. Keller knows it, too. I think that's why he is going to Fresno."

"Oh! That reminds me. He said he wanted to talk to you."

"I'll go see him." Shannon paused. "You know, Bowen was away from here for about six years. I wonder where he was?"

They left the bar and Shannon walked her to her car. They were standing on a side street when Steve Bowen walked up. Turning at the sound of steps, Shannon ran into a fist that caught the point of his chin. He was turned half around, and a second punch knocked him down.

"That'll teach you to mess around in other people's business!" Bowen said. He swung a kick at Shannon's face, but Shannon rolled over swiftly and got up. He ran into a swinging right and a left that caught him as he fell. He got up again and went tottering back into the car under a flail of fists. When he realized where he was again, he was seated in the car and Marjorie was dabbing at his face with a damp handkerchief.

"You didn't have a chance!" she protested. "He hit you when you weren't looking."

"Drive me to my car," he said.

Turning around a corner they stopped at a light, and alongside were Steve Bowen and his brothers. They were in a powerful Chrysler 300. The heavy car was stripped down for racing, and from the way the engine sounded they had hot-rodded it for even more horsepower. They looked at Shannon's face and laughed.

"Stop the car." Shannon opened the door and got out, despite her protests.

Ignoring the three, he walked to their car and studied the headlights. One had been replaced by glass from another make of car. When he straightened up, the grins were gone from their faces, and Joe Bowen was frightened.

"I see you've replaced a headlight," Shannon commented. "Was there any other damage?"

"Look, you . . . !" Tom Bowen opened the door.

"I'll handle this!" Steve Bowen interrupted. "You're looking for trouble, Shannon. If the beating you got didn't teach you anything, I'll give you worse."

Shannon smiled. "Don't let that sneak punch give you a big head. Is the paint on this fender fresh?"

There was a whine of sirens, and a car from the sheriff's department and also one of the city police cars pulled up.

"That's all, Shannon." Deputy Sheriff Clark stepped out. "It looks to me like you've had yours. Now get in your car and get out of town. You're beginning to look like a troublemaker and we don't want your kind around."

"All right, Clark. First, though, I want to ask if Tom has a permit for that gun he's carrying. Further, I want you to check the number on it, and check the fingerprints of all four of them. Don't try putting me off either, I'll be talking to the DA and the FBI about why certain vehicle identification tags are missing and who's been bought off and who hasn't. Bowen, by the time this is over you're going to look back in wonder at how stupid you were when you refused to tow those cars like John Shaw asked!"

Clark was startled. He started to speak, and the Bowens stared angrily at Shannon as he got back into Marjorie's car.

They drove off. "I've talked a lot, but what can I prove?" he said. "Nothing yet. . . . The Bowens could explain that broken headlight, even if the make checks out perfectly. What we need is some real law enforcement and a search warrant for those barns."

"What's going on? What are you talking about?" Marjorie asked.

"Hot cars . . . and I don't mean the kind you race."

Keller was not around when they rolled into the yard, but there was a telegram lying open on the table, addressed to Shannon. He picked it up, glanced at it, and shoved it into his pocket.

"That's it! Now we're getting someplace!"

Shannon seemed not to hear Marjorie's question about the contents. The message had been opened. Keller had read it. Keller was gone.

"Hide the car where we can get to it from the road, then hide yourself. No lights. No movement. The Bowens will be here as quick as they can get away from Clark. I don't have a thing on them yet, but they don't know it. Push a crook far enough and sometimes he'll move too fast and make mistakes."

There was little time remaining if he was to get to the barns before the Bowens arrived. They pulled the car behind the house, and Shannon made sure that Marjorie locked herself inside and turned out the lights. Then, careful to make no noise, he descended into the canyon and followed the path from near the junked cars through the wash and then an orchard to the barns back of the Bowen farmhouse.

By the time he reached the wall of the nearest barn, he knew he had only minutes in which to work. There was no sound. There were two large doors to the barn, closed as always, but there was a smaller door near them that opened under his hand.

Within, all was blackness mingled with the twin odors of oil and gasoline. It was not the smell of a farmer's barn, but of a garage. There was a faint gasping sound near his feet, then a low moan.

Kneeling, he put out a hand and touched a stubbled face. "Keller?" he whispered.

The old man strained against the agony. "I stepped into a bear trap. Get it off me."

Not daring to strike a light, Shannon struggled fiercely with the jaws of the powerful trap. He got it open, and a brief inspection by sensitive fingers told him Keller's leg was both broken and lacerated.

"I'll have to carry you," he whispered.

"You take a look first," Keller insisted. "With that trap off I can drag myself a ways."

Once the old man was out and the door closed, Shannon trusted his pencil flashlight.

Four cars, in the process of being stripped and scrambled. Swiftly he checked the motor numbers and jotted them down. He snapped off the light suddenly. Somebody was out in front of the barn, opposite from where he had entered.

"Nobody's around," Perult was saying. "The front door is locked and the bear trap is inside the back."

"Nevertheless, I'm having a look." That would be Tom Bowen.

The lock rattled in the door and Shannon moved swiftly, stepped in an unseen patch of oil, and his feet shot from under him. He sprawled full length, knocking over some tools.

The front door crashed open. The lights came

on. Tom Bowen sprang inside with his gun ready. But Shannon was already on his feet.

"Drop it!" he yelled.

Both fired at the same instant, and Bowen's gun clattered to the floor and he clutched a burned shoulder. Perult had ducked out. Shannon stepped in and punched Tom Bowen on the chin; the man went down. With nothing to shoot at Shannon put two rounds into the side of one of the cars just to make them keep their heads down and ran out back.

He was down in the canyon before he found Keller, and he picked the old man up bodily and hurried as fast as he could with the extra weight.

He was almost at the house when Keller warned him. "Put me down and get your hands free. There's somebody at the house!"

Marjorie cried out and Shannon lowered Keller quickly to the ground, and gun in hand went around the corner of the house.

Shannon saw Steve Bowen strike Marjorie with the flat of his hand. "Tell me," Bowen said coldly, "or I'll ruin that face of yours."

Perult came sprinting in the front gate. "Hurry, boss! Tom's been shot."

Shannon stepped into sight and Perult grabbed for the front of his shirt, and Shannon lowered the gun and shot him in the thigh. Jock screamed, more in surprise than pain, and fell to the ground.

"Fast with the gun, aren't you?" Steve Bowen said. "I suppose you'll shoot me now."

"We're going back to your place," Shannon said, and then he whispered to Marjorie. "Get on the phone and call the district attorney. After you've called him, call the sheriff. But the DA first!"

"What are you going to do?" Marjorie protested.

"Me?" Shannon grinned. "This guy copped a Sunday on my chin when I wasn't looking, and he beat up Johnny, so as soon as you get through to the DA I'm going to take him back to that barn, lock the door, and see if he can take it himself."

Twenty minutes later, Neil Shannon untied Steve Bowen and shoved him toward the door with his gun. They reached the barn without incident. Inside, Shannon locked the door and tossed the gun out of the window.

Bowen moved in fast, feinted, and threw a high, hard right. Shannon went under it and hooked both hands to the body. The bigger man grunted and backed off, then rushed, swinging with both hands. A huge fist caught Shannon, rocking his head on his shoulders, but Shannon brushed a left aside and hooked his own left low to the belly.

Getting inside, he butted Bowen under the chin, hit him with a short chop to the head, and then pushing Bowen off, hit him twice so fast, Bowen's head bobbed. Angry, the big man moved in fast and Shannon sidestepped and let Bowen trip over his leg and plunge to the floor.

Bowen caught himself on his hands and dove in a long flying tackle, but Shannon moved swiftly, jerking his knee into Bowen's face. Nose and lips smashed, the big man fell, then got up, blood streaming down his face.

Bowen tried to set himself, but Shannon hit him

with a left and knocked Bowen down again with a right.

Stepping in on Bowen, Shannon got too close and Bowen grabbed his ankle. He went down and Bowen leaped up and tried to jump on his stomach. Shannon rolled clear, got up fast, and when Bowen tried another kick, Shannon grabbed his ankle and jerked it high. Bowen fell hard and lay still.

There was a hammering at the door. Shannon backed off. "You're the tough guy, Bowen," he said, "but not that tough." Bowen didn't move.

The door opened and Clark came in followed by several deputies and a quiet man in a gray suit.

To the assistant district attorney he handed a telegram. "From the FBI. I checked on Bowen and found he had done six years in the federal pen for transporting a stolen car. I wired them on a hunch. I think you'll find that they were paying off certain people in county government to be left alone."

"Hey, now wait a minute!" Clark protested.

"Shut up," Shannon snapped. "They'll be looking at you, your boss, and a couple of commissioners, so you'd better start checking your hole card!

"Johnny Shaw got suspicious when he tried to get the county to make the Bowens move those derelict cars. He found out enough and Bowen ran him off the road. The headlight glass was a Chrysler lens and Bowen drives a 300. Perult and Steve Bowen walked over to the wreck afterwards to be sure Johnny was dead. The tracks are still there, but I made casts of them to be sure."

Steve Bowen moaned and sat up.

"Come on, Steve," Shannon said. "I think we're

all going to have to go to Ventura and answer a lot of questions."

Bowen winced as he stood up. "You broke my ribs," he growled.

"Count yourself lucky. If these boys hadn't come I'd still be at it. You beat up Johnny Shaw . . . he carried me out of a firefight in Korea when I was wounded. There were shells going off everywhere and he'd never even seen me before. They gave him a medal for it. Now, he wasn't a big guy like you, he didn't know how to box, and he'd become a medical corpsman because he knew he couldn't bring himself to kill. But when the chips were down he did what was necessary."

Shannon took a deep breath. "Plead guilty," he said. "Because if they don't have enough evidence to put you away, I'll find it. No matter how long it takes."

They were led to the waiting cars, and with the ambulances in the lead and Marjorie following, they headed for Ventura.

MAY THERE BE
A ROAD

Tohkta looked at the bridge suspended across the gorge of the Yurung-kash. After four years, the bridge hung again, and now, at last, he could go to his betrothed, to Kushla.

At this point the gorge was scarcely a hundred feet wide, but black cliffs towered into the clouds above it, even as they fell sheer away hundreds of yards below. Down those cliffs came the trails that approached the bridge on either side. From where the bridge came into view from above, it seemed the merest thread . . . a thin line for which the eye must seek and seek again.

Scarcely four feet wide, the bridge was built of their handmade rope, of slats cut from pine forests, and of thin planks laid across the slats. With every gust of wind the bridge swayed, but those who had built it hoped that it would be their lifeline to the outside world.

Tohkta's people were of the mountains, yet once

each year they had descended to the oasis towns at the desert's edge, taking the furs, the wool and hides, for which they were known. The gold they sometimes took was a secret thing. In the timeless kingdom of their mountain valleys the bridge was their link to the future.

Only once in all the years their tribal memory encompassed had the bridge not been there, hanging five hundred feet above the tumbling white water. And for too long had Tohkta's people been isolated by its loss.

Four . . . almost five years before there had come a great shaking of the earth when the mountains raised higher, and steam and hot water gushed from newly made cracks. There had been a grinding of rock when the teeth of the earth were gnashed together. In the midst of it, the pinnacle that supported their bridge had toppled from the far side of the Yurung-kash into the gorge below.

There followed years of struggle against the high rocks and the torrent, years of terrible work to replace their bridge. Fields still had to be tilled and flocks tended, but two men had been dashed to death on the jagged rocks below when they fell from their ropes. Yet now the bridge was done.

The Kunlun Mountains rim the northern edge of Tibet, hanging above the deserts of Sinkiang, and are among the loneliest of the world's mountain ranges. Long, long ago when Tohkta's grandfather was a boy, a rare caravan still ventured along the ancient track that led from Sinkiang across Tibet and through the Himalayas to India itself, passing close to Mount Kailas, sacred to Buddhists.

For centuries that ancient track had been almost abandoned. Only yak hunters, as wild and strange as the creatures they hunted, used it now, or an occasional herdsman taking his flock to secret pasturage in the high mountain valleys.

Tohkta sat his horse beside his grandfather, Batai Khan, chieftain of their small tribe of fifty-six tents. This was a proud day, for today Tohkta rode to claim his bride from her father, Yakub, a wealthy Moslem trader. He glanced at his grandfather with pride, for the old man sat his horse like a boy despite his almost one hundred years. Fierce and fiery as always, the Khan was the oldest among a people known for their great age and their great strength.

Few outsiders ever came to know the mountain Tochari, remnants of a proud, warlike race that had ruled most of eastern Turkestan and much of western China. In ages past they had carried their banners against Mongol and Chinese, against Tungan and Turk, against the Tatar and Hun.

Slowly the column of twenty riders and their pack animals crossed the swinging bridge, and Batai Khan did not start up the trail until all were safely across.

"Yol Bolsun!" he called out, waving to the people of the village who lined the switchback trail on the other side of the gorge. It was an old greeting to those who rode the mountain trails: "May There Be a Road!"

And now, for the first time in four long years, there *was* a road. The home of the Tochari was an island in mountains, cut off by the deep gorges of the Yurung-kash and the Keriya, and at its ends by impassable slopes. Within there lay more than one hundred square miles of grassy valleys, forest glades, waterfalls, and grass-covered mountain pastures. It was an isolated paradise among the snow-covered peaks, but now it was isolated no longer.

Tohkta was impatient. Kushla awaited in the ancient oasis town of Charklik, and how many were the nights he had remained awake to dream of her? Batai Khan and Yakub had arranged the match, but since their eyes first met, neither Tohkta nor Kushla had thoughts for another.

Yet four full years had gone by when no word could be received from her, nor sent to her.

"She will have forgotten me," Tohkta said gloomily. "It has been forever."

"She was a child," Batai Khan replied, "now she will be a woman, and so much the better. You are not forgotten, believe me." He glanced around at his handsome grandson. "I, who know women, say it. You have been a dream to her, and who can forget a dream?"

In the days that followed the finishing of the bridge Tola Beg, an ancient yak hunter, had been the first to cross, and he brought strange news. Chinese soldiers of a new kind had come to Sinkiang and to Tibet. The Dalai Lama had fled to India, and soldiers were in Khotan and Charklik as well as Lhasa. People had been driven from their farms and their flocks to work upon a new road, harnessed like yak or camels.

"Do not go, Batai Khan." Tola Beg peered across

the fire from his ancient, rheumy eyes, his skin withered and weathered by wind and cold, darkened by wind and sun. "They will imprison you and seize your goods."

"It is the time for the marriage of Tohkta."

"There is danger. The Chinese seek the ancient track to India but it is not India they want; it is the men of our mountains they would enslave." Tola Beg gulped his yak-butter tea noisily, as was the custom. "They respect nothing and they have no God. The mosques and lamaseries are closed and the lamas driven to work in the fields. The prayer wheels are stilled and there is a curse on the land."

"I can go alone," Tohkta said. "I will take the gold and go for Kushla."

"We are Tochari." Batai Khan spoke with dignity. "Does a khan of Tochari go like a thief in the night to meet his betrothed?"

They were Tochari. That was the final word among them. Tohkta knew the history of his people, and much more had been told him by an Englishman. In ages past it was said some of his people had migrated from Central Asia, going westward to become the Greeks and the Celts. Others had gone into northern India, to settle there, driven by the Hiung Nu, known to western nations as the Hun.

The Englishman had dug in ancient refuse piles along the ruins of the Great Wall, searching for bits of wood or paper on which there was writing. He had told Tohkta these fragments would piece together the history of the area, and of the Tochari. He glanced at Tohkta's dark red hair and green eyes, a coloring not uncommon among these people of the mountains, and said the Tochari were a people who made history.

Batai Khan had rebuked him gently. "We know our past, and need not dig in dung piles for it. If you would know it, too, come sit by our fires and our bards will sing for you."

And now they rode to claim the bride of Tohkta, for a khan of the Tochari must ride with warriors at his back and gold to consummate the union. Raw and cold was the weather, for the season was late. Soon the high passes would be closed, and the mountain basins would brim full with snow.

It was midnight on the third day when they reached the outskirts of the ancient town, crossing the road by which silk had once been carried to Greece and Rome. They drew up in a grove of trees and waited as the moon set beyond the desert hills. Tohkta was impatient to push on to the town, for eagerness rode his shoulders with sharp spurs. But Batai Khan had the caution of years.

Old as he was, he sat erect in his saddle, and the broadsword he carried slung between his shoulders was a mighty weapon in his hands. "The town has a different smell," he said, "there is trouble here."

"I must go to the house of Yakub," Tohkta said. "Tola Beg can come. If help is needed, he can return for you."

The Khan paused a moment, then nodded.

The house of Yakub was the largest in the oasis, and Tola Beg led the way on foot. Wind rustled among the tamarisks as they skirted an irrigation ditch. Beside Tohkta the old yak hunter moved, silent as a *djinn*. Tohkta, who had stalked wild sheep upon the highest peaks, was hard put to keep pace with the old man.

Outside the nearby *Ya-men,* which was the government house, stood vehicles that smelled of greasy smoke and petrol. Tohkta had seen them before, in Khotan. There were soldiers there also, reflected light gleaming from their gun barrels. They were fine rifles that filled Tohkta's mind with envy.

"The old wolf was right," Tola Beg breathed in his ear, "the town stinks of danger."

The town was different, very different. The fires in the foundry were out and the alley of the bazaar was dirty and neglected. Everywhere there were horses and trucks and soldiers and supplies. Even in the violent days after the murder of the old governor, when the fighting between the Nationalists and the Moslem generals was at its worst, there hadn't been this many armed men in Charklik.

"The forces of history are at work here," Tola Beg mumbled. "And that is something to avoid." They moved on through the darkness and then drew up.

Tohkta crouched in the shadows, listening. Before him was the wall of the compound of Kushla's father. Soon he would see her. His heart pounded with excitement.

Creeping like wild dogs to a sheepfold, they came into the yard. Here, too, they heard the language of the Han Chinese, and one voice that made Tohkta's hair prickle on his scalp . . . a voice with the harsh tone of command. Neither of them spoke Mandarin, for Sinkiang is a land of many tongues, Chinese the least of them, but both knew its sound.

The house of Yakub, yet filled with Han soldiers. Tola Beg tugged at his arm. They must steal away while they had the chance.

But where then was Yakub? And where was Kushla?

"We must go. They have taken it for their own use," Tola Beg whispered in his ear.

Tohkta moved back into the darkness, his thoughts racing over possible alternatives. Then it came to him, and he knew where they would be if they were alive and still in Charklik.

It was an ancient Buddhist temple, fallen to ruins, rebuilt, and ruined again. Sometimes Yakub had used it for a storehouse, and Kushla loved the ancient trees around it. There was shelter there, and a good spring nearby. They made their way through the dark town and approached with caution.

"Look!" Tola Beg caught his arm. "The spotted horse . . . it is the old one the girl loved. At least they left her that."

Why not? The horse was almost as old as Kushla herself, who would be eighteen this year.

Leaving Tola Beg, he moved swiftly, glancing each way, then listening. Like a wraith, Tohkta slipped past the yak hide that hung over the door.

In the vague light from the charcoal brazier he saw her, and on the instant he entered she looked up. She stood swiftly, poised like a young deer, ready for flight. And then she looked into his eyes and came into his arms without shame.

Yakub got to his feet. He was in rags. The one room of the temple that still possessed a roof held only a few sacks and some bedding. Yakub had been a proud and wealthy man, but was so no longer.

"Go, Tohkta! Go, quickly! If you are found here—!"

From his shirt, Tohkta drew the sack of gold. "The marriage price," he said. "I claim my bride."

How lovely she was! Her dark eyes glowed, her figure under the thin garments was so lithe and eager. The years he had waited had brought her to womanhood, and to a loveliness he could scarcely believe. He tried to say all this.

"If you think I am beautiful after all that has happened, then our parents have chosen well," she said.

"Please go!" Yakub seized his elbow. "For the sake of my daughter, take her and go. The gold also. If they find it they will take it, anyway."

"What has happened here?"

"The Red soldiers, the ones that we heard of but who never came, they have come at last. They take everything and say it is for the future. Whose future? What future? I do not understand them, for until they came, we were happy. All we wished was to tend our flocks in peace. Now they are moving into the mountains, more soldiers arrive every day."

"Batai Khan awaits us. Come, we will gather your flocks as we go, and you can live among us. I would not have my bride mourning her father on her wedding night."

Kushla handed him her bundle and they turned swiftly to the door. Then Kushla caught a cry in her throat, and Tohkta felt rage and despair crowding within him.

The man who stood in the doorway was small with square shoulders and a neatly perfect uniform. Slender, he seemed to have that whiplike strength that resists all exhaustion. His cold eyes inspected Tohkta with careful attention.

"Greetings." He stepped into the ruins of the room, and behind him were two soldiers armed with submachine guns. "Greetings to Yakub and his lovely daughter. Greetings to you, hillman. That is what you are, am I correct?" He spoke Tungan, and spoke it well. Tohkta said nothing.

"Answer me . . ." He pulled a small automatic from a holster. "Or I will shoot Yakub in the foot." He flicked the gun's safety off.

"Yes," said Tohkta. "I am from the hills."

"Very good. I am Chu Shih." He said this as if it were a fact that explained itself. "We have been waiting for you. Waiting quite awhile. We knew that this woman was betrothed to a young man from the Kunlun. I could have sent her and her father to a labor camp, but I wanted to meet you. Our destinies are intertwined, you see. Would you like to know how?"

Tohkta quietly assented. He was listening, listening to Chu Shih and listening for sounds from outside the building. There were more men out there, but how many he didn't know.

"You can have the opportunity of serving the people of China. I'm sure you do not care . . . but you will. There is a secret track over the mountains to India. It is the track used by Abu Bakr in the sixteenth century when he fled from Khotan. It is also my gateway to the mountain people. Do you know this track?"

"It is idle talk . . . bazaar talk. There is no track. There are only a few mountain pastures and fewer people. All you will find in the mountains are granite and ice, glaciers and clouds."

"If you were to show me the track, which is important to my future plans, I might permit you to keep your bride, and would let her father go free."

"Such stories are the talk of fools," Tohkta said. "They are the idle talk of goatherds."

To know men, Batai Khan had taught him, is the knowledge of kings. Tohkta looked into the eyes of Chu Shih and saw no mercy, only ruthless ambition. To refuse would mean torture and death. Torture he could stand; what he feared was torture for Kushla, or for her father.

"I do not believe," Chu Shih said, "that stories of the ancient route are talk. If you wish to go free, you will show me the track. If you do not show me, another will."

"I will show you what is there, but it may not be to your liking."

This man, Tohkta told himself, must die. I must kill him or return to kill him. If he lives our mountains will never be free. If need be Tohkta's people could wait for years before they came again to the oasis towns, and by that time, these might be overthrown, or their ideas changed. Young though he was, Tohkta had learned all things change; the Tochari had learned patience from their mountains.

Chu Shih's command brought in two more soldiers. Tohkta had a moment of sharp panic when he saw them, wanting to plunge at the door and fight his way free, but he fought down the feeling. He must think of Kushla and her father, who might be killed. Escape they must . . . somehow.

Out upon the street, the bridge of his wishing fell into the gorge of despair, for they had Tola Beg also. Two soldiers gripped the arms of the old yak hunter, and there was blood welling from an ugly cut on his cheekbone.

Turning, the Chinese colonel strode away. Kushla and Yakub being pushed ahead, Tola Beg and Tohkta followed surrounded by the six soldiers.

The Chinese who had searched them were coastal Chinese, unfamiliar with the customs of mountain Tochari. It was the custom in the hills to wear their hair long and their beards also. Tohkta's hair was wound about his head under his sheepskin hat, and into the hair was thrust a thin-bladed knife, as was also the custom.

Soldiers loitered before the *Ya-men,* several hundred yards away, but the street led through a narrow avenue of darkness bordered by a double row of tamarisks. In this darkness, Tohkta halted, and when the soldier behind him ran into him, Tohkta turned and drawing his knife, struck upward into the softness of the man's stomach.

Tohkta's hand drew Kushla behind him. Yakub, with more courage than Tohkta expected, seized the rifle of the soldier next to him, and then with a rush like a sudden gust of wind, Batai Khan and his riders swept through the tamarisks.

The horses were among the soldiers and all was confusion, pounding hooves, and flashing blades. Several of the soldiers had their rifles slung and Chu Shih was knocked sprawling by the shoulder of the horse of Batai Khan.

Lifting Kushla to the saddle of a lead horse, Tohkta leaped into his own saddle. A soldier slipped a rifle to his shoulder, but Tohkta rode him down, grasping the man's weapon as he fell. Then they were away in the darkness and riding hard for freedom and the hills.

There was shouting and a wild shot, but the attack had been sudden and with broadswords, the ancient Tochari way of fighting. In the darkness the soldiers had no chance against the charging horses and flashing blades. And it was only now that the force at the *Ya-men* was alerted.

Tohkta glanced back. Behind them there was confusion and wild shots but no roaring of motors coming to life, yet remembering the eyes of Chu Shih, Tohkta knew pursuit would come soon, and it would be relentless.

False dawn was cresting the peaks with gold when they reached the Valley of Rain where Yakub's last herd was held. This was the only one the Chinese had not seized, for, as yet, they had not discovered it. The people of the oasis were secretive about their pastures, as his people were about the mountain tracks.

Tohkta checked his captured rifle in the vague light. How beautiful it was! How far superior to their ancient guns! Six rifles had been captured, and two men had even taken bandoleers of cartridges. They shared them among the others.

"We must go," Batai Khan said. "The flock we drive will cause us to move slowly."

Tohkta watched the yaks and fat-tailed sheep bunched for the trail. The Tochari were men of flocks and herds, and could not easily leave behind the wealth of a friend.

He looked up at the mountain peaks, and in the morning light, streamers of snow were blowing like silver veils from under a phalanx of cloud. Now fear seized at his vitals. They must hurry. If snow blocked the passes, none would escape.

Hours ago they had left the desert and the threat of pursuit by trucks or cars. Only mounted men or those on foot could follow them now. But the Chinese had horses; Tohkta had seen many of them in town and they would follow, he knew that as well. Whether they liked it or not they were leading Chu Shih into the mountains, just as he had wished.

Hunched in their saddles against the wind, they pushed on, skirting black chasms, climbing around towering pinnacles, icy crags, and dipping deep into gorges and fording streams, until at last they came to a vast basin three miles above the desert. Here they rested into the coming night.

Far away to the west lay a magnificent range of glacier-crested mountains, their gorges choked with ice, splendid in the clear air that followed the snow of the morning and afternoon. Though the setting sun lit the peaks and ridges, close over them hung a towering mass of cloud like the mirror image of the mountains below.

Long before dawn they were moving again. Batai Khan pushed onward, fearful of the storms that come suddenly at high altitudes where there was no fodder for man or beast. Pushing up beside him, Tohkta noted that the old man's face was drawn by cold and weariness. Batai Khan was old . . . older even than Tola Beg.

"Batai Khan," Tohkta asked, "now that we are among our mountains we must fight the soldiers. They must not be allowed to return with knowledge of this trail. Their leader, most of all, must be killed." He explained what Chu Shih had wanted.

"Tohkta," the old man paused, "you will await them in the pass. You are right and the beasts move slowly; we must have time. These fifty yak and many fat-tailed sheep will mean wealth to your wife's father and food and comfort for our people. But do not fight so hard that you do not return to us. Let the mountains do their work and if these soldiers come to the Yurung-kash we will be waiting for them."

"I shall remain with him," Tola Beg spoke up.

All those with modern rifles stayed beside Tohkta, eager to test them on their former owners. Two others remained, hopeful of obtaining more rifles for themselves. The pass was a natural point for a surprise attack, and so the Tochari set their trap where it would be unexpected, in its narrowing approach.

Though they had little ammunition, each fired several ranging shots to check the sights of their new weapons. They then concealed themselves, all but two, along the walls of rock before the deep cleft that was the pass. There they waited, waited for their enemies to come.

And they came, the Chinese soldiers did. But they came slowly because of the great altitude, which bothered horses as well as the men.

Tohkta watched them from far across the elevated basin, and it began to snow once more. One of the horses slipped and fell, but the soldiers helped it up and came on.

How many were there? A hundred or more. But they were not dressed or provisioned for the high mountains. Tohkta could tell this because, though all were mounted, they had few packhorses, and these seemed to carry only weapons and ammunition.

At three hundred yards Tohkta and his hidden men opened fire. Instantly there was confusion. A milling of horses and men. For a moment only sporadic fire was returned, then Chu Shih rode into the midst of them on a tall gray horse and suddenly there was order. Soldiers dropped to the ground and sought cover, the bullets striking the rocks around Tohkta and his men were no longer random; it now seemed that the fire was seeking out each of them as separate targets.

"Be ready!" Tohkta called out as under the

covering fire a group of soldiers swarmed forward. "Now, run!"

Tohkta turned and ran himself. Before him, Basruddin spun and fired one last shot before entering the pass. The others followed as rifle fire cracked and whined off the rocks around them. Tohkta had known that they couldn't stand off a concerted attack, but he also knew that in the thin air of the mountains he and his men could outrun any lowland soldier.

Chu Shih's men paused in their rush to fire at the fleeing Tocharis, but their breath came too hard at fourteen thousand feet and their shots went wild. At a signal from their leader, soldiers on horseback charged into the pass to pursue the retreating tribesmen, but this was exactly what Tohkta had been planning for.

Tola Beg and a strong young boy had made their way up the steep walls of the pass and together they had found a precariously balanced boulder that the yak hunter had spotted years before. With their shoulders braced against the cliff behind them and their feet on the huge rock they waited. They waited until they heard the sound of firing stop and the sound of horsemen entering the pass. Then they pushed.

Nothing happened.

They eased up and Tola Beg looked at the boy and they pushed together then released and pushed again. Suddenly the boulder was rocking and Tola Beg pushed hard, pushed with all the strength he had in his old body and with all the strength he had in his mind. Something gave inside of him, something in his back, but he pushed on through the blossoming pain and then the boulder was rolling. It dropped from sight, and Tola Beg could feel its impact further down the mountain, then he heard the roar of other rocks falling with it and the screams of men and horses.

Tohkta, Ibrahim, and Basruddin turned and threw themselves back into the maelstrom of dust and flying rock that now choked the pass. They had seen little of it, for they had been running for their lives not only from the soldiers but from the landslide that nearly took them as well. It had only been the fast thinking of Ibrahim that had saved them, for as soon as they cleared the pass he had forced the running tribesmen into a corner of the hillside protected from the crashing torrent of rock.

Now they pushed their way back through the slide, and while Ibrahim mercilessly stripped the dead and wounded soldiers of guns and ammunition, Tohkta and Basruddin poured fire into the oncoming Chinese. Their lines wavered and fell back, the impact of this double ambush overcoming even Chu Shih's leadership. As soon as the soldiers had taken cover Tohkta and his followers fled back through the pass to where the others had brought up the horses.

Under a sky dense with cloud they started down the rocky slope. The men were excited by their victory, but Tohkta saw the look on the face of Tola Beg and knew that he was in pain. In the trees far below the pass they waited to see what the Han Chinese soldiers would do.

Chu Shih was taking no chances. After some time had passed there was activity around the mouth of the pass: a scouting party who had, no doubt, worked their way carefully through the rockfall alert for additional trouble. Then they watched as a squad moved into position on the hillside beside the entrance to the pass and set up a position with a machine gun unlimbered from one of the packhorses. Then, the area totally secure, mounted troops began to file out into the area controlled by the gun. Soon they would be ready to continue the pursuit.

Tohkta and his men filtered silently back into the trees. They had been very successful, counting many enemy dead or wounded, and Tola Beg was their only casualty. The old man had torn something in his back and could barely ride, being in constant pain.

By afternoon they were back up out of the trees and on a vast tilted plateau of snow and barren rock. The trail left by Batai Khan and his party was easily visible. The old warrior was pressing along as quickly as was possible, but Tohkta could tell that they were not far ahead. At the far edge of the plateau, just beyond their sight lay the beginnings of the trail down to the bridge. Remembering that trail and the bridge itself, Tohkta was suddenly frightened. However quickly his grandfather had been able to move the animals, once on the narrow trail their pace would slow to a crawl, and at the head of the bridge the beasts must be carefully managed or they would balk and panic. It might have been better to have turned them out into one of the mountain valleys on this side of the river, but as Tohkta galloped his horse along the path left by the horsemen and animals, he could see that was not the course that the old chieftain had taken.

Batai Khan was counting on the gorge of the Yurung-kash to protect the village. Since the beginning of time the approach to the bridge had been their village's greatest defense. The descending trail was exposed in every way, while the trail to the bridge from the side of the village wound between trees and rocks, the cover allowing the tribesmen to pour rifle and arrow fire into any attacker unlucky enough to start down the path.

Even though Tohkta had managed as successful an ambush as he could imagine in the pass, Chu Shih's management of the situation had been impressive. He had acted with courage, and once the officer had realized the danger he had carefully covered his men with the machine gun and then organized his column before proceeding. Even on the exposed approaches of the bridge trail Tohkta feared the effect that the rapid firer would have. Chu Shih must not be allowed to cross the gorge to their village and pastures, but he must not be allowed to return to report of this mountain route either. Something had to be done and it had to be done soon.

At the edge of the plateau the dark canyon of the Yurung-kash became visible in the distance. Looking back, Tohkta could see the first of the Han Chinese scouts fanning out as they discovered themselves facing open ground. There was one more thing that the young Tochari could see and it was this that gave him hope. The high ridges behind the soldiers were invisible . . . invisible because of falling snow. The storm was headed toward them, but what was more important was the amount of snow that would build up in the pass. At fourteen thousand feet it wouldn't take long for the way back to Sinkiang to be closed for the season. Perhaps the weather would take care of one of their troubles.

He reined around and whistled to his men. "The invaders must not be allowed to return to the desert," he told them. "God brings a storm to answer our prayers, but they will try to reach our village. Even now Batai Khan may be crossing with Yakub's herds. We must hold the Chinese here to give our men time to clear the bridge, and we must hold them here to give the father of storms time to fill the pass."

They tied their horses where the trail dipped into the gorge. The bridge was a long way down and beyond a bend, but through the trees and rock Tohkta could see animals straggling up the trail on the other side. Good. If they could hold out for an hour Batai Khan would have the resistance organized and the trail to the bridge would become a trail of death for the Chinese. All Tohkta would have to do is get down the trail and across the bridge with four score soldiers at his heels.

Tohkta called for the boy who had helped Tola Beg and one other. He gathered up the nine rifles that Ibrahim had taken from the fallen troops in the pass; he weighed them heavily with ammunition also.

"Go to Batai Khan," he said. "Have him give these rifles to the best marksmen among our people. We must guard the bridge like in the stories of old, he will know what to do. Now go!"

He turned to the remaining men. "Go with them and prepare. Basruddin, Ibrahim, and Loshed; these I would keep with me."

"And I," said Tola Beg. When Tohkta began to protest he raised a hand. "Do not tell me I am hurt. It is only pain, I can still shoot farther than any man here and my hands are steady."

"All right." Tohkta shook his head but smiled. "Let us go see at what distance your lightning can strike."

Basruddin and Ibrahim crawled, flat to the ground, into the plain of ice and boulders. Tohkta, Loshed, and Tola Beg found their way to a group of rocks and carefully prepared a shooting position for the old hunter. Just over a hundred yards behind them they set up another position at the head of the Yurung-kash trail.

Though the plateau was flat, it angled downward away from them. The oncoming Chinese were clearly visible, and while they had some cover available, they could not use it and advance at the same time.

When they were nine hundred yards off, Tola Beg squeezed off his first shot. It struck at the ground just before the first horse, which reared and panicked.

"It was low. Six or seven feet." Tohkta, watching through the hunter's spyglass, advised him.

The rider had fallen from the horse even as the others scattered out, dismounting. As the fallen rider got to his feet, Tola Beg shot him through the thigh.

"The leg . . . two feet low."

The fallen rider, the man shot through the leg, was lucky, for Tola Beg now had their range. The yak hunter's next three targets died instantly, felled by bullets they didn't even hear.

Soldiers dove for cover; in moments the top of the plateau was empty but for standing horses. Tohkta had spotted where Chu Shih had gone to ground, and from that shallow depression he saw a flicker of movement and, a moment later, could hear the distant sound of a barked order. The hand of Chu Shih went up and gestured right and left. Instantly, six soldiers moved the one way, and six the other, advancing to flank Tohkta's small party.

But Tohkta had planned for this. He opened up on the men to the right and Loshed joined him. While they lacked the practice of the old hunter, both had good eyes, and soon they forced their targets further off down the top of the plateau, out of range.

Occasionally shots clattered in the rocks around them, but their cover was good and the range extreme. Several of the main party had pushed the advance and were struggling to set up a machine gun. "They have come far to die," Tola Beg said, and squeezed off two shots.

Out upon the granite a man screamed and died.

And then the six flankers to the left ran into Ibrahim and Basruddin, belly down in the snow. Tohkta could not see all that happened, but within a moment five of the Chinese were dead; the last shot down as he ran panic-stricken back toward the main body.

Tohkta and Loshed cheered . . . and then the machine gun opened up. Tracers flew, like flickering meteors, the snow and earth around Basruddin shredded, the bullets throwing up gouts of mud then blood as the gun crew expertly worked their weapon. The heavy throbbing of shots ended, then the bullets were striking around them!

Tracers flashed toward the rocks. Loshed howled, a bright red line appearing on the back of his hand. Tola Beg twisted out of the way, grimacing as his back spasmed. Three times dust jumped from his heavy sheepskin coat and then there was blood on his lips. Tohkta dropped behind a rock trembling. He glanced at Loshed.

"The old hawk is dead." Scattered flakes of snow drifted from the dark sky.

"Basruddin too, and maybe Ibrahim," Tohkta said. Behind them the machine gun lashed the rock, and ricochets whined off into the clouds like banshees. Then the fire tore high into the air to drop down and the end of its arc spattering like heavy rain inside their fort of rock. The gunner worked the falling bullets back and forth.

How can you fight this weapon? Tohkta damned himself for a fool. You couldn't raise your head, you couldn't even take cover. It took the random inaccuracy of rifle ammunition at long range and used that to its advantage, peppering a whole area with fire. Under its protection Chu Shih's soldiers would be advancing.

"Run to the horses," Tohkta commanded. "Our other position is useless. Get to the bridge. We will put our trust in God and Batai Khan. Let us hope that one or the other is ready for us."

They ran. First Loshed, then Tohkta, who paused a moment to scoop up the ammunition of Tola Beg and to touch his cold form once on the back. They ran with bullets hitting all around them, but the light was going and with the oncoming storm, snow filled the air. Then a rifle opened up seeking out the oncoming soldiers from the rocks at the head of the trail, covering them as they ran. They came to the horses, sliding down the hillside, landing in trampled snow. Ibrahim was waiting for them. He grinned. "I killed two more. They will be Basruddin's servants in heaven!"

Stepping into the saddle, Tohkta could clearly see the advancing Chinese, spread out in a skirmish line. The squad with the machine gun was struggling forward with the heavy weapon, the altitude weighing them down as much as the ammunition and tripod. Behind them, almost hidden by the swirling veils of snow, Chu Shih was bringing the horses up.

They came on, relentlessly. They had passed the point where they could retreat through the pass; in the time it would take to get back to that notch in the mountains it would be too late. Chu Shih's only hope for either victory or survival was to press on, find the Tochari village with its warm felt tents, its supplies of fuel and food. Nothing could survive upon the high plateaus. Tohkta knew then that he hated them, hated them with a wild hatred mingled with fear, for that slender, whiplike man was relentless as a hungry wolf, fierce as a cornered tiger. His men might whimper and wish to go back, but he drove them on.

A group of mounted soldiers thundered forward, through a gap in the line of advancing troops. Tohkta wheeled his horse, and the three of them plunged down the switchbacked trail. The horses skidded on the icy gravel; Ibrahim's mount slid and its shoulder struck Tohkta in the leg, sending both horses and riders into a painful collision with the rock wall.

Then the firing began from the head of the trail. With a wild glance thrown back up the slope Tohkta saw a knot of soldiers gathered there, rifles aimed almost vertically down at them. Flame stabbed from the gun muzzles, but then the soldiers were pushed aside and a squad of Han horsemen with Chu Shih in the lead took to the trail.

Tohkta, Ibrahim, and Loshed clattered through a straight stretch. The bridge was only one hundred yards off to their right, but it was still far below them. A bullet snapped past him and, looking up, Tohkta saw the first switchback lined with kneeling soldiers all firing down at them. Closer still, Chu Shih and his band of horsemen came on, less than a half dozen switchbacks above.

Bullets ricocheted off the rocks. One caught Loshed across the top of the arm and he laughed, smearing his wounded hand with blood and waving it at Tohkta as they turned their horses into another level. Then a bullet caught him in the side and another pierced the spine of his horse and he was falling, the horse was falling, from the narrow trail and disappearing into the rocks hundreds of feet below.

At that moment a fusillade of rifle fire exploded from concealed points along the trail leading up to the Tochari village. Soldiers fell from the top of the trail, and in a moment the Chinese and the villagers were pouring volley after volley into each other in the thundering confines of the gorge.

Reaching the shelf where the bridge stanchions had been fastened to the rock, Tohkta dropped from his horse and was met by Batai Khan and four warriors armed with old rifles. Ibrahim turned his horse tightly in the narrow space.

"They follow us closely, Grandfather!" Tohkta pointed up the trail. But the four men had pressed forward, and as the first of Chu Shih's horsemen came into sight they fired, sending the first horse screaming over the cliff edge, its rider still astride, and collapsing two more in a struggling mass, blocking the trail.

Above, the machine gun opened up, forcing the defenders on the trail to cover and allowing soldiers to crowd their way onto the trail again. In the gray light of the gorge tracers whipped like hellfire, streaking in all directions as the burning bullets bounced from the rock and whirled away into the oncoming night.

The nearest soldiers were advancing again; using the dead horses as cover, they rained fire on the shelf, leaving few areas of even partial safety. Chu Shih was, whatever else he might be, a leader. Yet better than any of them he knew how desperately he must cross the bridge and take the village.

Tohkta nestled the stock of the rifle against his cheek, measuring the distance. He squeezed off his shot, and the man at whom he fired froze, then fell. The snow fell faster. Blown particles stung like bits of steel upon their cheeks. The Chinese above moved in. One paused to crouch against the rock wall. Ibrahim shot him, and he rolled down the trail to their feet.

At the top of the trail more soldiers made their way down the switchbacks, covered by the machine gun. They came in short, quick dashes, utilizing the slightest bits of cover. Ever they drew closer. Occasionally there would be the crack of one of the captured rifles or the dull boom of a muzzle-loader from the villager's side of the gorge and often a soldier would fall, but always this would instantly attract a lash of resumed fire from the machine gun.

"We must go, Batai Khan," said Tohkta. "We cannot hold out here."

"Yes," agreed the old man, and motioned to his companions to cross the bridge. He dropped into their place and, as they ran into the open, dropped the first soldier to raise a rifle. Ibrahim shot and Tohkta was beside him firing and reloading, but the second Tochari on the bridge was down and as the others bent to pick him up another was shot and fell into the crevasse. Then Ibrahim ran, pounding across the swaying bridge.

The old man put his hand on Tohkta's arm. "Go," he said. "Go, Tohkta Khan. I will stay."

It was not lost on Tohkta that Batai Khan had used the leader's title. He shook his head.

"No," Tohkta protested. "Our people need you."

"Go, I say!" He glared at Tohkta from his fierce cold eyes. Then in a softer voice, he said, "Would you have me die as an old horse dies? I cannot stop them," he said, "but the bridge can."

Tohkta stared at him, uncomprehending. Then it came to him, and he was astonished. For an instant he was filled with despair as he realized what tremendous cost had gone to the building of this bridge, the long struggle with the mountain and the river, the backbreaking toil. "You would destroy our bridge? It cost four years to build!"

"What are four years of work against four thousand years of freedom. In time, you can build another bridge." Even as his grandfather spoke, he knew it was what they must do. The despair left him.

Together they knelt and fired, retreated a few steps, then fired again. An icy wind roared down the tunnel of the gorge, and the bridge swayed before it. Down the cliff trail they could see them coming now, many dark figures, blossoming with fire. Bullets struck about them.

Batai Khan was hit, and he fell, losing his grip upon the rifle, which fell into the void. Tohkta bent to lift him but there was a gleam in the old man's eye. "Leave me here! You must destroy the bridge and silence the devil gun."

"Yes, Grandfather."

"Tohkta Khan, go with God!"

Batai Khan tore loose and fell to the stone. Snow

drove down the gorge, obliterating all before them. And Tohkta ran though his heart was crushed.

On the bridge the howling wind caught him. The ropes flexed and jumped with every step and bullets tore through the rope and wood around him. Soldiers depressed the muzzle of the machine gun, holding the tail of the tripod high, and tracers tore at him. One left a smoldering hole in his sheephide jacket, another left a slice like that of a knife upon his calf.

Then he was across, he fell, and was struggling to rise when he felt small hands lift him. It was Kushla. Ibrahim was there, reloading his Chinese rifle.

"Go!" He grabbed her by the shoulders. "Have men bring axes. We must cut the bridge!"

Ibrahim was next. "Come on!" Tohkta said. "We must stop the machine gun!"

The three of them ran. They ran up the narrow trail, and though there was cover it was scant enough. Bullets flew. Tocharis fired back from behind rocks or trees. Men on both sides of the gorge died.

As he went Tohkta gathered up the few men with stolen rifles, and when he could wait no longer they took cover behind a boulder. There were five of them.

"We must destroy the devil gun!" Tohkta ordered them. "We must kill those who use it and any who are close, we must keep firing though we all may die. With that gun, the Hans can take the bridge before we can cut it. Are you ready?"

Together they rose and as one fired up and across the crevasse and into the group of soldiers around the gun. Several fell, and as Tohkta worked the bolt on his rifle, the gunner began to swing the muzzle. Fire sliced toward them and they fired again and again. Bullets bounded into the rock, into Ibrahim, tore Tohkta's rifle from his grasp and ripped his thigh. But as he fell so did the Chinese gunner, and the two tribesmen left standing shot the next nearest man too.

Tohkta lurched to his feet. The gun was silent, the crew a struggling mob of the dead and dying. He lifted Ibrahim's rifle and shot a man who lifted himself from the trail near the gun. The man fell, clutched at the edge of the trail and, as the rock crumbled in his fingers, clutched at the barrel of the machine gun.

A moment later the man was spinning down into the gorge and the gun was falling fast behind him. Tohkta felt like crying out in triumph, but the day had been too expensive in lives and a dozen or more soldiers had poured onto the shelf where the stanchions of the bridge were fastened. Chinese and Tochari defenders alike were firing into each other at near point-blank range.

Then the roar of guns dropped to an occasional shot as tribesmen fled up the trail toward Tohkta. Across the river, at the turn of the last switchback, a slim figure astride a gray horse moved. Chu Shih rode forward. His mount leaped the mound of dead horses and men as if they were a low gate and not sprawled bodies on a narrow trail with a sheer drop on one side.

The soldiers parted as their commander rode amongst them; then, with riflemen in the lead, he started out onto the bridge.

Tohkta boiled with rage. He would never let them cross! He stumbled into a prone position and taking careful aim at Chu Shih's head squeezed the trigger.

The rifle clicked on an empty chamber. He was out of ammunition!

Down on the shelf there was flickering movement. The form of Batai Khan stood and drew the broadsword from the scabbard across his back. The razor-sharp blade flashed as he brought it down on one of the two ropes that held the right side of the bridge. The blade bit and bit again. Then the rope gave way and suddenly the bridge sagged and swung.

Chu Shih turned in his saddle, the horse rearing as the weakened bridge bucked and twisted like a living thing. There was a shot and Batai Khan jerked. More soldiers came running down the trail, firing their rifles. The first of these skidded to a stop, working the bolt of his gun, and Batai Khan's great sword struck, disemboweling the man. Suddenly Han soldiers on all sides were firing. The men on the tilting, swaying bridge, the soldiers on the trail, all fired as the ancient Tochari leader turned, his massive body pierced by a half dozen bullets, and brought his blade down on the other right-hand rope.

The ends of the second tether, not cut through, spun and twisted as they unraveled. There was a frozen moment, then the soldiers ran panic-stricken back toward the rock shelf. For a moment the eyes of the Tochari chieftain and the Chinese officer locked, then Batai Khan raised his sword and bellowed, *"Yol Bolsun!"*

A single shot brought him down. The sword clattering to the rocks beside him. A single shot from an unknown trooper on the bridge . . . a shot that did no good at all, for the primitive rope shredded and the floor of the bridge peeled away, hanging twisted almost a thousand feet over the roaring waters.

Chu Shih's horse fell, sliding, taking four soldiers with it. The officer grabbed for one of the ropes on the high side of the bridge, held for a moment, then tumbled toward the river far below.

Tohkta struggled to stand as two villagers ran past him, axes at the ready. In a moment the villagers reformed their positions along the trail and, with scathing fire, drove the remaining Han soldiers up the switchback trail. Following them down to the bridgehead Tohkta watched as the axmen cut the bridge away. It collapsed with a crash against the far wall of the gorge. On the rock shelf above it lay the body of Batai Khan.

"Yol Bolsun," Tohkta whispered as Kushla came to stand beside him.

"What was that, my love?" she said.

"It means good-bye or good luck . . . May There Be a Road." After a moment Tohkta laughed. For even though Batai Khan had destroyed their bridge he had bought them time. Time to live, to raise another generation in freedom, time to plan . . . if necessary time to escape. This, in its own way, was as much of a road as that once joined by their bridge. He had a vision of a Buddhist's spinning prayer wheel. Even as they had once been connected to their future by the bridge, now they were connected to the future by the lack of it. A season? A year? A decade? Who could tell, but, as the Tochari know, nothing but the mountains lasts forever.

By torchlight, Tohkta Khan gathered his dead and returned to the village with his bride. The future given them by Batai Khan would begin tomorrow, and there was much to do.

FIGHTER'S FIASCO

G ood heavyweights are scarcer than feather
pillows in an Eskimo's igloo, so the first time
I took a gander at this "Bambo" Bamoulian,
I got all hot under the collar and wondered if I was
seeing things. Only he wasn't Bambo then, he was
just plain Januz Bamoulian, a big kid from the
Balkans, with no more brains than a dead man's heel.
But could he sock! I'm getting ahead of myself. . . .

I am walking down the docks wondering am I going to eat, and if so, not only when but where and
with what, when I see an ape with shoulders as
wide as the rear end of a truck jump down off the
gangway of a ship and start hiking toward another
guy who is hustling up to meet him. It looks like
fireworks, so I stand by to see the action, and if the
action is going to be anything like the string of cuss
words the guy is using, it should be good.

This guy is big enough to gather the Empire State Building under one arm and the Chrysler Tower under the other, and looks tough enough to buck rivets with his chin, so I am feeling plenty sorry for the other guy until he gets closer and I can get a flash at him. And that look, brother, was my first gander at the immortal Bambo Bamoulian.

He is about four inches shorter than the other guy, thicker in the chest, but with a slim waist and a walk like a cat stepping on eggs. He is a dark, swarthy fellow, and his clothes are nothing but rags, but I ain't been in the fight racket all these years without knowing a scrapper when I see one.

Me, I ain't any kind of a prophet, but a guy don't need to be clairvoyant to guess this second lug has what it takes. And what is more, he don't waste time at it. He sidles up close to the big guy, ducks a wide right swing, and then smacks him with a fist the size of a baby ham, knocking him cold as a Labrador morning!

Old Man Destiny doesn't have to more than smack me in the ear with a ball bat before I take a hint, so I step up to this guy.

"Say," I butt in. "Mightn't you happen to be a fighter?"

"How would you like to take a walk off the pier," he snarls, glaring at me like I'd swiped his socks or something. "You double-decked something-or-other, I am a fighter! What does that look like?" And he waves a paw at the study in still life draped over the dock.

"I mean for money, in the ring. You know, for dough, kale, dinero, gelt, sugar, geetus, the—"

"I get it!" he yelps brightly. "You mean for money!"

What would you do with a guy like that?

"That's the idea," I says, trying to be calm. "In the ring, and with the mitts."

"It's okay by me. I'll fight anybody for anything! For money, marbles, or chalk, but preferably money. Marbles and chalk are kind of tough on the molars!"

"Then drop that bale hook and come with me. I am the best fight manager in the world, one of the two smartest guys in the universe, an' just generally a swell guy!"

"That's okay. I like you, too!" he says.

Ignoring what sounds faintly like a crack, I say, "They are wanting a fighter over at the Lyceum Club. And we'll fight whoever they got, we don't care who he is."

"We? Do both of us fight one guy? Mister, I don't need no help."

"No, you fight. I'm the brains, see? The manager, the guy that handles the business end. Get it?"

"Oh, so you're the brains? That's swell, it gives you somethin' t' do, an' we'll manage somehow!"

I looks at him again, but he is walking along swinging those big hooks of his. I catch up, "Don't call me mister. My name is McGuire, 'Silk' McGuire. It's Silk because I'm a smooth guy, see?"

"So is an eel smooth," he says.

A few minutes later, I lead my gorilla into Big Bill Haney's office and park him on a chair in the outer room with his cap in his mitts. Then I breeze inside.

"Hello, Bill!" I says cheerfully. "Here I am again!

You got that heavyweight for the four-rounder tonight?"

"What d' you care?" he says, sarcastic. "You ain't had a fighter in a year that could punch his way out of a paper bag!"

"Wrong," I says coldly. "Climb out of that swivel chair and cast your lamps over this—" And I dramatically swing the door open and give him a gander at my fighter, who has parked his number tens on the new mahogany table.

"Hell," he says, giving Bambo the once-over. "That ain't no fighter. That chump is fresh off the boat."

"No wisecracks. That guy is the greatest puncher since Berlenbach and faster than even Loughran. He's tougher than a life stretch on Alcatraz, and he ain't never lost a battle!"

"Never had one, either, huh?"

Big Bill looks Januz over with a speculative glint in his eyes, and I know what he sees. Whatever else he may have, he does have color, and that's what they pay off on. My bohunk looks like a carbon copy of the Neanderthal man, whoever he was, only a little tougher and dumber.

"Okay," Haney says grudgingly. "I'll give him the main go tonight with 'Dead-Shot' Emedasco. Take it or leave it."

"With who?" I yelps. "Why, that guy has knocked over everyone from here to China!"

"You asked for a fight, didn't you?" he sneers. "Well, you got one. That clown of yours would've dragged down about twenty bucks for getting bounced on his ear by some preliminary punk; with the Dead-Shot he'll get not less than five centuries. Why are you kicking?"

"But this guy's a prospect. He can go places. I don't want him knocked off in the start, do I? Chees, give a guy a chance, won't you?"

"Forget it. That's the only spot open. I filled that four-rounder yesterday, and then Hadry did a run-out on the main event, so I can shove your boy in there. If he lives through it, I'll give him another shot. What do you call him?"

"Hey, buddy?" I barks at him. "What d' you call yourself?"

"Me? I come without calling," he grins. "But my name is Bamoulian. Januz Bamoulian. J-a-n-u-z—"

"Skip it!" I says hastily. "We'll call you Bambo Bamoulian!"

I touch Haney for a fin, so we can eat, and we barge down to Coffee Dan's to hang on the feed bag. While Dan is trying to compose a set of ham and eggs, I go into a huddle with myself trying to figure out the answers. This big tramp Dead-Shot Emedasco is poison. Or that's the way he sounds in the papers. I have never seen him, but a guy hears plenty. I usually get all the dope on those guys, but this is one I missed somehow. He has been touring the sticks knocking over a lot of guys named Jones, and on paper looks like the coming heavyweight champ.

The way Bambo charges them ham and eggs, I decide we better fight early and often, and that I'd rather buy his clothes than feed him. But while I am on my third cup of coffee, me not being a big eater myself as I'm nearly out of money again, I look up and who should be steering a course for our table but "Swivel-Neck" Hogan.

Now, I like Swivel-Neck Hogan like I enjoy the galloping cholera, and he has been faintly irritated with me ever since a poker game we were in. He had dealt me a pair of deuces from the bottom of the deck, and I played four aces, which relieved him of fifty bucks, so I know that whenever he approaches me there is something in the air besides a bad smell.

"Hey, you!" he growls. "The skipper wants ya."

"Say, Bambo," I says, "do you smell a skunk or is that just Swivel-Neck Hogan?"

"Awright, awright," he snarls, looking nasty with practically no effort. "Can dat funny stuff! The chief wants ya!"

As I said, I like Swivel-Neck like the seven-year itch, but I have heard he is now strong-arming for "Diamond-Back" Dilbecker, a big-shot racketeer, and that he has taken to going around with a gat in every pocket, or something.

"Act your age," I says, pleasant-like. "You may be the apple of your mother's eye, but you're just a spoiled potato to me." Then I turns to Bambo and slips him my key. "Take this and beat it up to the room when you get through eating, an' stick around till I get back. I got to see what this chump wants. It won't take long."

Bambo gets up and hitches his belt up over his dinner. He gives Swivel-Neck a glare that would have raised a blister on a steel deck. "You want I should bounce this cookie, Silk?" he says, eagerly. "Five to one I can put him out for an hour."

"It'd be cheap at twice the price," I chirps. "But let it ride."

When we get to Dilbecker's swanky-looking apartment, there are half a dozen gun guys loafing in the living room. Any one of them would have kidnapped and murdered his own nephew for a dime, and they all look me over with a sort of professional stare as though measuring up space in a cornerstone or a foundation. This was pretty fast company for yours truly, and nobody knows this better than me.

Dilbecker looks up when I come in. He is a short, fat guy, and he is puffy about the gills. I feel more at home when I see him, for Diamond-Back Dilbecker and me is not strangers. In fact, away back when, we grew up within a couple of blocks of each other, and we called him Sloppy, something he'd like to forget now that he's tops in his racket.

"McGuire," he says, offhand. "Have a cigar." He shoves a box toward me, and when I pocket a handful I can see the pain in his eyes. I smile blandly and shove the stogies down in my pockets, figuring that if I am to go up in smoke it might just as well be good smoke.

"I hear you got a fighter," he begins. "A boy named Bamoulian?"

"Yeah, I got him on for tonight. Going in there for ten stanzas with Emedasco." Now, I wonder as I size him up, what is this leading up to? "And," I continue, "he'll knock the Dead-Shot so cold, he'll keep for years!"

"Yeah?" Dilbecker frowns impressively. "Maybe so, maybe no. But that's what I want t' see you about. I got me a piece of Emedasco's contract, and tonight I think he should win. I'd like to see him win by a kayo in about the third round."

Dilbecker slips out a drawer and tosses a stack of bills on the desk. "Of course, I'm willing to talk business. I'll give you a grand. What do you say?"

I bit off the end of one of his cigars, taking my time and keeping cool. Actually, I got a sinking feeling in my stomach and a dozen cold chills playing tag up and down my spine.

Dilbecker's at a loss for patience. "Take it, it's a better offer than you'll get five minutes from now," he growls. "Things could happen to you, bad things . . . if you know what I mean."

He's right, of course. He's got a room full of bad things on the other side of the door. I hate to give in to this kid I used to know on the old block but what the hell . . . lookin' at him I realize it may be my life on the line. Nevertheless, a man's got to have his pride.

"Don't come on hard with me, Dilbecker. You may be a tough guy now because you got a crowd o' gun guys in the next room but I remember when the kids from St. Paul's used to chase you home from school!"

"Yeah? Well you forget about it!" he says. "Set this fight and don't make me mad or both you and the Slavic Slugger'll wake up to find yourselves dead!"

Now, I'm not bringing it up but I helped him escape from the parochial school boys a time or few and I took my lumps for it, too. I'm not bringing it up but it's got my blood pressure going anyway.

"Awright, you said your piece," I says, as nasty as I can make it. "And now I'm sayin' mine. I'm sending my boy out there to win and you can keep your money and your gunsels and your damned cigars!" I tossed the load from my pocket on his desk. "I got connections, too. You want to bring muscle? I'll bring muscle, I'll bring guns and sluggers, whatever it takes."

He laughs at me, but it's not a nice laugh. "Muscle? You? You're a comedian. You should have an act. You bum, you been broke for months. You know better than to put the angle on me. Now get out of here, an' your boy dives t'night, or you'll get what Dimmer got!"

Only a week ago they dragged "Dimmer" Chambers out of the river, and him all wound up in a lot of barbed wire and his feet half burned off. Everybody knows it is Dilbecker's job, but they can't prove nothing. I am very sensitive about the feet, and not anxious to get tossed off no bridges, but Bamoulian will fight, and maybe—a very big maybe—he can win!

Also, I don't like being pushed around. So, am I brave? I don't know. I get out of there quick. I got the rest of my life to live.

So we go down to the Lyceum and I don't tell the big ape anything about it. He's happy to see me and raring to go; I don't want to distract him any. I'm bustin' a sweat because I've got no connections, no muscle, no gun guys and Sloppy Dilbecker has. I do, however, call in some favors. There's an old car, which is sitting right outside the dressing-room door, and a pawnshop .38, which is in my pocket. And running shoes, which is on my feet.

Now it's nearly time and I am getting rather chilled about those feet by then, although it looks like they'll be warm enough before the evening is over. Several times I look out the dressing-room door, and every time I stick my head out there, there is a great, big, ugly guy who looks at me with eyes like gimlets, and I gulp and pull my head in. I don't want Bambo worried going into the ring, although he sure don't look worried now, so I says nothing. He is cheerful, and grinning at me, and pulling Cotton's kinky hair, and laughing at everybody. I never saw a guy look so frisky before a battle. But he ain't seen Dead-Shot Emedasco yet, either!

Once, I got clear down to the edge of the ring, looking the crowd over. Then I get a chill. Right behind the corner where we will be, is Sloppy Dilbecker and three of his gun guys. But what opens my eyes and puts the chill in my tootsies again is the fact that the seats all around them are empty. The rest of the house is a sellout. But those empty seats . . . It looks like he's saving space for a whole crew of tough guys.

It is only a few minutes later when we get the call, and as we start down the aisle to the ring, I am shaking in my brand-new shoes. Also, I am wondering why I had to be unlucky enough to get a fighter stuck in there with one of Dilbecker's gorillas. And then, all of a sudden I hear something behind me that makes my hair crawl. It is the steady, slow, shuffling of feet right behind me.

When I look back, I almost drop the water bottle, for right behind me is that big dark guy who has been doing duty right outside our door, and behind him is a crowd of the toughest looking cookies you ever saw. They are big, hard-looking guys with swarthy faces, square jaws, and heavy black eyebrows.

While Bambo takes his stool, I see them filing into the empty seats behind Sloppy, and believe me they are the toughest crowd that ever walked. I ain't seen none of them before. And except for one or two, they ain't such flashy dressers as most of Dilbecker's usual gun guys, but they are bigger, tougher, and meaner looking and when Cotton touches me on the arm, I let a yip out of me and come damn near pulling a faint right there. Who wouldn't, with about fifty of those gun guys watching you?

When I look around, Emedasco is already in the ring. He is a big mug weighing about two hundred and fifty pounds and standing not over six feet seven inches!

We walk out for instructions, and as the bunch of us come together in the center of the ring, Bambo hauls off and takes a swing at Dead-Shot's chin that missed by the flicker of an eyelash. Before we can stop them, Emedasco slammed a jarring right to Bambo's head, and Bambo came back with a stiff left to the midsection! Finally we got them separated, and I tell Bambo to hold it until the fight starts, and when the bell rings we are still arguing.

Emedasco charged out of his corner like a mad bull and takes a swing at Bamoulian that would have torn his head off had it landed, but Bambo ducked and sank a wicked left into the big boy's stomach. Then, as Emedasco followed with a clubbing right to the head, he clinched, and they wrestled around the ring until the referee broke them. They sparred for a second or two, and then Bambo cut loose with a terrific right swing that missed, but hit the referee on the side of the head and knocked him completely out of the ring and into the press benches.

Then those two big lugs stood flat-footed in the center of the ring and slugged like a couple of maniacs with a delirious crowd on its feet screaming bloody murder. Emedasco was a good sixty pounds heavier, but he was in a spot that night, for if ever a man wanted to fight, it was my Bambo Bamoulian.

I was so excited by the fight that I forgot all about Dilbecker, or what might happen if Bamoulian won, which looked like could happen now.

When the next bell sounded, Bambo was off his stool and across the ring with a left he started clear from his own corner, and it knocked Emedasco into the ropes. But that big boy was nobody's palooka, and when he came back, it was with a volley of hooks, swings, and uppercuts that battered Bambo back across the ring, where he was slammed to the floor with a powerful right to the beezer.

The dumbfounded crowd, who had come to see

Emedasco knock over another setup, were on their chairs yelling like mad, seeing a regular knock-down-and-drag-out brawl like everybody hopes to see and rarely finds. Bambo was right in his element. He knocked Dead-Shot Emedasco staggering with a hard left to the head, slammed a right to the body, and then dropped his hands and laughed at him. But Emedasco caught himself up and with one jump was back with a punch that would have shook Gilbraltar to its base. The next thing I know, Bambo is stretched on his shoulder blades in my corner, as flat as a busted balloon.

I lean over the ropes and yell for him to get up, and you could have knocked me cold with an ax when he turns around and says, grinning, "I don't have to get up till he counts nine, do I?"

At nine he's up, and as Emedasco rushes into him, I yell, "Hit him in the wind! Downstairs! In the stomach!"

Holding the raging Emedasco off with one hand while the big guy punches at him like a crazy man, my prize beauty leans over and says, "What did you say, huh?"

"Hit him in the stomach, you sap!" I bellowed. "Hit him in the stomach!"

"Oooh, I get it!" he says. "You mean hit him in the stomach!" And drawing back his big right fist, he fired it like a torpedo into Emedasco's heaving midsection.

With a grunt like a barn had fell on him, Emedasco spun halfway around and started to drop. But before he could hit the canvas, Bambo stepped in and slammed both hands to the chin, and Emedasco went flying like a bum out of the Waldorf, and stayed down and stayed out.

We hustled back to the dressing room with the crowd cheering so loud you could have heard them in Sarawak, wherever that is, and believe me, I am in a sweat to get out of there.

As we rush by, I hear a wild yell from the big ugly guy who has had his eye on me all evening, and when I glance back that whole crowd is coming for me like a lot of madmen, so I dive into the dressing room and slam the door.

"Hey, what's the idea?" Bambo demands. "Somebody might want to come in!"

"That's just what I'm afraid of!" I cry. "The hallway is full of guys that want to come in!"

"But my brother's out there!" Bambo insists, and jerks the door open, and before you could spell Dnepropetrovak, the room is full of those big, tough-looking guys.

I make a break for the door, but my toe hooked in the corner of Bambo's bathrobe, which has fallen across a chair, and I do a nosedive to the floor. The gun goes sliding. Then something smacks me on the dome, and I go out like a light.

When I came to, the Bambo is standing over me, and the guy with the black eyes is holding my head.

"Awright, you got me! I give up!" I said. "You got me, now make the most of it."

"Say, you gone nuts?" Bambo squints at me. "What's eatin' you, anyway? Snap out of it, I want you t' meet my brother!"

"Your who?" I yelps. "You don't mean to tell me this guy is your brother?"

"Sure, he came to see me fight. All these guys, they my people. We come from the Balkans together, so they come to see me fight. They work on the docks with me."

I am still laughing when we drop in at the Green Fan for some midnight lunch, and it isn't until we are all set down that I remember it is one of Sloppy Dilbecker's places. Just when I find I am not laughing anymore from thinking of that, who should come up but Swivel-Neck Hogan. Only he is different now, and he walks plenty careful, and edges up to my table like he is scared to death.

"Mr. McGuire?" he says.

"Well, what is it?" I bark at him. I don't know why he should be scared, but bluff is always best. And if he is scared, he must be scared of something, and if a gun guy like Swivel-Neck is calling me mister, he must be scared of me, so I act real tough.

"Sloppy—I mean Diamond-Back—said to tell youse he was just ribbing this afternoon. He ain't wantin' no trouble, and how would youse like to cut in on the laundry an' protection racket with him? He says youse got a nice bunch of gun guys, but there is room enough for all of youse."

For a minute I stare at him like he's nuts, and then it dawns on me. I look around at those big, hard-boiled dock workers, guys who look like they could have started the Great War, because, when it comes right down to it . . . they did. I look back at Swivel-Neck.

"Nothing doing, you bum. Go an' tell Sloppy I

ain't wanting none of his rackets. I got bigger an' better things to do. But tell him to lay off me, see? And that goes for you, too! One wrong crack an' I'll have the Montenegran Mafia down on you, get me?"

He starts away, but suddenly I get an inspiration. Nothing like pushing your luck when the game is going your way.

"Hey!" I yells. "You tell Sloppy Dilbecker that my boys say they want the treats on the house t'night, an' tell him to break out the best champagne and cigars he's got, or else! Understand!"

I lean back in my chair and slip my thumbs into the armholes of my vest. I wink at Bambo Bamoulian, and grin.

"All it takes is brains, my boy, brains."

"Yeah? How did you find that out?" he asks.

THE
CACTUS KID

Pausing at the head of the four steps that led to the floor of the dining room, the Cactus Kid surveyed the room with approval. In fact, he surveyed the world with approval. For the Cactus Kid, christened Nesselrode Clay, had but an hour before he closed a sale for one thousand head of beef cattle, and the check reposed in his pocket.

Moreover, the Kid was young, the Kid was debonair, and the Kid walked the earth with a light-hearted step and song on his lips. His suit was of tailored gray broadcloth, his hat of spotless white felt, his shirt was white, his tie black, and his black, perfectly polished hand-tooled boots were a miracle of Spanish leatherwork. Out of sight behind the black silk sash was a Smith & Wesson .44, one of the guns for whose skillful handling the Kid was renowned in places other than this.

He was handsome, he was immaculate, he was alive in this best of all possible worlds, and before him lay the expected pleasure of an excellent meal and a bottle of wine, and afterward a cigar. Surely, this was the life!

The wild grass ranges of Texas, Arizona, and Nevada were a dim memory, and lost with them was the smell of dust and cattle and singed hair and all the memories that attended the punching of cows.

Only one seat remained unoccupied, and the Cactus Kid descended to the main floor with the manner of a king entering his domain, and wove his way among the crowded tables, then paused briefly, his hand on the back of the empty chair. "You do not object, gentlemen?"

The two men who occupied the table lifted black, intent eyes and surveyed him with a cool and careful regard. Their faces were stern, their manners forbidding. "You are," one of them said, "the Americano?"

"As you can tell"—the Kid gestured with both hands—"I am most definitely an Americano."

"Be seated then, by all means."

Had they meant to emphasize that "the"? Or was it his imagination? The menu took his attention from such mundane matters, and he looked upon the gastronomic paradise suggested by the card with satisfaction. A far cry, this, from beef and beans cooked over an open fire with rain beating down on your back while you ate! As the waiter drew near, the Kid looked up, and found the two men regarding him intently.

He returned their attention with interest. Both men were prosperous, well-fed. The waiter spoke, and the Kid turned and in flawless Spanish he ordered his meal. He was conscious, as he did so, that he had the undivided attention of his companions.

When the waiter had gone they looked at him and one spoke. "You speak Spanish."

"As you see."

"It is unexpected, but fortunate, perhaps."

Something in their tone gave him the feeling they would have been more pleased had he not known their language.

"So"—it was the first man again—"I see you arrived all right."

There was no reason for argument on that score. Despite various difficulties he had succeeded in bringing his herd of cattle through, and he had, he decided, arrived all right. "Yes," he admitted.

"You are ready?"

A good question, the Kid decided. He decided, being in fine fettle, that he was undoubtedly ready. "Of course," he said carelessly. And then he added, "I am always ready."

"Good! The hour will be at six, in the morning."

Their meals came, giving the Kid time for thought. Now what the deuce had he run into, anyway?

"That's mighty early," he suggested.

They looked at him sternly. "Of course. It must be early. You will be waiting outside?"

Perhaps, if he agreed, more information would be forthcoming.

"Yes, I'll be waiting."

Instead, they finished their meals in silence and left him, and he stared after them wondering. Oh, well. It was an entertaining dinner, anyway, and that was that. Catch him getting up at six in the morning! This was the first time in months that he'd had a chance to sleep late.

He scowled. What was it all about? Obviously, they thought he was someone else. Who did they think he was? His boss had told him to go ahead and enjoy himself for a couple of days after the cattle were delivered, and the Cactus Kid meant to do just that. And one way he planned to enjoy himself was sleeping late.

He was sitting over a glass of wine and a cigar when the door opened and he saw a tall, fine-looking old man come in with a girl—a girl who took his breath away.

The Cactus Kid sat up a little straighter. She was Spanish, and beautiful. Her eyes swept the room and then came to rest on him. They left him, and they returned. The Kid smiled.

Abruptly her glance chilled. One eyebrow lifted slightly and she turned away from him. The Kid hunched his shoulders, feeling frostbitten around the edges of his ego. The two seated themselves not far away, and the Kid looked at the older man. His profile was what is called "aristocratic," his goatee and mustache were purest white. The waiters attended them with deference, and spoke to them in muted voices. Where one nonchalant waiter had drifted before, now a dozen of them rushed to and fro, covering the table with dishes, lavishing attention.

One waiter, and suddenly the Kid was aware that it was the same who had served him, was bending over the table talking to them in a low voice. As he talked, the girl looked toward the Cactus Kid, and after the waiter left, the older man turned and glanced toward him.

That he was an object of some interest to them was plain enough, but why? Could it have some connection with the two odd men he had just shared his meal with? In any event, the girl was undoubtedly the most beautiful he had ever seen—and quite aware of it.

Calling the waiter, he paid his bill, noting the man's surreptitious glances. "Anything wrong?" he asked, studying the waiter with a cold glance.

"No, no, señor! Only . . ." He paused delicately.

"Only what?" the Kid demanded.

"Only the señor is so young! Too young," he added, significantly, "to die so soon!"

Turning quickly, he threaded his way among the tables and was gone. The Cactus Kid stared after him, then walked to the dining-room steps and climbed them slowly. At the door he glanced back over his shoulder. The girl and the older man were watching him. As he caught their glance the girl made a little gesture with her hand and the Kid walked out of the room.

Whatever was happening here was too much for him. Unfortunately, he knew nobody in this part of Mexico except the man to whom he had delivered the cattle, and that had been more miles to the south. Somehow he had become involved in a plot, some development of which he knew nothing at all.

An hour of fruitless speculation told him nothing. He searched back through the recent weeks to find a clue, but he found no hint. And then he remembered the mysterious appointment for six tomorrow morning.

"At six?" he asked himself. "Nothing doing!"

An old Mexican loitered at the gate that led from the patio into the street. Casually, the Kid drifted across the patio to him, and there he paused. Taking his time, he built a cigarette, then offered the makings to the old Mexican.

The man glanced up at him out of shrewd old eyes. "*Gracias,* señor," he said softly. He took the makings and rolled a cigarette, then returned the tobacco and papers to the Kid, who was about to strike a match. "No, señor," he whispered, "behind the wall. It is not safe."

The Cactus Kid scowled. "What isn't safe?" he asked. "I don't understand."

"You have not been told? The man has many friends; they might decide it is safer to kill you now. The señor," he added, "has a reputation."

"Who do you think I am?" the Kid asked.

"Ah?" The peón looked at him wisely. "Who am I to know such a thing? It is enough that you are here. Enough that you will be here tomorrow."

The Kid studied it over while he smoked, taking his time. The oblique angle seemed best. "Who," he said, "was the beautiful señorita in the dining room?"

"What?" The old peón was incredulous. "You do not know? But that is she, señor! The Señorita Marguerita Ibanez." With that the old peón drifted off into the street and the Kid turned and walked back to the inn and climbed to his room. He opened the door and stepped inside, closing it carefully after him.

Then he struck a match and lighted the candle. "Señor?" It was a feminine voice, but he turned sharply around, cursing himself mentally for being so careless. He was wearing but one gun, in position for a right-hand draw, and the candle was in that hand.

Then he stared. Before him, a vision of loveliness, was the señorita from the dining room.

"I have come to tell you," she said hastily, "that you must not do this thing. You must go, go at once! Get your horse, slip out of the compound tonight, and ride! Ride like the wind for the border, for you will not be safe until you cross it."

The Cactus Kid chuckled suddenly. Puzzled as he was, he found himself enjoying it. And the girl was so beautiful. He put the candle down and motioned for her to be seated. "We've some talking to do," he said. "Some explanations are in order."

"Explanations?" She was plainly puzzled at the word. "I know of nothing to explain. I cannot stay, already my uncle will have missed me. But I had to warn you. I had not expected anyone so—so young! An older man—no, it cannot be. You must go! I will not have you killed because of me."

"Look, ma'am," he said politely, "there's something about this I don't understand. I think you've got the wrong man. You seem to believe I am somebody I am not."

"Oh!" She was impatient. "Do not be a fool,

señor! It is all very well to conceal yourself, but you have no concealment. Everyone knows who you are."

He chuckled again and sat down on the bed. "Everyone but me," he said, "but whatever it is, it does not matter. No matter what happens I shall always be able to remember that I was visited once by the most beautiful girl in Mexico!"

"It is not time for gallantry," she protested. "You must go. You will be killed. Even now it may be too late!"

"What's this all about?" he protested. "Tell me!"

"Oh, don't be a fool!" She was at the door now and there was no mistaking her sincerity. Her face was unusually pale, her eyes enormous in the dim light from the candle. "If you kill him, they will kill you. If you do not kill him—then he will kill you." Turning quickly, she was gone.

"Well of all the fool . . ." He stopped speaking. What was happening, he could not guess, but somehow he was right in the middle of a lot of trouble, and trouble of which he knew nothing. Now the Cactus Kid was no stranger to trouble, nor to gunplay, but to go it blind and in somebody else's country, that was a fool's play. The girl was right. The only way was to get out. If he stayed he was trapped; to kill or be killed in a fight of which he understood nothing.

He hesitated, and then he looked suddenly toward his saddlebags and rifle. There was a back stairs—it would be simple to get to the stable . . . and he could be off and away. It wasn't as if he was running. It simply wasn't his fight. He had stumbled on a lot of trouble, and . . .

There was no moon and the trail was only a thin white streak. He walked his horse until he was a mile away from the town, and then he lifted into a canter. He glanced back just once. The señorita had been very lovely, and very frightened.

He frowned, remembering the man in the shadows. For he had not escaped without being seen. There had been a man standing near the wall, but who he had been, the Kid had no idea. There had been no challenge, and the Cactus Kid had ridden away without trouble.

Steadily he rode north, slowing at times to walk. Remembering the trail on the way down, he recalled a village not far ahead, and he was preparing to run out and skirt around it when he heard a rider coming. He slowed and started to swing his horse, then the other horse whinnied.

The Cactus Kid shucked his six-gun. "Who is it?" he asked in Spanish.

"I ride to the inn with a message for Señorita Ibanez, have you been there?"

"You will find her," the Kid paused for a second, "but be careful, there is trouble."

The man sat on his horse, a dark shape against the stars. "Much trouble, yes? You speak like an American, I think."

"Yes, I am. Why?"

"At my house there is a wounded man, an American. He tries to tell me things I do not understand." He rode closer and peered at the Kid from under a wide sombrero. "He is dying. It is better, perhaps, that you talk to him, rather than a gentle lady."

They rode swiftly, but the distance was short. It was an isolated cabin of adobe off the main trail and among some huge boulders. Swinging down from their horses, the Mexican led the way into the house.

The man on the pallet was finished, anyone could see that. He was a big man, and his hard-drawn face was pale under what had been the deep brown of his skin. Nearby on a chair was a pair of matching Colts and the man's bloody clothing. Yet he was conscious and he turned his head when the Kid came in.

"I'm . . . I'm a lousy coyote if it ain't . . . ain't a Yank," he said hoarsely.

The Kid, with the usual rough frontier knowledge of treating wounds, bent over him. It required no expert skill to see these simple Mexican folk had done all that could be done. The amazing thing was that the man was alive at all. He had been shot at least six times.

"I'm Jim Chafee," he whispered. "I guess they got me this time."

The Cactus Kid stared at the dying man. Chafee! General in at least two Mexican revolts, almost dictator in one Central American country, and a veteran soldier of fortune. Even in his dying hours, the man looked ten years younger than he must have been.

"Hey!" Realization broke over the Kid. "I'll bet you're the guy they thought I was." Bending over the wounded man he talked swiftly, and Chafee nodded, amused despite his condition.

"He's bad," Chafee whispered. "I was dry-gulched . . . by her uncle and six gunmen."

"Her uncle?" The Kid was startled. "You mean . . . what do you mean?"

The Mexican interposed. "Bad for him to talk," he objected.

Chafee waved the man aside. "I'm through," he said. "I only wish I could get even with those devils and get that girl out of there!" He looked at the Kid. "Who're you?"

"They call me the Cactus Kid," he replied.

Chafee's eyes gleamed. "I've heard of you! You're that hell-on-wheels gunfighter from up Nevada way." He sagged back on the pallet. "Kid," he whispered, "go back there an' help that girl. But don't trust nobody."

The Cactus Kid stared down at the wounded man. His face was relaxing slowly, yet his eyes were still bright. . . . "Knew her father," he whispered, "good man. That old devil . . . the uncle, he killed him . . . she don't know that."

While the Kid sat beside him, the dying man fumbled out the words of the story, but only a part of it, for he soon stopped talking and just lay there, breathing heavily.

Slowly, the Kid got to his feet. He had gone to his room at about nine o'clock. He had been riding north for almost three hours . . . if he started now and rode fast, he could be back in half that time. From his pocket he took a handful of silver pesos, more money than this peón would see in three months. "Take care of him," he told him, "keep him alive if you can, if not, see there is a priest. I will come by again, in a few weeks."

"He shall be my brother, señor," the Mexican said, "but take your money. No money is needed to buy care in the house of Juan Morales."

"Keep it," the Kid insisted. "It is my wish. Care for him. I'll be back."

With a leap he was in the saddle, and the horse was legging it south toward the town. As he rode, the Kid was suddenly happy again. "I never rode away from a fight before—nor a girl that pretty!" he added.

It seemed he had been in bed no more than a few minutes when he was called. Yet actually he had crawled into bed at two o'clock and had all of four hours' sleep behind him. He dressed swiftly and went down the stairs. The Mexicans in the kitchen looked at him wide-eyed, and one huge woman poured him a brimming bowl of coffee, which he drank while eating a tortilla and beans. He was saddling up when the two men from the dinner table appeared.

"Ah, you are still here," one said. "Did you sleep well?"

"Oh, very well!" the Kid replied glibly. He turned to them grinning. "Now just who are you?"

"I am Pedro Sandoval! This man is Enrique Fernandez. We rode with the old general, and you must have heard of us. Surely, Señor Chafee—!"

They mounted up and rode around the inn and started out the road. Nothing was said for almost a mile, and he was puzzled. Both Sandoval and Fernandez seemed unusually quiet, yet he did not dare ask any questions.

Without warning the two men beside him swung their horses into the woods and he turned with them. On the edge of a clearing, they swung down. On the far side were several men, and now one of them came hurrying toward them.

"You are late!" he said impatiently. "We have been waiting. Señor DeCarte is most angry."

"It was unavoidable," Fernandez replied shortly. "Señor Chafee slept late."

"Slept?" The man stared at the Kid in astonishment. "That soundly?"

"Why not?" The Kid shrugged, and then glanced across the clearing. A big man on the far side had taken off his coat and was now selecting a pistol from a box.

The Cactus Kid stopped in his tracks . . . it was ridiculous . . . it couldn't be!

But it was. Fernandez was beside him. "Your jacket, señor?" he said. "You will remove it?"

The Kid slipped out of the jacket, then asked, "By the way, you know in the States we don't do this quite the same way. Would you mind telling me the rules?"

Fernandez bowed. "I am sorry. I thought this had been done. You will face each other at a distance of twenty paces. At the word, you will lift your pistols and fire. If neither scores a hit, you will advance one step closer and fire a second time."

Fernandez's eyes searched the Kid's anxiously. "I . . . hope you will win, señor. This is all very strange. Somehow you do not seem . . . if I did not know I would think . . . you will pardon me, of course, but . . ."

"You don't think I'm Jim Chafee?" The Kid chuckled. "You're right, amigo, I'm not." Before the startled man's words could come, the Kid said quickly, "Chafee was ambushed. He is either dead by now, or dying. I am taking his place, and you may be sure I'll shoot as straight.

"Now tell me: Who am I shooting, and what for?"

Fernandez stared. He gulped, and then suddenly, he laughed. "This is most unbelievable! Preposterous! And yet . . . amusing.

"This man is Colonel Arnold DeCarte. He is one of certain deadly enemies of General Francisco Ibanez, the father of Marguerita. In fact, he is believed to be their leader and one of those in a plot to dispossess the señorita of her estates.

"He challenged Ibanez and was to have fought him today but Ibanez was slain by assassins. Now you tell me that Jim Chafee, who took up the fight, has also been slain, or badly wounded, at least."

The Cactus Kid looked at the pistol in his hand. It would have to serve, but he would have preferred his own Smith & Wesson .44. DeCarte was advancing to position, but now he stopped, staring at the Cactus Kid.

The Frenchman turned abruptly. "What farce is this? This is not Señor Chafee . . . it is a child!"

As the others turned, the Kid stepped forward, interrupting the excited babble of their voices. "What's the matter, DeCarte? Afraid? Or do you prefer to shoot your men down from ambush, as General Ibanez and Chafee have been shot?"

DeCarte's face turned dark with angry blood. "You accuse me of that?" he roared. "By the—!"

"Control yourself, señor!" Fernandez said sternly. "The duel is arranged. If you wish to retire from the field, say so. This gentleman is taking the place of Señor Chafee."

DeCarte stared at the Kid angrily, yet as he looked, his expression changed. The Cactus Kid stood five feet eight in his socks, and weighed one hundred and fifty pounds. His hair waved back from his brow and his face looked soft. He was deceptively boyish looking, a fact that had cost more than one man dearly. The Kid could almost see the thought in DeCarte's mind. This boy . . . I will shoot him down. . . .

"Take your place!" DeCarte snapped. "Let the duel commence!"

Coolly, the Cactus Kid walked to his place. This was different from the gun duels he was accustomed to where men met in the street or elsewhere and moved and shot as they wished. For this sort of thing there was a ritual, a ceremony, and he wished to conform. He glanced down at the heavy pistol. It was a good pistol, at that. It was a single-shot gun, and a second was thrust into his belt.

The third man stepped to his position. "One!" he barked.

The Cactus Kid stiffened and stood, his right side turned toward DeCarte. The man seemed very near.

"Two!"

They lifted their pistols. The guns were heavy, but the Kid's wrists were strong from the endless hours of roping, riding, and range work. He held it steady and looked along the barrel at DeCarte.

"Three!"

Flame stabbed at him and something brushed at his face. DeCarte stood very still, then turned slowly toward the Kid and fell flat on his face. He had been shot through the right eye.

The Kid put his hand to his cheek and brought it away bloody. He touched his cheek again. The bullet had burned him, so near he had been to death. Excited men gathered about DeCarte, and the Kid picked up his jacket and slipped into it. His own .44 was still behind the sash where he had carried it since his arrival in Mexico.

Fernandez came to him. "A splendid shot!" he said. "A remarkable shot! But we must go, at once! He has many friends. You must leave Mexico."

"Leave?" The Cactus Kid shook his head. "I can't do that," he said quietly. "I must stay. And I want to see the señorita."

"That is impossible." Sandoval had come up to them. "It is not to be considered. If you are not out of Mexico in a matter of hours, his friends will have you arrested."

"That I'll gamble on," the Kid said shortly. "I'm staying."

Sandoval's face stiffened slightly. "As you wish," he said, and turned abruptly.

As they swung into their saddles, Fernandez leaned closer to the Kid. "I will take you to her. We ride now to the hotel. Go at once to your room!"

They rode swiftly over the road back to town and then to the inn. The Kid stabled his horse and then checked his gun. Swiftly, he mounted the stairway. In his room he changed at once into range clothes and belted on both his guns. That there would be further trouble, he did not doubt. What lay behind all this he did not know, nor exactly who his enemies were. Chafee had warned him to trust no one, and had said that Marguerita's uncle was one of those trying to grab the vast estate of which he had heard only hints.

Waiting irritated him. He packed his few things into his saddlebags and the small carpetbag in which he carried his gray suit. From the window he looked down into the patio. There was nobody in sight, although it was well along toward midday. Nor was there any sound of anyone approaching his room.

Suddenly, through the gate came a half dozen mounted soldiers and an officer. Four of the soldiers swung down and started for the entrance. The Kid wheeled to rush to the door, then heard a faint sound from without—the merest scrape of a foot!

He hesitated, picked up a chair in one hand, and laid the other on the doorknob, stepping back as far as he could while still retaining his grip. Then he swung the door wide and hurled a chair into the hall!

Yet as he jerked wide the door and swung the chair, a shotgun blasted and the heavy charge smashed into the chair bottom, some of the shot ricocheting from the doorjamb. Leaping out, gun in hand, he was just in time to see a man rushing down the hall. The Kid stepped out of the door and shot from the hip.

The running man seemed to stumble and then he sprawled headlong to the floor. From below there was a shout, and he heard the soldiers rushing toward the stair. Grabbing his saddlebags and carpetbag, he darted out of the door, slamming it after him, and turning down the hall, ran past the fallen man and through a door that waited beyond. It led down a narrow stair to the ground outside the inn.

He hit the bottom running and charged into the open, seeing a horse standing there. Instantly, he sprang into the saddle, swung the horse wide, and spurred it into the brush. In two jumps it was running all out. Behind him there were yells and running feet, but he was already out of sight.

Instantly, he drew up. No need to let them hear the running horse to know his direction. Turning at right angles to his original course, he swung around the town and headed into the chaparral. It was rough going and there was no trail, but he worked his way back through the brush, heading toward the mountains. It was scarcely noon now, and he had many daylight hours ahead of him. He paused a moment to fasten down his saddlebags. He patted the horse's flank.

What had become of Fernandez? And of Marguerita?

. . .

The Cactus Kid saved his horse but worked, on a zigzag trail, back into the roughest kind of country, yet avoiding the canyons that led into the Sierra Madre. It would be his luck to ride into a box canyon and be trapped.

Several times he studied his back trail from the summits of ridges he crossed, taking precautions so as not to be seen. He saw no dust or evidence of pursuit.

Finding a faint cattle trail, he followed it, winding along the slope of the hills. The trail suddenly divided, and one path led higher up into the rugged mountains. He chose this way and dismounted to save his horse. It was not his own, but it would do, and was a powerful gray gelding with the deep chest and the fine legs of a runner and stayer.

At the crest of the range, with several miles of terrain exposed below him, he turned into the trees and stopped, slipping the bit from the gelding's mouth so it could feed properly. Then he picketed the horse and sat down on the slope.

Almost an hour had passed before he saw any sign of life, and then it was only a peón driving a goat. The man was coming up the trail and making a hard time of it. When almost to the Kid, the goat suddenly stopped and shied away. The peón straightened and looked at the trees. "It is all right, old one," the Kid said softly, "I am a friend."

He saw then that the man's face was bleeding from a cut across the cheek. The peón did not come toward him but stood there, holding his hand against his face. "If you are he they seek," he said, "may you go with God. Those others—they are devils!"

"They struck you?"

"With a whip." The peón turned his head now and stared at the Kid, who was visible to him but out of sight of anyone below. "They asked me if I had seen a gringo. I told them no and they swore I lied. I had not seen you, señor. Then they struck me."

"Where are they now?"

"In the canyon below. They search for tracks."

The Kid nodded. They would find them, of course. Then they would be on his trail. He gathered up his picket rope and put the bit back in the gelding's mouth.

"Old one," he said, "do you know the hacienda of Ibanez? Is it near?"

"It is north," the old man said, "you are pointing for it now. It is thirty miles from east to west, and fifty miles from north to south. If you ride straight on, you can reach there for dinner. But they are there also, the devils."

"Ibanez was killed."

"*Si*, we know this, but those who come in his place, ah!"

The Cactus Kid mounted. "They won't have it so good, old-timer," he said grimly. "I'm looking for some of them now."

The worst of it was, he reflected as he rode on, that he did not know whom he was looking for. What he intended to do was to find Marguerita and talk to her. She would put him straight, and he grinned at the thought; talking with her would cause him no pain. If one had to be trapped into defending or aiding a girl, it was pure luck that she turned out to be so beautiful.

The Ibanez hacienda was something to look at, and the Kid studied the place thoughtfully. The house was surrounded by a wall on three sides, the back of the house making up most of the fourth side. There were orchards and meadows, irrigation ditches and row crops. The fields were not small, but stretched on for acres and acres. On a far hill he could see cattle grazing; white-face cattle such as they were now bringing into Texas.

Keeping to back trails, he rode for the house itself and finally stopped under some eucalyptus trees a hundred yards off. No pursuit was in sight, and he doubted if they would find him soon, for they would still be hunting him in the mountains. He was about to mount up when he saw a peón standing under the trees, watching him.

He was gambling on the dislike the peóns seemed to have for his own enemies, and he said, "I am a friend to the Señorita Marguerita. I have just killed in a duel an enemy of the old general. I need a fresh horse and to see the señorita. She is here?"

The man had a thin face and large, hot eyes. He came forward quickly, showing beautiful teeth in a quick smile. "She is here, señor. She has come within the hour. And already the story is told that you . . . you must be the one . . . who killed DeCarte. We are happy, amigo!"

The Mexican came forward and took the horse. "I will prepare for you a fine horse, señor, who runs like the wind and never stops! And I will warn you if they come. Go down to the house . . . but be careful."

Taking nothing with him but what he wore, the Cactus Kid turned and walked swiftly toward the gate. Now he would find out what this was all about and there need be no more going it blind. That he was far from out of the woods, he knew. Whoever these enemies of the old general were, they seemed to have influence enough to employ the army, and they would certainly want him dead. Yet the Kid knew that he was relatively unimportant and what they feared was that he might try to aid the señorita.

He walked through the gate and across to the door of the house. When he stepped through he became immediately conscious of his dusty, disheveled appearance. His boots sounded loud on the worn stone floor and he walked on into the large room with dark panels on the walls.

The whisper of a footstep startled him and he turned. It was Marguerita, her magnificent eyes wide and frightened. "Señor! You must leave at once! They are searching for you everywhere. Here they will look, and we, my uncle and I, we are suspect."

"Your uncle?" His eyes searched her face. "He is here?"

"Yes, of course. He was so pleased when he heard of your victory. It was magnificent, señor. But," she hurried on, "you must not stay. DeCarte had powerful friends and they are searching for you. My uncle says you must not come here."

"He didn't see me come now?" the Kid asked hastily. "If he didn't, don't tell him."

"And why not?" The voice was cool. "You think me ungrateful, my young friend?"

The Cactus Kid half turned to face the tall, aristocratic man with the white goatee and mustache. Certainly, he had never seen a finer appearing man, and yet as the uncle drew nearer, the Kid could see the hard lines around his mouth, half concealed by the mustache, and the coldness in the man's eyes.

"I am Don Estaban," he said, "the master here. We are at your service."

"You own the ranch?" The Cactus Kid looked surprised. "It was my impression that it belonged to the señorita."

Don Estaban's lips tightened and his eyes flashed hard and cold. This man, the Kid reflected, had a mean temper. "So it does," Don Estaban said quietly. "I am but the manager, the master in function, if you will."

The Kid turned to Marguerita. "May I talk with you? There is much to say."

Before she could reply, Don Estaban interrupted. "It is not the custom in Mexico," he said, "for young ladies to talk to gentlemen unchaperoned. I cannot permit it."

"Perhaps he would like to bathe and prepare for dinner, Uncle Estaban," Marguerita said quickly. "If you would show him to a room. Or I can call Juana."

Turning, she called out and a slender girl came quickly into the room, and the Kid followed her away. Behind him he heard low conversation.

Once in the room, he glanced suspiciously about. It was spacious, with a huge four-poster bed. Throwing his hat on a hook, he poured water into a basin and unfastened his neckerchief and started unbuttoning his shirt. Then the door opened quickly and the señorita stepped into the room. "Always I come to your room!" she whispered. "It is most improper!"

"I like it." The Kid looked at her appreciatively. "I like it very much. I wish you'd make a habit of it. Now tell me what this is all about, and quickly."

The story was simple enough, and she told it rapidly with no time wasted on details. The ranch was part of a grant that had been in the hands of her family since the Conquest, but of late it had become more and more valuable. During the reign of Maximilian—who had been shot only a short time before—it had been taken from their family and given to the DeCartes, who were adventurous followers of the French king.

When he was thrown out, the estate had been returned to its original owners, but by that time DeCarte had married into an influential Mexican family and he had continued to claim the estate. There had been some furious words between the old general and DeCarte, and the resulting challenge. The fact that the general had been a renowned pistol shot might have had something to do with his assassination. Jim Chafee had been planning to take up the challenge when he himself had been shot, and the arrival of the Cactus Kid at the time Chafee was expected had led Fernandez and Sandoval to believe he was their man.

DeCarte was dead . . . the bullet had killed him instantly, but the trouble was only just begun.

"You must not stay here," Marguerita told him quickly. "It is not safe. You must return to your own country."

"What about you?" he asked. "How will you deal with your uncle?"

"My uncle?" She turned on him quickly. "What do you mean?"

"Your uncle is one of them, Marguerita. He is trying to get your estate for himself, to divide it with DeCarte and someone else."

Her face paled. "Oh, no! You don't mean that! You can't!"

Yet even as she spoke he could see the dawning of belief in her eyes. She turned on him. "Where did you get that idea? Who would suggest it?"

"Chafee told me it was he who killed your father. He said it was your uncle who had him ambushed."

She stood very still, and then suddenly she sat down on the chair near the table. "What am I to do? He was the only one . . . there is no one, nobody to help me."

"Why not me?" The Cactus Kid sat down on the bed and began to build a cigarette. "Marguerita," he said quietly, "I'm in this up to my ears. Even for my own safety, I would be better off staying here and licking it than trying to beat them to the border. Go on, we don't want you to get caught here . . . I'll see you at dinner."

• • •

It was a long tall room but there were only three places set at the big table. As the Cactus Kid ate and talked, he also listened, his ears attuned to the slightest sound from without. Yet Don Estaban seemed not to be expecting anything. Later, as Marguerita played the piano, the Kid stood nearby, watching her.

How lovely she was! How fine was this life! How simple and easy! Good food, good wine, quiet hours in this wonderful old Spanish home, the stillness and coolness inside the house that seemed so far from the fevered air outside, or the work and struggle of the cattle trails to which he had been born. Yet beneath it all, there were the stirrings of evil, plotting men who wished to take all this from a slender, lovely girl, robbed of her father by the man who now sat in that high-backed chair, so certain everything would soon be his.

Don Estaban spoke suddenly. "You are an excellent shot, señor. It was most unexpected, your victory."

"I think it surprised a lot of people."

"Do you always wear two guns?" queried his host.

"When I am expecting trouble."

"You expect trouble here? Now?" Don Estaban permitted his voice to carry a note of surprise. "In this house?"

The Cactus Kid turned his head slowly and looked to the older man. "I sure do," he said quietly. "I expect it everywhere. The hombres who killed the general, who shot down Chafee, they expected me to be killed by DeCarte. Now that I'm here they'll try to kill me."

The Cactus Kid opened his eyes and sat bolt upright in bed. It was dark and still. But outside in the hall, there was a faint footfall. Like a cat he eased into his trousers without a whisper of sound . . . he got his guns belted around him . . . reached for his boots . . . and then the door opened!

In the doorway stood Sandoval, and in his hands was a shotgun, half lifted to point toward the empty bed. Sandoval spoke softly, "Señor?"

"Hand that gun to me," the Kid said softly, "butt first."

Sandoval hesitated, then took a gamble. Springing back through the door, he swung the shotgun into position and the Kid fired. It was a wild gamble, for Sandoval's leap had carried him back out of range, but the Kid fired his shot through the wall.

Sandoval cried out and the shotgun fell with a clatter to the floor. Instantly, the Kid swung around into the doorway. Sandoval had backed up against the wall and was clutching his stomach with both hands.

Along the balcony on the other side of the great hall, there was a scuffle of sound and the Kid ran in his stocking feet toward it. He reached the turn that led to Marguerita's quarters and skidded to a halt. Two men stood at the door of the girl's room, rattling the latch. Beyond them was Don Estaban.

"Open up," Estaban called. "Open up, or we'll break the door!"

The Cactus Kid swung around the corner and instantly, the two men whirled and lifted their rifles to fire. They were slow . . . much too slow!

The Kid dropped to a half crouch and fired three rapping, thundering shots. The nearest man cried out and fell against the shoulder of Don Estaban, disturbing his aim. The Kid's second shot smashed the second rifleman, and his third was a clear miss. Don Estaban leaped forward and swung up his gun. In the close confines of the hall the Kid swung the barrel of his pistol. It thudded against the don's skull, and he wilted to the floor.

"Marguerita?" He stepped quickly to the door. "It's the Kid. Better come out."

She came quickly, her eyes wide at the carnage. Swiftly they ran down the hall to the Kid's room, where he got into his boots. He said, "Do the peóns like you?"

She nodded.

"Take me to the best one," he said. "We'll arm them and be ready for trouble. If somebody wants a fight, we'll give them one!"

He was the same young Mexican whom the Kid had seen on his arrival, the one who had promised him the horse that so far had not been needed. Briefly, Marguerita explained and he listened attentively. "I will have twenty men within the hour," he said then, "men who will die for the daughter of Ibanez!"

Swiftly they walked back through the trees, then stopped. A half dozen riders were around the main gate, and there were as many empty saddles. More men had arrived. Suddenly a tall, slightly stooped man came through the gate and threw a cigarette into the dirt. He wore leather trousers, tight fitting and flaring at the bottoms, and he wore two guns, tied down. His jacket was velvet and embroidered in red and gold, his sombrero was weighted with silver.

Only his chin was visible, a sharp-boned chin with a drooping mustache. Marguerita caught his arm. "It is Bisco!"

The Kid looked again, his skin tightening over his stomach, his scalp crawling. So . . . now it was Bisco!

Three times the man had been across the border to raid and kill; he was the most feared gunman in Mexico. Half Yaqui, he was utterly poisonous. "They've brought him here for me," he said quietly. "They know who I am."

"Who are you?" Marguerita turned toward him, her eyes wide.

"My right name is Clay. I'm nobody, Marguerita, but he's a man who is brought in to take care of trouble."

"You are modest, I think. Yes, you are too modest. I heard you sold cattle here for your employer. That he trusts you to do this. I think you are brave, good, and I think you are most handsome!"

He chuckled. "Well, now. After that I should be up to almost anything. Right now I've got an urge to go out there and brace that Bisco."

"No"—her face was white—"you must not! You must not be killed by him. Or by anybody."

He looked down into her wide eyes and something seemed to take away his voice, so he stood there, with the cool wind on his face, and then almost without their own volition, they were in each other's arms.

Then he stepped away, shaking his head. "You take a man's mind off his business," he said softly, "and if we expect to get out of this alive, we can't have that happening."

Behind them there was a light footfall. "No," said a voice, "we cannot!"

The Cactus Kid froze where he stood. The voice was that of Don Estaban.

The Kid felt his guns lifted from their holsters, and then Don Estaban said quietly, "Now walk straight ahead . . . to the gate."

Anger choked the Kid as they started forward, the girl beside him. The Kid saw Bisco turn and stare toward them, then come forward with long strides, grinning widely. "So! It is the Cactus Kid! I have long hoped we will one day meet, but—what is this? Perhaps I am not necessary."

"If I had a gun," the Kid replied, speaking Spanish, "you'd be necessary, all right! I'd take you right now!"

Bisco laughed.

The Kid looked past him and saw Fernandez standing in the gateway, his face puzzled. The young Mexican came forward swiftly. "Don Estaban! What does this mean? This man is our friend!"

The older man shook his head. "No, Enrique, he is not."

Enrique's face was stiff. Then he shrugged. "*Pardoneme*," he said, "you know best." He turned and strolled indifferently away.

The Kid stared after him, his eyes blazing. Watch yourself and trust nobody! That was what Chafee advised, and he had certainly been right!

"We'll get this over at once!" Don Estaban turned to a man that stood near him. "Pedro, I want a firing squad of four *vaqueros*. We are going to execute this man—and then"—he smiled—"we will say he was plotting against the government, that he was executed formally."

"You're a white-livered thief." The Cactus Kid spoke without violence. "With the heart of a snake and the courage of a coyote."

Don Estaban's face whitened and his eyes glittered. "Speak what you will," he said contemptuously. "Soon you will be dead."

Four men came into the yard with rifles, and the Cactus Kid was immediately led to the wall. Unbelievingly, Marguerita stared, and then she whirled to her uncle. "You cannot do this thing!" she cried out. "It is murder!"

Don Estaban smiled. "Of course. And unless you obey me you shall join him. What do you think?" He turned on her suddenly. "Am I to turn all this over to you? A foolish girl? Why do you suppose your father died? What do you think that—?" He went on, his tirade growing louder. He was speaking in English, which only Bisco and the Kid could understand.

Suddenly, from behind the wall where he stood, the Kid heard a whisper:

"Amigo, if I make trouble, can you get over the wall?" It was Enrique Fernandez!

"Yes!"

"Your guns are here. Below the wall."

Don Estaban turned away from the girl. "Enough!" he said. "Bisco, hold her. Now"—he turned to the man who had brought the riflemen—"tie his hands and shoot him."

"Wait!" All eyes swung toward the gate. It was Fernandez. "You must not do this thing!"

At the word "wait," the Kid spun on his heels and leaped at the wall. He had gauged it correctly and he caught both hands on the top. With a powerful jerk upward, he pushed himself belt high to the top of the wall, and then swung his feet over.

Fernandez had succeeded even better than he expected, for the Kid was swinging over the wall before he was seen. A snap shot missed, and as he hit ground the Kid went to all fours. The guns were not three feet away, and he caught up the belt and swung it about him, buckling it hastily.

Inside there was a chorus of yells and a shot. The Kid raced around the corner of the wall to see Fernandez staggering back against the wall with a bullet through his shoulder, and then the riflemen poured from the gate.

They expected to find an unarmed man—instead they found a deadly gunfighter, and the range was less than twenty feet.

Four men came through the gate, and in the first burst of firing, three spilled over the ground. The last sprang back, and the Kid, turning abruptly, raced back the way he had come. There was a small wooden door in the far corner of the wall. He had noticed it earlier, and now he raced to it and jerked it open. Inside, a heavily constructed two-wheeled cart stood between him and the confusion in the courtyard. Bisco had let go of the girl who was standing near the door to the house. Don Estaban, gun in hand, was shouting orders to Sandoval, Bisco and the remaining guard, and the leader of the firing squad.

Suddenly, from outside there was a clatter of hoofs and wild shouts, "*Viva* Ibanez! *Viva* Ibanez!"

Don Estaban turned and started for the door, then stopped. "Bisco!" he said hoarsely.

The gunman turned at the word, then froze, his hands lifted and poised.

The Cactus Kid stood beside the wooden cart, facing them. His guns were in his holsters. "You can all give up," he said quietly, his eyes on Bisco, "if you want to. Those are Ibanez men out there."

"I never give up!" Bisco's eyes held eagerness and challenge. His hands dropped and grasped his gun butts, the guns lifted and the black muzzles opened their eyes at the Kid, and suddenly the Cactus Kid's guns bucked in his hands, and Bisco crumpled to the dust.

Music sounded softly from the patio, and Marguerita stood close beside him. "You are going then?" she asked him.

"I've got to," he said. "I've got to go back north

to deliver that money. I wouldn't fit in here. This life is pleasant, but it's not for me."

"You won't miss me?"

Sure I will, he thought, but sometimes ropin' a girl was like ropin' a grizzly. There might be great sport in the catching but it was hard to figure out what to do with one once caught. Later, as he turned his horse into the road that led to the border he laughed. Once you'd had your fun puttin' a loop on a bear, the best thing to do was to shake loose and run.

MAKING IT
THE HARD WAY

U nder the white glare of the lights, the two
fighters circled each other warily. Finn Downey's eyes were savagely intent as he stalked
his prey. Twice Gammy Delgardo's stabbing left
struck Downey's head, but Finn continued to move,
his fists cocked.

As the lancelike left started once more, Downey
ducked suddenly and sprang in, connecting with a
looping overhand right. Delgardo's legs wavered,
and he tried to get into a clinch.

Finn was ready for him, and a short left uppercut
to the wind was enough to set Delgardo up for a
second right. Delgardo hit the canvas on his knees,
and Downey wheeled, trotting to his corner.

Gammy took nine and came up. His left landed
lightly, three times, as Downey pushed close; then
Finn was all over the game Italian, punching with
both hands. Gammy staggered, and Finn threw
the high right again. He caught Delgardo on the

point of the chin, and the Italian hit the canvas, out cold.

Jimmy Mullaney had Finn's robe ready when he reached the corner.

"That's another one, kid," Mullaney said. "Keep this up an' you'll go places."

Downey grinned. He was a solidly built fellow, brown and strong, with dark, curly hair. When the crowd broke into a roar, he straightened to take a bow, then he saw the cheers were not for him. Three men were coming down the aisle, the one in the lead a handsome young fellow in beautifully fitting blue gabardine. His shoulders were broad, and as he waved at the crowd, his teeth flashed in a smile.

"Who's that?" Finn demanded. "Some movie actor?"

"That?" Mullaney said, startled. "Why, that's Glen Gurney, the middleweight champion of the world!"

"Him?" Downey's amazed question was a protest against such a man even being a fighter, let alone the champion of Downey's own division. "Well, for the love of Mike! And I thought he was tough!"

Gurney looked up at Finn with a quick smile. "How are you?" he said pleasantly. "Nice fight?"

Sudden antagonism surged to the surface in Finn. He stepped down from the ring and stood beside Gurney.

So this was the champ! This perfectly groomed young man with the smooth easy manner. Without a scar on his face! Why, the guy was a *dude*!

"I stopped him in the third, like I'll do you!" Downey blurted.

Mullaney grabbed his arm. "Finn, shut up!"

Boiling within Finn Downey was a stifled protest against such poised and sure fellows who got all the cream of the world while kids like himself fought their way up, shining shoes or swamping out trucks.

Gurney's smile was friendly, but in his eyes was a question.

"Maybe we will fight someday," he agreed, affably enough, "but you'll need some work first! If I were you, I'd shorten up that right hand!"

Eyes blazing, Downey thrust himself forward. "You tell *me* how to fight? I could lick you the best day you ever saw!"

He started for Gurney, but Jimmy grabbed him again. "Cut it out, kid! Let's get out of here!"

Gurney stood his ground, his hands in his pockets. "Not here, Downey. We fight in the ring. No gentleman ever starts a brawl."

The word "gentleman" cut Finn like a whip. With everything he had, he swung.

Gurney swayed and the blow curled around his neck as men grabbed the angry Downey and dragged him back. And the champ had not even taken his hands from his pockets!

Mullaney hustled Downey to the dressing room. Inside, Jimmy slammed the door and turned on him.

"What's got into you, Finn? You off your trolley? Why jump the champ, of all people? He'd tear your head off in a fight, and besides, he's a good guy to have for a friend!"

Downey closed his ears to the tirade, all the more irritated because there was justice in it. He showered, then pulled on his old gray trousers and his shirt. Getting his socks on, he worked the tip of the sock down under his toes so that no one could see the hole.

He was angry with himself, yet still resentful. Why did a guy like Gurney have to be champion? Well, anyway . . . when they fought he would put his heart into it.

The fight game must be going to the dogs, or no snob like Glen Gurney could ever hold a title.

Of course, there were ways of getting there by knocking over a string of handpicked setups. That, however, meant money and the right sort of connections. With money improving the challenger's odds, no wonder Gurney was champ.

Mullaney pulled out bills and paid him eighty dollars.

"That's less my cut and the twenty you owe me. Okay?"

"Sure, sure!" Finn stuffed the bills into his pocket.

Jimmy Mullaney hesitated. "Listen, Finn. You've got the wrong idea about Gurney. The champ's a good egg. He never gave anybody a bad break in his life."

Downey thrust his hands in his pockets.

"He's got a lot of nerve telling me how to throw a right! Why, that right hand knocked out seven guys in a row!"

Mullaney looked at Downey thoughtfully. "You've got a good right, Finn, but he was right. You throw it too far."

Downey turned and walked out. That was the way it was. When you were on top everybody took your word. His right was okay. Only two punches in three rounds tonight, and both landed.

He fingered the bills. He would have to give some to Mom, and Sis needed a new dress. He would have to skip the outfit he wanted for himself. His thoughts shifted back to the immaculate Glen Gurney and he set his jaw angrily. Just let him get some money! He'd show that dude how to dress!

That wouldn't be easy, but nothing in his life had been easy. From earliest childhood all he could remember were the dirty streets of a tenement district, fire escapes hung with wet clothing, stifling heat and damp, chilling cold.

Never once could he recall a time when he'd had socks or shoes without holes in them. His father, a bricklayer, had been crippled when Finn was seven, and after that the struggle had been even harder. His older brother now was a clerk for a trucking firm, and the younger worked in the circulation department of a newspaper. One of his sisters worked in a dime store, and the other one, young and lovely as any girl who ever lived, was in high school.

"Hey, Finn!"

Downey glanced up, and his face darkened as he saw a fellow he knew named Stoff. He had never liked the guy, although they had grown up on the same block. These days Stoff was hanging around with Bernie Ledsham, and the gambler was with him now.

"Hi," he returned, and started to pass on.

"Wait a minute, Finn!" Stoff urged. "You ever meet Bernie? We seen your fight tonight."

"How's it?" Finn said to Bernie, a thin-faced man with shrewd black eyes and a flat-lipped mouth. Finn had seen him around, but didn't like him either.

"How about a beer?" Bernie said.

"Never touch it. Not in my racket." Downey drew away. "I've got to be getting on home."

"Come on. Why, after winnin' like you did tonight, you should celebrate. Come with us."

Reluctantly, Finn followed them into a café. Norm Hunter, a man he also knew, was sitting at a table, and with him was a short, square-built fellow with a dark, impassive face. When Finn Downey looked into the flat black eyes, something like a chill went over him, for he recognized the man as Nick Lessack, who had done two stretches in Sing Sing, and was said to be gunman for "Cat" Spelvin's mob.

"You sure cooled that guy!" Norman Hunter said admiringly. "You got a punch there!"

Pleased but wary, Finn dropped into a seat across the table from Nick Lessack.

"He wasn't so tough," he said, "but he did catch me a couple of times."

"He got lucky," Bernie said. "Just lucky."

Downey knew that was not true. Those had been sharp, accurate punches. The lump over his eye was nothing, for black eyes or cut lips were the usual thing for him, but it bothered him that those punches had hit him. Somehow he must learn to make them miss.

Stoff had disappeared, and Finn was having a cup of coffee with Hunter, Bernie, and Nick Lessack.

"That blasted Gurney!" Bernie sneered. "I wish it had been him you'd clipped tonight! He thinks he's too good!"

"I'd like to get in there with him!" Finn agreed.

"Why not?" Bernie asked, shrugging. "Cat could fix it. Couldn't he, Nick?"

Lessack, staring steadily at Downey, spoke without apparently moving his lips. "Sure. Cat can fix anything."

Finn shrugged, grinning. "*Okay!* I'd like to get in there with that pantywaist."

"You got to fight some others first," Bernie protested. "We could fix it so you could fight Tony Gilman two weeks from tonight. Couldn't we, Nick? After he stops Gilman, a couple of more scraps, then the champ. Anybody got any paper on you, kid? I mean, like this Mullaney?"

"He just works with me." Downey felt shame at what that implied, for whatever he knew about fighting, Jimmy had taught him. "I got no contract with him."

"Good!" Bernie leaned closer. "Listen, come up and have a talk with Cat. Sign up with him, an' you'll be in the dough. Tonight you got maybe a hundred fish. Cat can get you three times that much, easy. He can give you the info on bets, too."

"Sure," Hunter agreed. "You tie up with us, and you'll be set."

"Let's go," Nick said suddenly. "We can drop the kid by his home."

Bernie paid the check and they went outside where there was a big black car, a smooth job. "Get in, kid," Nick said. "Maybe Cat'll give you a heap like this. He give this one to me."

When they left Finn Downey on the corner, the street was dank, dark, and still, and he kicked his heel lonesomely against the curb. He was filled with a vague nostalgia for lights, music, comfort, and warmth, all the fine things he had never known.

Spelvin had money. Bernie and Hunter always had it, too. Finn was not an innocent; he had grown up in the streets, and he knew why Bernie and Hunter had always had money. When they were kids, he had watched them steal packages, flashlights, and watches from parked cars or stores. Twice Bernie had been in jail, yet they had more and better clothes than he'd ever had, and they had cars and money.

Finn's sister, Aline, was waiting up for him.

"Oh, Finn! You were wonderful! The rest of them had to get up early, so they went to bed, but they told me to tell you how good they thought you were!"

"Thanks, honey." He felt for the thin wad of bills. "Here, kid. Here's for a new dress."

"Twenty dollars!" She was ecstatic. "Oh, Finn, thank you!"

"Forget it!" He was pleased, but at the same time he felt sad that it took so little money to make so much difference.

He would give Mom forty for rent and groceries. The other twenty would have to carry him until his next fight. If he fought Gilman, he'd get plenty out of that, and a win would mean a lot.

Yet there was a stirring of doubt. He wasn't so sure that beating the hard-faced young battler would be easy. Yet if Spelvin was handling him, he would see that Finn won. . . .

In the morning, Jimmy Mullaney was waiting for him at the gym. He grinned. "I'm going to get you lined up for another one right away if I can, boy."

"How about getting me Tony Gilman?"

"Gilman?" Jimmy glanced at him quickly. "Kid, you don't want to fight him! He's rugged!"

"Cat Spelvin can get him for me." Finn squirmed as he saw Jimmy's face turn hard and strange.

"So?" Jimmy's voice was like Finn had never heard it before. "He's a sure-thing man, kid. You tie in with him an' you'll never break loose. He's a racketeer."

"I ain't in this game for love!" Downey said recklessly. "I want some money."

"You throwin' me over, kid?" Mullaney's eyes were cold. "You tyin' in with Spelvin?"

"No." The voice that broke in was even, but friendly. "Let's hope he's not."

Finn Downey turned and faced Glen Gurney.

"You again?" he growled.

Gurney thrust out a hand and smiled. "Don't be sore at me. We're all working at this game, and I came down to the gym today on purpose to see you."

"Me? What do you want with me?"

"I thought I might work with you a little, help you out. You've got a future, and a lot of guys helped me, so I thought I'd pass it on."

Downey recognized the honesty in the champion's voice, but flushed at the implied criticism of his fighting ability. "I don't need any help from you," he said flatly. "Go roll your hoop."

"Don't be that way," Gurney protested. "Anything I say, it's coming from respect."

"He don't need your help," drawled another voice behind them.

Gurney and Downey turned swiftly—and saw Cat Spelvin, a short man with a round face and full lips. Beside him were Bernie and the inevitable Nick Lessack.

"We'll take care of Finn," Cat said. "You do like he said, champ. Roll your hoop."

Coolly, Gurney looked Cat over, then glanced at Nick. "They're cutting the rats in larger sizes these days," he said quietly.

"That don't get you no place," Spelvin said. "Finn's our boy. We'll take care of him."

Finn felt his face flush as he looked at the champion. For the first time he was seeing him without resentment and anger. In Gurney was a touch of something he hadn't seen in many men. Maybe that was why he was champion.

"Downey," Gurney said, "you have your own choice to make, of course, but it seems to me

Mullaney has done pretty well by you, and I'm ready to help."

"I promised Spelvin," Downey said.

Gurney turned abruptly and walked away. Jimmy Mullaney swore softly and followed him.

Spelvin smiled at Downey. "We'll get along, kid. You made the smart play. . . . Bernie, is the Gilman fight on?"

"A week from Monday. Finn Downey and Tony Gilman."

"You'll get five hundred bucks for your end," Spelvin said. "You need some dough now?"

"He can use some," Bernie said. "Finn's always broke."

Finn turned resentful eyes on Bernie, but when he walked away there was an advance of a hundred dollars in his pockets.

Then he remembered the expression on Mullaney's face, and the hundred dollars no longer cheered him. And Glen Gurney . . . maybe he had been sincere in wanting to help. What kind of a mess was this anyway?

The arena was crowded when Finn Downey climbed into the ring to meet Tony Gilman. Glancing down into the ringside seats, he saw Mullaney, and beside him was the champ. Not far away, Aline was sitting with Joe, the oldest of the Downey family.

When the bell sounded, he went out fast. He lashed out with a left, and the blond fighter slammed both hands to the body with short, wicked punches.

He clinched, they broke, and Finn moved in, landing a left, then missing a long right.

Gilman walked around him, then moved in fast and low, hitting hard. Downey backed up. His left wasn't finding Gilman like it should, but give him time. One good punch with his right was all he wanted, just one!

Gilman ripped a right to the ribs, then hooked high and hard with a left. Downey backed away, then cut loose with the right. Gilman stepped inside and sneered:

"Where'd you find that punch, kid? In an alley?"

Finn rushed, swinging wildly. He missed, then clipped Gilman with a short left and the blond fighter slowed. Gilman weaved under another left, smashed a wicked right to the heart, then a left and an overhand right to the chin that staggered Downey.

Finn rushed again, and the crowd cheered as he pushed Gilman into the ropes. Smiling coldly at Finn, Gilman stabbed two fast lefts to his face. Finn tasted blood, and rushed again. Tony gave ground, then boxed away in an incredible display of defense, stopping any further punches.

The bell sounded, and Finn walked to his corner. He was disturbed, for he couldn't get started against Gilman. There was a feeling of latent power in the fighter that warned him, and a sense of futility in his own fighting, which was ineffective against Gilman.

The second round was a duplicate of the first, both men moving fast, and Tony giving ground before Downey's rushes, but making Finn miss repeatedly. Three times Finn started the right, but each time it curled helplessly around Gilman's neck.

"You sap!" Gilman sneered in a clinch. "Who told you you could fight?"

He broke, then stabbed a left to Finn's mouth and crossed a solid right that stung. Downey tried to slide under Gilman's left, but it met his face halfway, and he was stopped flat-footed for a right cross that clipped him on the chin.

The third and fourth rounds flitted by, and Downey, tired with continual punching, came up for the fifth despairing. No matter what he tried, Gilman had the answer. Gilman was unmarked, but there was a thin trickle of blood from Finn's eyes at the end of the round, and his lip was swollen.

In the ringside seats he heard a man say, "Downey's winning this," but the words gave him no pleasure, for he knew his punches were not landing solidly and he had taken a wicked pounding.

Gilman moved in fast, and Downey jabbed with a left that landed solidly on Tony's head, much to Finn's surprise. Then he rushed Gilman to the ropes. Coming off the ropes, he clipped Tony again, and the blond fighter staggered and appeared hurt. Boring in, Finn swung his right—and it landed!

Gilman rolled with the punch, then fell against Finn, his body limp. As Downey sprang back, Tony fell to the canvas.

The referee stepped in and counted, but there was no movement from Gilman. He had to be carried to his corner. As Finn lowered him to a stool, Tony said hoarsely:

"I could lick you with one hand!"

Flushing, Finn Downey walked slowly back across the ring, and when the cheering crowd gathered around him, there was no elation in his heart. He saw Gurney looking at him, and turned away.

As he followed Bernie and Norm Hunter toward the dressing room, the crowd was still cheering, but inside him something lay dead and cold. Yet he had glimpsed the faces of Joe and Aline; they were flushed and excited, enthusiastic over his victory.

Bernie grinned at him. "See, kid? It's the smart way that matters. You couldn't lick one side of Gilman by rights, but after Cat fixes 'em, they stay fixed!"

Anger welled up in Downey, but he turned his back on them, getting on his shoes. When he straightened up, they were walking out, headed for the local bar. He stared after them, and felt disgust for them and for himself.

Outside, Aline and Joe were waiting.

"Oh, Finn!" Aline cried. "It was so wonderful! And everyone was saying you weren't anywhere good enough for Tony Gilman! That will show them, won't it?"

"Yeah, yeah!" He took her arm. "Let's go eat, honey."

As he turned away with them, he came face-to-face with Glen Gurney and two girls.

Two girls, but Finn Downey could see but one. She was tall, and slender, and beautiful. His eyes held her, clinging.

Gurney hesitated, then said quietly, "Finn, I'd like you to meet my sister, Pamela. And my fiancée, Mary."

Finn acknowledged the introduction, his eyes barely flitting to Mary. He introduced Joe and Aline to them, then the girl was gone, and Aline was laughing at him.

"Why, Finn! I never saw a girl affect you like that before!"

"Aw, it wasn't her!" he blustered. "I just don't like Gurney. He's too stuck-up!"

"I thought he was nice," Aline protested, "and he's certainly handsome. The champion of the world . . . Do you think you'll be champ someday, Finn?"

"Sure." His eyes narrowed. "After I lick him."

"He's a good man, Finn," Joe said quietly. "He's the hardest man to hit with a right that I ever saw."

The remark irritated Finn, yet he was honest enough to realize he was bothered because of what Glen Gurney had said about his fighting. Yet he could not think of that for long, for he was remembering that tall, willowy girl with the lovely eyes, Pamela Gurney.

And she had to be the champ's sister. The man he would have to defeat for the title!

Moreover, he would probably tell her about tonight, for Finn knew his knockout of Tony Gilman would not fool a fighter of Gurney's skill. The champion would know only too well just what had happened.

Somehow even the money failed to assuage his bitterness and discontent. A small voice within told him Gilman and Bernie were right. He was simply not good enough. If Gilman had not taken a dive, he could never have whipped him, and might have been cut to ribbons.

Then, he remembered that he hadn't hit Gilman

with his right. He had missed, time and again. If he could not hit Gilman, then he could not hit the champ, and the champ was not controlled by Cat Spelvin. Finn had a large picture of himself in the ring with Glen Gurney, and the picture was not flattering.

Spelvin had told him he would be fighting Webb Carter in two weeks, and Webb was a fairly good boy, though not so good as Gilman. The knockout of Gilman had established Finn Downey as a championship possibility. Now a few more knockouts, and Cat could claim a title bout.

At daybreak the next morning, Finn Downey was on the road, taking a two-mile jaunt through the park. He knew what he wanted, and suddenly, as he dogtrotted along, he knew how to get it.

He wanted to be champion of the world. That, of course. He wanted the fame and money that went with it, but now he knew he wanted something else even more, and it was something that all of Cat Spelvin's crookedness could not gain for him—he wanted the respect of the men he fought, and of Jimmy Mullaney, who had been his friend.

He was jogging along, taking it easy, when from up ahead he saw Pamela Gurney. She was riding a tall sorrel horse, and she reined in when she saw him.

"You're out early, aren't you?" she asked.

He stopped, panting a little from the run.

"Getting in shape," he said. "I've got another fight comin' up."

"You did well against Tony Gilman," she said, looking at him thoughtfully.

He glanced up quickly, trying to see if there had been sarcasm in her voice, but if she knew that had been a fixed fight, she showed no sign of it.

"My brother says you could be a great fighter," she added, "if you'd work."

Finn flushed, then he grinned. "I guess I never knew how much there was to learn."

"You don't like Glen, do you?" she asked.

"You don't understand; I have to fight for what I get. Your brother had it handed to him. How can you know what it's like for me?"

Her eyes flashed. "What right have you to say that? My brother earned everything he ever had in this world!"

Suddenly, all the unhappiness in him welled to the surface. "Don't hand me that! Both of you have always had things easy. Nice clothes, cars, money, plenty to eat. Gurney is champ, and how he got it, I don't know, but I've got my own ideas."

Pamela turned her horse deliberately. "You're so very sure of yourself, aren't you?" she said. "So sure you're right, and that you know it all! Well, Mr. Finn Downey, after your fight with Tony Gilman the other night, you haven't any room to talk!"

His face went red. "So? He told you, didn't he? I might have known he would."

"Told me?" Pamela's voice rose. "What kind of fool do you think I am? I've been watching fights since I was able to walk, and you couldn't hit Tony

Gilman with that roundhouse right of yours if he was tied hand and foot!"

She cantered swiftly away. Suddenly rage shook him. He started away, and abruptly his rage evaporated. Pamela was the girl he wanted, the one girl above all others. Yet what right did she have to talk? Glen Gurney certainly was no angel. But burning within him was a fiery resolution to become so good they could never say again what they were saying now. Pamela, Gilman, Bernie. How cheap they must think him!

He recalled the helplessness he had felt against Gilman, and knew that no matter what Glen Gurney thought of him, once in the ring he would get no mercy from the champ. He had begun to realize how much there was to learn and knew that he would never learn, at least while he was being handled by Spelvin.

What he should do was go to see Jimmy Mullaney. But he hated the thought of admitting he was wrong. Besides, Jimmy might not even talk to him, and there was plenty of reason why he should not. Still, if he could learn a little more by the time he fought Carter, he might make a creditable showing.

He found Mullaney in the cheap hotel where he lived. The little man did not smile—just laid his magazine aside.

"Jimmy," Finn said, "I've made a fool of myself!"

Mullaney reached for a cigarette. He looked past the lighted match and said, "That's right. You have." Jimmy took a deep drag. "Well, every man has his own problems to settle, Finn. What's on your mind now?"

"I want you to teach me all you know."

Jimmy stared at him. "Kid, when you were my fighter that was one thing. Now you belong to Cat. You know what he'd do to me? He might even have the boys give me a couple of slugs in the back. He's got money in you now. You think Gilman did that dive for fun? He got paid plenty, son. Because Cat thought it would be worth it to build you up. Not that he won't see Gilman work you over when the time is ripe. Spelvin wants you for a quick killing in the bets."

"Jimmy," Finn said, "suppose you train me on the side? Then suppose I really stop those guys? Then when Spelvin's ready to have me knocked off, suppose I don't knock off so easy?"

Mullaney scowled and swore. "It's risky, kid. He might get wise, then we'd both be in the soup." He grinned. "I'd like to cross that crook, though."

"Jimmy—give it to me straight. Do you think I can be good enough to beat Gurney or Gilman?"

Mullaney rubbed out the cigarette in a saucer. "With hard work and training, you could beat Gilman, especially with him so sure now. He'll never figure you'll improve, because nobody gets better fighting setups. Gurney is a good kid. He's plenty good! He's the slickest boxer the middleweight division has seen since Kid McCoy."

Mullaney paced up and down the room, then nodded. "All right, kid. That brother of yours, he's got a big basement. We'll work with you there, on the sly." He flushed. "You'll have to furnish the dough. I'm broke."

"Sure." Finn pulled out the money from the Gilman fight. "Here's a C. Buy what we'll need, eat on it. I'll cut you in on the next fight."

When he left Mullaney, he felt good. He ran down the steps into the street—and came face-to-face with Bernie Ledsham.

Bernie halted, his eyes narrow with suspicion.

"What you doin' down here? Ain't that where Mullaney lives?"

"Sure is." Finn grinned. "I owed the guy dough. I wanted him paid off. No use lettin' him crab about it."

Ledsham shrugged. "If he gives you any trouble, you just tell me or Cat."

Downey believed Bernie's suspicions were lulled, but he didn't trust the sallow-faced man.

"Come on," he said, "I'll buy a beer!"

They walked down the street to a bar, and Finn had a Pepsi while Bernie drank two beers and they talked. But there was a sullen air of suspicion about the gangster that Finn Downey didn't like. When he could, he got away and returned home. . . .

Downey's knockout over Tony Gilman had made him the talk of the town. Yet Finn knew everyone was waiting to see what he would do against Webb Carter.

Carter had fought Gilman twice, losing both times, and he had lost to Gurney. He had been in the game for ten years and was accepting his orders unhappily, but was needing money.

The bell rang in the crowded arena on the night of the fight. Finn went out fast. Coached by Mullaney, he had worked as never before, shortening his right hand, sharpening his punches, developing a left hook. Yet he showed little of it at first.

Carter met him with a fast left that Finn managed to slip, and smashed both hands to the rock-ribbed body of the older fighter. Carter stiffened a left hook to Finn's face, and Finn threw a wicked left uppercut to the wind. Carter backed away cautiously, studying Finn with new respect, but Downey moved on in, weaving and bobbing to make Carter's left miss. Then Finn feinted and smashed a right to the ribs. In a clinch, he hammered with that right three times, and broke.

He wasted no time, but walked in close, took a chance, and deliberately missed a couple of punches. Carter was making him miss enough, anyway. More than ever, Downey realized how much he had to learn, yet he felt that even the short period he had trained for this fight had improved him.

Mullaney had warned him that he must be careful with Carter. The fighter could punch, and while it was in the bag for him to dive, Carter might slip over a couple of hard ones. A cut eye now would do Finn no good.

The second and third went by swiftly, with Finn working with care. He missed punches, and seemed clumsy, and at times was clumsy, despite his efforts, yet his hard work had done him more good than he had realized.

In the fourth round he came out fast, and Carter moved around him, then led a left. Downey went under it and smashed that right to the ribs again, then followed it into a clinch behind two trip-hammer blows to the wind. Carter looked pale, and he glared at Finn.

"What's the matter, kid? Ain't it enough to win?"

Downey broke before the referee reached them, jabbed a left that caught Carter high on the head, then stepped in, feinting a right to the body and throwing it high and hard. It caught Webb on the cheekbone, and his face went white and his lips looked numb. He went into a clinch.

"You take it easy, kid," he growled, "or I'll lower the boom on you!"

"Anytime you're ready!" Finn snapped back.

Carter jerked free and smashed a right to Downey's head that made his knees wobble. Then he plunged in throwing them with both hands. Sensing a rally, the crowd came to its feet, and Finn, instead of yielding before the storm of blows, walked right into it, swinging with both hands.

Webb stabbed a left to Finn's mouth that made him taste blood, and Finn slid under another left and jammed a right to the heart, then a left to the wind and a right to the ear. He pushed Carter away, took a light punch going in, and smashed both hands to the body, throwing the hooks with his hip behind them.

The fifth round was a slugfest, with the fans on

their chairs screaming themselves hoarse. In the sixth, as Carter came out of his corner, Finn moved in, feinted a left, and smashed a high hard right to the head. This was the round for Carter's dive, but Finn had no intention of letting him take it, and the right made Carter give ground. Finn pressed him back, weaving in under Carter's punches and winging them into the other fighter's body with all the power he had.

He broke clean and backed away, looking Carter over. There was amazed respect in Webb Carter's eyes. Finn circled, then feinted, and Carter threw a right. Downey countered with a lifting right to the solar plexus that stood Carter on his tiptoes, and before Webb realized what had happened, a whistling left hook cracked on his chin and he hit the canvas on his face, out cold!

Finn trotted back to his corner, and Bernie held up his robe, staring at Carter. Finn leaned close.

"Boy!" he whispered. "He made it look good! Better than Gilman! He stuck his chin into that punch and just let go!"

"Yeah," Bernie agreed dolefully. "Yeah, it almost fooled me!"

It was after the end of the fight that Finn Downey saw Pamela Gurney and her brother. They were only a few seats from his corner. Pamela's face was cold, but there was a hard, curious light in Glen's eyes.

Finn didn't show that he noticed them, but he knew that Gurney wasn't fooled. The champ knew that knockout was the McCoy. And it would puzzle him.

Well, let it! The only one Finn was worried about was Cat, but when the gambler came into his dressing room he grinned at Downey.

"Nice going, kid! That was good!"

Evidently, Spelvin knew little about fighting. He didn't know an honest knockout when he saw it.

In the month that followed, Finn spent at least four days a week in the basement gym with Mullaney. They were not training sessions. Finn just listened to Jimmy and practiced punches on the heavy bag. When he went to the regular gym for his workout, he was the same as ever. In ring sessions he worked carefully, never showing too much, but with occasional flashes of form and boxing skill. His right, always a devastating punch, was traveling less distance now, and he was hitting even harder.

In that month he had two fights, and both opponents went into the tank, but not until after a brisk, hard workout. In each fight he knew he could have stopped the man had the fight been on the level.

Now he and Jimmy had a problem, for a return match with Gilman was to be scheduled in a short time.

"They'll figure to get me this time," Finn agreed with Mullaney. "I've been scoring knockouts right and left, and Gilman has only fought once, and looked bad. The boys are saying he's through, so the betting should be at least two to one that I repeat my kayo. Cat will figure to clean up."

The writer of a sports column, a man named Van

Bergen, offered the judgment of most of the sports-writers:

> Tony Gilman is seeking a return match with young Finn Downey, the hard-socking battler who stopped him two months ago. If Gilman is wise he will hang them up while he has all his buttons. In his last two fights, Tony showed that he was through. Formerly a hard-hitting, tough middleweight, Gilman lacked all of the fire and dash that characterized his earlier fights. He may never be his old self again.
>
> Downey continues to come along. After his surprise knockout over Gilman, he went on to stop tough Webb Carter, and since has followed with knockout wins over Danny Ebro and Joey Collins.
>
> If the match is made, Downey should stop Gilman within six rounds.

Cat Spelvin called Downey in on a Tuesday morning. He was all smiles.

"Well, kid, one more fight, then I think we can get Gurney for you. The fans still like Gilman, so we'll feed him to you again. From there on, you walk right into the title."

Finn grinned back at him. "Well, I've got you to thank for it, Cat. If you hadn't helped, I'd probably still be fighting prelims."

Cat lit a cigar. "Just take it easy, kid. Gilman will be a setup for you!"

Bernie and Nick Lessack walked outside with Downey.

"Let's go get a beer," Bernie suggested. "No use killin' yourself workin' for fights that are in the bag."

"Yeah." Secretly, Finn ground his teeth. They thought he was so stupid they weren't even going to try to buy him off.

In his gym workouts, he fooled along. At times, when he worked hard in the ring, he told Bernie or Nick: "I've got to look good here! If the sportswriters thought I was stalling, they might smell something!"

This was reported to Cat and he chuckled. "The kid's right!" he said. "We want him to look good in the gym! The higher the odds, the better!"

In the gym in Joe's basement, Finn worked harder than ever. Then, three days before the battle, he met Pamela again. She was riding the sorrel and started to ride on by, but when he spoke, she stopped.

"Hello, Pam," he said softly.

She looked down at him, his face flushed from running, his dark hair rumpled. He looked hard and capable, yet somehow very young.

"I shouldn't think you'd train so hard," she said coolly. "Your fights don't seem to give you much trouble."

"Maybe they don't," he said, "and maybe they give me more than you think."

"You know," she said, "what you said about Glen's fights was untrue. Everything Glen won, he fought for."

"I know," he admitted. "I took too much for

granted, I guess." He hesitated. "Don't you make the same mistake."

Their eyes held, and it was suddenly hard for her to believe what her brother had said—that Cat Spelvin was framing Finn Downey's fights. He looked too honest.

"If I did take a few the easy way," he said, "you couldn't blame me. My sis never had clothes like yours in her life, but she's goin' to have them, because I'm goin' to see she does—ahh, you wouldn't understand how we feel."

"Wouldn't I?" She smiled at him suddenly. "Finn, I like you. But don't start feeling sorry for yourself or making excuses. Glen never did."

"Glen!" Finn growled. "All I hear is Glen! I'd like to get in there with him sometime! Glen never felt sorry for himself or made excuses! Why should he?"

"Finn Downey," Pamela said quietly, "I hope you never get in the ring with Glen. If you do, he'll give you such a beating as you never saw! But before this goes any further, I want to show you something. Will you go for a ride with me this afternoon?"

He stared at her for a moment.

"No, I won't," he said. He looked away angrily because he was feeling such a strange emotion that something came into his eyes and into his throat when he looked at her. "I won't go for a ride with you because I think about you all the time now. I'm just a boxer from the wrong side of town. If I was to be around you too much it would tear my heart out. You'd never take a guy like me seriously, and I can't see why you should."

Pamela shook her head. "Finn, my brother is a fighter. I've nothing against fighters, it's just the kind of fighters they are. I like fighters that win their fights in the ring, not in some smoke-filled back room with a lot of fat-faced men talking about it." Her face grew grave. "You see, something's going on. I shouldn't mention it to you, but it's some sort of an investigation. It started over your fight with Gilman. One of the sportswriters, Pat Skehan, didn't like it. I don't know much, but if you should be mixed up in it, it will come out."

"So you're warning me. Why?"

"Because I like you. Maybe because I understand how you feel about your sister, about clothes and money and things."

And then, before he could say another word, she had cantered away.

Jimmy Mullaney was in a ringside seat when Finn Downey crawled through the ropes for his return bout with Tony Gilman. Jimmy was where they had planned for him to be. His eyes were roving over the other ringsiders with a curious glint in them. Jimmy had been around for a long time and he knew pretty much what was happening tonight.

Glen Gurney had come in, and with him were his sister, Pamela, Pat Skehan, the sportswriter, and another man. When Jimmy saw him, he began to whistle softly, for the man was Walt McKeon—and in certain quarters his name meant much.

Cat Spelvin and Nick Lessack were there, too. Every few minutes Norm Hunter would come up to

Cat and whisper in his ear. Spelvin would nod thoughtfully, sometimes making a notation on a pad. Jimmy understood that, too.

Two hours before, the odds quoted on the fight had been three to one, with Finn a strong favorite, and thirty minutes before, the odds had fallen, under a series of carefully placed bets, to six to five. Norm Hunter was one of Cat's legmen, and he had been actively placing bets.

Finn felt good. He was in the best shape of his life, but he also knew he was facing the fight of his life. Regardless of the fact that he had been told Gilman was going to take a dive tonight, that had never been Spelvin's plan. Tonight he was going to cash in by betting against Finn Downey. Gilman had never liked taking that dive for him, and he was going to get even if he could by giving Finn a thorough beating. Downey understood that clearly enough. He also knew that Tony Gilman was a fighting fool, a much better fighter than any he had ever faced. Even in that previous match when Tony had been under wraps, he had made a monkey out of Finn most of the way.

Bernie Ledsham leaned on the ropes and grinned at Finn, but the grin was malicious.

"You going to take him, kid?"

Downey grinned back at him. "You can bet your last dime I am!"

The bell sounded suddenly, and Finn went out fast. The very look of Tony Gilman told him what he already knew. Gilman was out to win! Tony lanced a left to the head that jarred Finn to his heels, then crossed a whistling right that Finn slipped by a hair. Finn went in with a left and right to the body.

"All right, you pantywaist," Gilman hissed in his ear. "I'm goin' to tear you apart!"

Downey chuckled and broke free, clipping Gilman with a quick left as they moved together again. Gilman slammed a right to the body and they circled, trading lefts. Gilman rushed, throwing both hands, and the punches hurt. Finn went back to the ropes, but slid away and put a fast left to Gilman's face. He circled, watching Tony.

Gilman was anxious to get him; he was a tough scrapper who liked to fight and who was angry. He ripped into Downey with both hands, landing a hard left to the head, then a jolting right that smashed home twice before Finn could get into a clinch. His mouth felt sore and he could taste blood. Tony shook him off, feinted a left, then hooked with it. The fist clipped Finn flush on the chin, and his knees wobbled.

The crowd broke into cheers, expecting an upset but the bell rang.

Returning to his corner, Finn Downey saw the fat, satisfied smile on Spelvin's face. He dropped on the stool. For the first time he was doubtful. He had known Tony was good, but Gilman was driven by anger now and the desire for revenge, and he was even better than Finn had suspected.

The second round was a brannigan from bell to bell. Both men went out for blood and both got it. Finn took a stabbing left that sent his mouthpiece sailing. The next left cut his lips, then he took a solid right to the head that drove him to the ropes.

He came off them with a lunge and drove a smashing right to Gilman's ribs. Tony wrestled in the clinches and tried to butt, but Finn twisted free, then stepped in with a quick, short hook to the chin that shook Gilman to his heels.

In a clinch in the third round, after a wicked slugfest, Downey whispered to Gilman: "What's the matter? Can't you dish it out any better than that?"

Gilman broke away from him. His blue eyes were ugly now, and his face hard. He moved in behind a straight left that Finn couldn't seem to get away from until he had taken three on his sore mouth. Then he did get inside and drove Gilman back.

He could taste blood and there was the sting of salty sweat in the cuts on his face, and beyond the ropes there was a blur of faces. He ripped into Gilman with a savage two-fisted attack that blasted the older fighter across the ring.

"Thought I was a sap, huh?" he snarled in Gilman's ear. "You win this one, bud, you fight for it!"

Gilman smashed him with a right cross that knocked him back on his heels. Before he could get set, Tony was on him with two wicked hooks, and the first thing he knew he had hit the canvas flat on his back!

He rolled over and got his knees under him, his head buzzing. Beyond the ropes was a vast roar of sound, but there was a roar within his skull also.

At nine he made it to his feet, but he was shaky, and when he tried to bicycle away, Tony was on him with a stiff left, then another, then a right hook.

The terrific punch lifted him up and smashed him to the floor on his shoulder blades. In his skull the roaring had grown to a vast drumming sound. He shook his head to clear it, but the roaring continued. He crawled to his knees, and when he saw the referee's lips shaping nine, he came up with a lunge.

Before him he saw the red gloves of Tony Gilman, saw the punch start. He felt it hit his skull. He tried to catch his balance, knowing that a whistling right hook would follow, and follow it did. He rolled to miss the punch, but it caught him and turned him completely around!

Something caught him across the small of the back and he felt his feet lift up. Then he was lying flat on his face on the apron of the ring, staring through a blue haze at the hairy legs of Tony Gilman. He had been knocked out of the ring!

He grabbed a rope, and half pulled, half fell through the ropes into the ring, then lunged to his feet. He saw Gilman coming, ducked under the punch, then dived across the ring and brought up against the ropes.

Then Gilman was there. Tony's first punch was wild and Finn went under it and grabbed the blond fighter like a drowning man.

Then he was lying back on his stool and Mullaney was working on his eye.

"What round?" he gasped.

"The seventh, coming up!" Mullaney said quickly.

The seventh? But where—? He heard the warning buzzer and was on his feet, moving out toward Gilman.

Tony was disturbed. He had been sure of this fight; however, the clumsy, hard-hitting, but mostly ineffectual fighter he had met before had changed. Gilman was having the fight of his life. What had happened to Bernie Ledsham he didn't know, but Mullaney now was in Finn's corner.

A double cross? Was Spelvin going to cross him this time? Or was it *Spelvin* who was being crossed up?

He circled warily, looking Downey over. This called for some cool, careful boxing. He was going to have to cut Finn up, then knock him out. He would get no place slugging with him. How anything human could have survived that punch that took him out of the ring, he didn't know, to say nothing of the half dozen he had thrown before and after.

Finn, on his part, knew he was going to have to slow Tony down. Gilman was still too experienced for him, and plenty tough. He was beginning to realize how foolish he must have sounded to Glen Gurney when he told the champ how he was going to knock him out. For Gurney had beaten Gilman, and badly.

Gilman circled and stabbed a left. Finn weaved under it and tried to get in close, but Gilman faded away from him, landing two light punches.

Finn crouched lower, watching Tony. Gilman sidestepped quickly to the right and Finn missed again. He circled. Twice he threw his right at Gilman and missed. Tony was wary, however, and did not seem to be inclined to overconfidence.

Downey went under a left, then let a right curl around his neck, and suddenly he let go in a long dive at Gilman! They crashed into the ropes. Gilman whipped free, but Finn smashed a left to the body, whipped a cracking left hook to the chin, and crossed a right to Gilman's head.

Tony broke free and backpedaled, but Finn followed him relentlessly. He landed a left, took a blow, then caught Gilman in a corner.

Tony turned loose both hands; toe to toe, they stood and slugged like wild men while the huge arena became one vast roar of sound.

Finn was watching his chance, watching that left of Gilman's, for he had noticed only a moment before that Gilman, after landing a left jab, sometimes moved quickly to the right.

The left came again—again, and a third time. Gilman fell away to the right—and into a crashing right hook thrown with every ounce of strength in Finn Downey's body!

Gilman came down on his shoulder, rolled over on his face.

At nine, he got up. Finn Downey knew what effort he used to make it, but make it he did. Finn walked in, feinted a right, then whipped a left hook into Gilman's solar plexus and crossed a right on his jaw.

Tony Gilman hit the canvas flat on his face. Downey trotted to his corner. This time, Gilman didn't get up.

Mullaney threw Finn's robe around his shoulders, and he listened to the roar of sound. They were cheering him, for he had won. His eyes sought the ringside seats. Pamela was struggling through the crowd toward him.

When she reached him, she caught his arm and squeezed it hard.

"Oh, Finn, you won! You really won!"

"Nice fight, man!" Gurney said smiling. "You've shortened up that right!"

Finn grinned back. "I had to," he said, "or somebody would have killed me! Thanks for the tip."

"Yeah," Pat Skehan said, "it was a nice fight." He grinned fleetingly, then brushed by.

"Will you take that ride in the morning?" Pamela asked.

"Okay, yeah," Downey said. His head was spinning and the roaring in his ears had not yet died away.

In the dressing room, Mullaney grinned at Finn as he cut the strings on the gloves.

"Pal," he said, "you should have seen Cat! He dropped sixty G's on this fight! And that ain't all! Walt McKeon was here tonight. Walt's an investigator for the state's attorney. He was curious as to why Bernie was in your corner when Bernie works for Cat and Cat owns Gilman's contract. After some discussion, we rectified the situation!"

The morning sun was bright, and Finn leaned back in the convertible as it purred over the smooth paved roads.

He had no idea where he was going, and didn't care. Pamela was driving, and he was content to be with her.

The car turned onto gravel, and he rode with half-closed eyes. When the car came to a halt, he opened them and looked around.

The convertible was in a lane not far from a railroad track. Beyond the track was a row of tumbled-down, long-unpainted shacks. Some housed chickens. In one was a cow.

At several of the houses, the wash hung on the line and poorly clad youngsters played in the dust.

"Where are we?" he demanded.

"In Jersey," Pamela said. "There's a manufacturing town right over there. This is where a lot of mill hands and railroad workers live, many not too long on this side of the water."

Not over fifty yards away was a small house that once had been painted green. The yard was littered with papers, sticks, and ashes.

A path led from the back door into a forest of tall ragweed.

"Let's get out," Pamela said. "I want to walk around." There was an odd look in her eyes.

It was hot and close in the jungle of ragweed. Pamela stepped carefully over the spots of mud. Finn moved carefully; he was still cut and bruised from the fight. The path led to a ditch that was crossed by a dusty plank. On the other side, the ragweed finally gave way to a bare field, littered with rusty tin cans, broken boxes, and barrels.

Pamela walked swiftly across it and into the trees that bordered the far edge. Here the path dipped to a small open space of green grass. A broken diving board hung over what had been a wide pool. Now the water was discolored by oil.

Pam sat down on a log in the shade. "Like it?" she asked curiously.

He shrugged, looking around. "How'd you know all this was here?"

Her smile vanished. "Because I used to live here. I was born in that house back there. So was Glen. Glen built that diving board. In those days, the water was still clean enough to swim in. Then the mill began dumping there and spoiled it. Even after that, I used to come here and sit, just like this. We didn't have much money, and about all we could do was dream. Glen used to tell me what he would do someday. He did it, too. He never went to school much, and all the education he got was from reading. All he could do was fight, so that's how he made it—by fighting. He paid for my education, and helped me get a job."

Finn Downey got up suddenly. "I guess I've been a good deal of a sap," he said humbly. "When I looked at you and at Glen, I figured you had to be born that way. I guess I was mighty wrong, Pam."

Pamela got up and caught his hand. "Come on! Let's go back to the car. There's a drugstore in town where we used to get cherry sodas. Let's go see if it's still open!"

They made their way back across the polluted ditch and through the overgrown lot. The convertible left a haze of dust on the road for some minutes after it departed.

Far off there was the sound of a ball bouncing,

then a pause and the sound of a backboard vibrating and the *whiff* as the ball dropped through the net. A gangly youngster dribbled down an imaginary court and turned to make another shot.

The crowd went wild.

THE HAND
OF KUAN-YIN

There was no sound but that of the sea whispering on the sand and the far-off cry of a lonely gull. The slim black trunks of the sentinel palms leaned in a broken rank above the beach's white sand, now gray in the vague light. It was the hour before dawn.

Tom Gavagan knelt as Lieutenant Art Roberts turned the body over. It was Teo.

"It doesn't make sense," Roberts said impatiently. "Who would want to kill *him*?"

Gavagan looked down at the old man and the loneliness of death was upon him, and a sadness for this old man, one of the last of his kind. Teo was a Hawaiian of old blood, the blood of the men who had come out of the far distances of the Pacific to colonize these remote islands before the dawn of history.

Now he was dead, and the bullet in his back

indicated the manner of his going. Seventy-five years of sailing the great broken seas in all manner of small craft had come to this, a bullet in the back on the damp sand in this bleak hour before daybreak. And the only clue was the figure beside him, that of a god alien to Hawaii.

"It's all we have," Roberts said, "unless the bullet gives us something."

The figure was not over fifteen inches in height, and carved from that ancient ivory that comes down to China from the islands off Siberia. The image was that of Kuan-yin, the Chinese goddess of mercy, protector of shipwrecked sailors, and bringer of children to childless women. It lay upon the sand near Teo's outstretched fingers, its deep beige ivory only a shade lighter than the Hawaiian's skin.

Wind stirred the dry fronds of the palms, whispering in broken sentences. Somewhere down the coast a heavier sea broke among the rocks.

"What would he want with a Kuan-yin?" Roberts was puzzled. "And where did he get it?"

Gavagan got to his feet and brushed the sand from his hands. He was a tall man with a keen, thoughtful face.

"You answer that question," Gavagan said, "and you'll be very close to the man who killed him."

Roberts indicated the Kuan-yin. "What about that? Anything special?"

"The light isn't good," Gavagan said, "but my guess is you'll find nothing like it outside a museum." He studied the figure in the better light from Roberts's flash. "My guess is that it was made during the T'ang dynasty. See how the robe falls? And the pose of the body? It is a superb piece."

Roberts looked up at him. "I figured it was something special, and that's why I called you. You would know if anybody would."

"Anytime . . ." He was thinking that Teo had called and left a message with his service just two days ago. Odd, not because they had spoken only rarely in recent years, but because Teo had never liked using the telephone. He was a man at home with the sea and the winds and not comfortable or trusting around modern conveniences. Gavagan had intended to stop by and see the old man the night before but had gone to a luau up in Nanakuli instead.

Gavagan indicated the statue. "After you've checked that for prints, I'd like another look at it. You may have stumbled into something very big here."

"Like what?" Roberts pushed him. "Teo was just an old fisherman. We both knew him. Tell me what you're thinking."

"I don't know, but it's a rare piece, whatever it's doing here . . . no doubt it's why he was killed."

A car from the police lab had drawn up on the highway skirting the beach, and Tom Gavagan walked back to his convertible. In the eastern sky the clouds were blushing with a faint rose, and Gavagan sat still in his car, watching the color change, thinking.

To most things there was a semblance of order, but here everything was out of context. What would an old fisherman like Teo be doing in the middle of the night on a lonely beach far from his home? And with a museum-quality ivory statue, of all things?

Roberts had said little, for he was not a talkative man when working on a case, but Gavagan had noticed there was scarcely any blood upon the sand. The bullet wound must have occurred somewhere else, and Teo had evidently staggered out upon the beach and died.

If so, why had he gone to that beach? And why would anyone shoot an old fisherman who was without enemies?

The only answer to that must be that Teo had something somebody wanted.

The Kuan-yin?

It was a valuable piece, a very valuable piece, but not many people would be in a position to know that. Kuan-yin figures, inexpensive ones, could be picked up in almost any curio store, and only an expert or someone with a rare appreciation for art would know this was something special.

It was a starting point, at least, for no one in the islands owned such a piece or Tom Gavagan would have known of it. Most of the islanders knew of his interest in art, and from time to time he had been asked to view almost every collection in Hawaii, sometimes to evaluate a piece for the owner, sometimes merely to share the pleasure in something beautiful.

Tom Gavagan was a curious man. He also was more than casually interested. His first voyage on deep water had been in old Teo's ancient schooner, the *Manoa,* and much of his own knowledge of the sea had been acquired from Teo aboard that vessel.

Gavagan had grown up with Teo's three sons, one lost at Pearl Harbor, a second at Iwo Jima. Kamaki was the only one left, the last of his family now, for Kamaki had no children.

The sun was a blast of flame on the horizon when Gavagan reached the deck of the *Manoa*. For a minute or two he stood very still, looking around.

There was no sound but the lazy lap of water against the hull, yet he felt uncomfortable, and somehow wary. Teo had lived on his boat, and for years had moored it at this abandoned pier down the shore from the village. Gavagan stood listening to a car go by on the highway a quarter of a mile away, and then he walked forward, his footsteps echoing on the deck. Suddenly, he paused. On the deck at his feet lay some splinters of wood.

He had seen such wood before. It was aged and had a faint greenish tinge. Squatting on his heels, he felt of the fragments. They still seemed faintly damp. These might be slivers from the pilings of the old pier, although there was no reason for their presence here.

Or they might be wood brought up from the bottom of the sea. They looked as wood does when it has been immersed in salt water for a long time.

He dropped the fragments and walked to the companionway. Hesitating there, he looked down into the darkness below, and then once more he looked around.

There was no one in sight. At the village a half mile away, there seemed to be some movement, and across the deep water a fishing boat was putt-putting out to sea. The mooring lines creaked lone-somely, and Gavagan put a foot down the ladder, then descended sideways because of the narrow-ness.

The small cabin was empty, but nothing seemed unusual unless it was a pulled-out drawer. He started to go on into the cabin, then stopped.

There were indications here that the *Manoa* had recently been out to sea. There were coiled ropes against the wall, not a place that Teo would store such things but, perhaps, a place he might put them while reorganizing his gear. Sacks of food lay in the galley, opened; rice, salt, both partly used. In the forward locker Teo's ancient copper helmet and diving dress lay crumpled, still wet where the rub-berized fabric had folded. Kamaki was not around and there seemed no indication of why Teo had placed the call.

Somewhere within the schooner or against the outside hull, there was a faint bump. His scalp prickled. . . .

Turning swiftly to climb the ladder, he glimpsed something on the deck to the left of and slightly be-hind the ladder. He picked it up, startled and unbe-lieving. It was a bronze wine vessel in the form of an owl or a parrot, and covered with the patina of time. He had seen one like it in the Victoria and Albert Museum; behind it there was another one. It was . . . the hatch darkened and when he looked up, Al Ribera was standing up there, looking down.

"Hello, Gavagan. Looking for something?"

There had never been anything but active dislike

between them. Al Ribera had been a private detective in San Francisco and Honolulu until he lost his license first in one place, then the other. He was an unsavory character, and it was rumored that he was a dangerous man. Tom Gavagan did not doubt it for a minute.

"I was looking for Kamaki."

"Kamaki?"

"Old Teo's son. I came to tell him about his father."

Al Ribera's face was only mildly curious. "Something wrong?"

"He's dead . . . murdered."

"Tough." Ribera glanced around. "Son? I didn't know he had a son. Friend of mine over from the coast wanted to charter a schooner for some deep-sea fishing."

"Teo doesn't charter . . . didn't charter, I mean."

Ribera shrugged. "My friend wanted a Hawaiian. You know how these mainlanders are."

Gavagan thought swiftly. Not for a minute did he believe Ribera's story. There were too many dressed-up charter boats around Honolulu, boats that would appeal to a tourist much more than this battered schooner of Teo's.

Gavagan went up the ladder, and Ribera reluctantly stepped aside, glancing down the ladder as he did so. It was obvious to Gavagan that Ribera very much wanted to get below and look around.

"Where were you last night?" Gavagan asked.

Ribera's features chilled, and he measured Gavagan

with cold, hard little eyes. "Are you kiddin'? What's it to you?"

"Teo was a friend of mine and Art Roberts grew up with Teo's boys, like I did."

"What's that got to do with me? If it makes any difference," he added, "I was with a doll last night."

Taking a cigarette from a pack, Ribera put it between his lips, then struck a match. He was stalling, not wanting to leave.

Gavagan leaned back against the deckhouse. "Hope Kamaki gets back soon. I've got to be back at the Royal Hawaiian to meet a guy in a couple of hours."

"I think I'll go below and have a look around." Al Ribera threw his cigarette over the side.

"No."

"What?" Ribera turned on him, angrily. "Who's telling who around here?"

"I'm telling you." Gavagan studied the man coolly. "The police want nothing disturbed . . . especially"—he glanced over—"the bronze owl."

Al Ribera stiffened sharply, then slowly let his muscles relax, but Gavagan knew he had touched a nerve. "Who's interested in owls? I don't get it."

"A lot of people are going to be interested," Gavagan explained, "especially when a man who has fished all his life suddenly turns up with a bronze owl of the Chou dynasty which any museum would cheerfully pay thousands of dollars for."

Al Ribera spread his legs slightly and lit another cigarette. He showed no inclination to leave, and

Gavagan began to grasp the idea that somehow Ribera intended to get below before he left the schooner, even if it meant trouble. There was something here he wished to cover up, to obtain, or to find out.

"That owl," Gavagan said, "is a particularly fine specimen of Chinese bronze. I'd like to own it myself."

"You're welcome to it, whatever it is. I'll not say anything."

"Somewhere," Gavagan suggested, "Teo came upon several valuable pieces of art. There's nothing like any of this in the islands, and pieces like this can't very well be stolen. Or if they were stolen the thief would get nowhere near the real value from them . . . they're known pieces."

Ribera's hard eyes fastened on Gavagan. "I expect," he said slowly, "from what you say there aren't many people in the islands who would know these pieces for what they are. Am I right?"

"Maybe two . . . there might be a half dozen, but I doubt it."

"You're wasting time." Gavagan stood up. "The *Manoa* isn't for charter."

Ribera turned angrily and started for the gangway, but at the rail he paused. "Suppose I decided to go below anyway?"

"I'd stop you." Gavagan was smiling. "What else?"

Ribera threw his cigarette into the water. "All right," he said, more mildly, "another time, another place."

The big man walked to his car, and when he started off, the wheels dug into the gravel, scattering it behind him like a volley.

He got back to the gallery around five. It was a dim, tunnel-like shop that displayed African and Oceanic art by appointment only. A long canoe with outriggers hung from the ceiling, primitive drums, carved life-sized human forms, and cases of stone idols lined the walls. He snapped on the light over his desk and called his service.

He had waited several hours for Kamaki to show up, but there was no sign of him. The bronze owl he had given a quick once-over and it was as fine a piece as the Kuan-yin. He hesitated to call Roberts about this new find and the fact that Ribera had been by until he had spoken with Kamaki . . . something was up and he had no intention of getting his old friend in trouble. Finally, he'd walked down to the village and asked a couple of people to tell Kamaki to call if they saw him. He also asked them to keep an eye on the boat, suggesting that they might call the police if they saw anyone lurking about.

There were two messages: Art Roberts wanting to know if he'd had any further thoughts and a woman named Laurie Haven. She'd been by the shop, got the phone number off the door, and would be waiting until six at a place down the street called Ryan's.

. . .

The girl at the table was no one he had ever known, and not one he would have forgotten. She was beautiful, and she dressed with a quiet smartness that spoke of both breeding and wealth. He walked to her table and seated himself. "I'm Tom Gavagan," he said.

Her eyes, in this light at least, were dark blue, and her hair was brown. "I am Laurie Haven. I wanted to know if you had any information regarding the Madox collection."

"Those were some fabulous pieces." He was surprised and immediately cautious. Madox had once had a superb collection of Chinese art. *Once,* however, was the operative word. Both the man and his artifacts had disappeared. "A man who would take such a collection to sea was a fool," Gavagan said.

"Not at all." Laurie's eyes measured him coolly. "My uncle was an eccentric man, but he was also a good sailor."

"My apologies," Gavagan said. "That was insensitive."

"He's been missing four years. And there are probably many that share your opinion . . . all of which is beside the point." She opened her purse and took from it a ring, a dragon ring made of heavy gold and jade. "Have you ever seen that before?"

Tom Gavagan fought to keep the excitement from his voice. "Then this was not in the collection when it was lost? It is the Han ring, of course."

"It *was* lost."

Somehow this was beginning to make sense. The

Kuan-yin, the bronze owl, and now this. "So how—?"

"I bought the ring, Mr. Gavagan, two days ago in Pearl. I bought it for sixty dollars from a man who believed he was cheating me."

Gavagan turned the heavy ring in his fingers. If this ring had been in the collection when lost, yet had turned up for sale in Pearl Harbor, it meant that either all of the artifacts had not been lost, or all of them had been stolen.

From the moment he had seen the bronze owl, he had begun to grasp at the edges of an explanation. He had been sure he had heard of that owl, yet there could have been more than one . . . there could have been many. Still . . .

"Why did you come to me?"

"Because I believe you can help me. You know the people who understand such things, Mr. Gavagan, and I do not believe my uncle's collection was stolen before he was lost at sea."

"Come along," he told her, "we're going to see a man about an owl."

All was dark and still when the car drew up alongside the old pier where the *Manoa* was moored. There was no light on the schooner, looming black and silent upon the dark water. "I hope he's aboard," Gavagan said, "or in the village. Anyway, there's something here I want you to see. You should stay in the car, though, there've been some rough characters about."

At the plank, he hesitated. There was a faint stirring aboard the schooner. Swiftly, Gavagan went up the gangway. As his feet touched the deck, a man loomed suddenly before him.

"Kamaki?" It was too tall to be Kamaki. Gavagan heard a shoe scrape as the man shifted his feet to strike.

Gavagan lunged forward, stepping inside the punch and butting the man with his shoulder. The man staggered and started to fall, but Gavagan caught him with a roundhouse right that barely connected.

The hatch opened suddenly and Al Ribera stood framed in the light holding a pistol. "All right, Gavagan. Hold it now."

Tom Gavagan stood very still. The man he had knocked down was getting up, trying to shake the grogginess out of his head. Realization suddenly dawned on the man and he cocked himself for a swing.

"Stop it!" Ribera said harshly. "Don't be a damned fool. He can help, if he wants to live. The guy's an expert in this stuff."

Gavagan measured the distance to Ribera, but before he could move, the man he had hit was behind him and he had no chance. Ribera stepped aside, and Gavagan was shoved toward the ladder.

There had been no sound from Laurie Haven, and suddenly he realized they thought the car to be empty.

Kamaki was lying on the deck with his hands tied behind him. As Gavagan reached the bottom of the ladder, the Hawaiian succeeded in sitting erect.

Al Ribera came down the steps. There was another man, a Chinese with a scarred face whom Gavagan recalled having seen about town.

Three of them, then . . . and Ribera had a gun.

Kamaki had blood on his face from a split in his scalp and there was a welt on his cheekbone. The stocky Chinese had a blackjack in his fist. Gavagan was bound, hands behind his back, ankles tight together.

"What's the matter, Al?" Gavagan asked. "Did your perfect crime go haywire?"

Ribera was not disturbed. "*Crime?* It's a salvage job. The skipper just wouldn't cooperate with his new partners. You ever been down in a helmet and dress?"

"The word is out, Ribera, those pieces are known. They know where they came from and, soon enough, they'll know who you are."

"There's nothing to connect us with this! And for your information, when we get the rest of this stuff up we're not coming back. We took on enough provisions tonight to get to San Francisco."

"What about the ring?"

Ribera's head turned slowly. "What ring?"

"The jade and gold ring from the collection. Somebody peddled it."

Ribera stared hard at Gavagan, trying to decide whether this was a trick, yet as he stared, Gavagan could almost see his mind working. There was enough larceny in Ribera that he would be quick to suspect it of another.

Ribera turned to look at the big man Gavagan

had fought with on the deck. The man's eyes shifted quickly, but he tried to appear unconcerned.

"Nielson, did you—?"

"Aw, he's lyin'!" Nielson declared. "There ain't no ring I know of."

Ribera's eyes were ugly. "Yes, there was. By the lord Harry, one of you is lyin', and I'll skin the . . ." He stopped and motioned his men out of the cabin. "Come on, let's take this on deck."

They locked the door to the cabin, and Gavagan could hear footsteps on the ladder. "What's going on here, Kamaki?"

"Sounds like you know more than I do. . . . Pops found this wreck, we brought some stuff up. He called you and was asking around about the sunken boat when Ribera showed up. He knew all about what we'd found and wanted to cut himself in. When we said no, they took over. They were going to force us to go back out. They let me go with the Chinese guy to get supplies. I guess that's when Pops escaped." He was quiet for a moment then. "Almost escaped," he said.

"He had the Kuan-yin with him when he died," Gavagan said.

Kamaki shook his head, tears showed in his eyes. "He wanted to give it to my wife . . . to help us have kids. Can you believe that? He has a chance to get away but he takes the time to steal a hunk of ivory because he thinks it might help her. He got shot and he still carried it down the beach with him. . . ." There was no sound for a moment but Kamaki quietly crying.

Then the Hawaiian took a long slow breath. "They are getting ready to cast off," he said.

"What!"

"The tide is turning, they're going to take the *Manoa* out."

Tom Gavagan heard feet moving on the deck, lines being let out, the slap of filling canvas. "Can these guys sail?" he asked.

"Yeah. The Swede and the Chinaman . . . the Chinaman can dive, too."

Soon enough they could feel the roll of the deep ocean, and Gavagan inched his way over to where Kamaki was tied.

"Let's figure a way to get loose. I don't fancy being tied up and I don't fancy going down in a helmet and dress with these guys running my lines."

"They took all the knives when they tied me up . . . even the one on the weight belt of the diving dress," Kamaki said.

"What about that?" Gavagan jerked his head at a long nail driven into the crosspiece just above the door. It was at least six inches long but had been driven into the wood only about an inch. "If we could get it out I think I could use it to get the knots untied."

"Yeah?" Kamaki suddenly grinned. "Watch me."

He wormed his way over to the bulkhead and maneuvered himself so that he was on his back with his legs extending up the wall. He arched his back until his weight was on his shoulders and his heels scooted almost a foot higher, closer to the nail. But the boat was rolling constantly now, and no sooner had he tried to hook the ropes binding his legs over the nail than the deck heeled over and he fell, his heels hitting the deck with a thud.

"Help me." Kamaki squirmed back into position. Gavagan soon got the idea. He got to his feet and, leaning against the bulkhead, blocked Kamaki's legs from sliding to the right. A locker blocked them from going too far left. Kamaki hunched, his powerful torso straining. Hunched again . . . he slipped one of the ropes binding his feet over the nail. Then he tightened his stomach muscles and fearlessly hung all of his two hundred and twenty pounds from the nail.

There was a moment where nothing happened. Then the *Manoa* listed, Kamaki's weight shifted, and with a groan the nail pulled free from the wood. Kamaki crashed to the deck.

"You okay?" Gavagan whispered.

"I'll pay for that later. I think they heard us." Kamaki tried to get back to where he had been as footsteps crossed the decking above them.

"Get down!" Kamaki demanded. But Tom Gavagan shook his head.

Al Ribera opened the hatch and came partway down the companionway, gun drawn. He saw Gavagan standing unsteadily at the bottom of the steps.

"You tryin' something?"

"Cut us loose!" Gavagan demanded.

Ribera laughed. "No chance." He leaned out and gave Gavagan a shove. Gavagan tottered on bound feet and fell to the deck. "That'll teach you to stay sitting down," Ribera smirked, and closed the hatch behind him. He never saw, or didn't pay attention to, the six-inch nail lying at Gavagan's feet.

Kamaki grunted. "You are one cool customer, Tom."

It took ten minutes of finger-numbing work for Gavagan to loosen the knots on Kamaki's wrists. Less than a minute later they were free. Free but still locked in the cabin. Kamaki went to the small table protruding from one side of the locker. He pulled up on it and removed the single leg underneath. The table hinged up and fastened against the locker. They now had a weapon.

Some sort of diversion was in order, but before they could discuss what to do there came more sounds of feet on the deck over their heads and then the sound, far off but approaching rapidly, of powerful engines. There was the crackle and squawk of a bullhorn announcing words that sent relief flooding through Tom Gavagan.

"This is the United States Coast Guard! Drop your sails and heave to!"

There was no change in the motion of the *Manoa*. Suddenly the hatch was thrown open. Before Kamaki could set himself there were footsteps on the stairs and Ribera appeared, gun in hand.

"Got loose, did you? Well, tough. Get out on deck, we need hostages."

Suddenly Kamaki swung the table leg. It hit Ribera's forearm and the gun went off into the deck. Gavagan rushed him, getting inside and hitting him with a right to the jaw. The man staggered back and Gavagan wrenched the gun away. The Swede stepped into the hatch, and Gavagan pointed the gun at him and forced him back onto the deck.

They were at sea and the *Manoa* had fallen away from the wind; she was pitching erratically in the troughs of the waves. Off to the port side a powerful searchlight cut through the night. Silhouetted behind it a Coast Guard cutter stood ready, the barrel of a machine gun picking up the edge of the beam.

Kamaki dragged Ribera, none too gently, up onto the deck, and Gavagan collected the Chinese. They waited as a boat from the cutter pulled up alongside. The third man off the boat after a Coast Guard lieutenant and an ensign was Art Roberts. The fourth person out of the boat was Laurie Haven.

"Well, Tom," said Roberts, "imagine meeting you here."

"Where are we?" Gavagan located a faint glow in the sky that must be the beginnings of dawn. "And how did you get here?"

"The middle of the ocean, it seems. It looked like you were heading for Molokini Island." Roberts had a faint smile on his face.

Laurie spoke up. "I took your car and went for the police as soon as the boat left the dock."

"With a little help from Lieutenant Cargill we caught you on radar," Roberts told him.

"Here." Tom Gavagan handed the policeman Ribera's pistol. "I think the chances are pretty good that ballistics will prove this is the gun that shot Teo."

He took the pistol, produced an evidence bag, and dropped it in. "You will all have to come in to headquarters, there are a lot of questions that need answering. A Coast Guard crew will bring this boat back to port."

The sky was just going from gray to blue and the lights of the island were appearing in the distance when Tom Gavagan found Laurie Haven on the deck of the cutter.

"I haven't really thanked you for saving us," he said.

"I haven't thanked you for finding where my uncle's ring came from. It's a relief just to know what ultimately happened to him. We all wondered for so long."

"With luck, Kamaki can recover much more from the wreck."

"I should pay you something. . . . I never dreamed I'd get such fast results."

"No need. But if you want to sell any of the Madox collection, I'd be honored to handle it for you." He glanced at her appraisingly. "There is a favor you could do for me . . . when the police are finished with it I would like it if you gave that Kuan-yin to Kamaki as a partial payment for recovering your uncle's collection."

Laurie looked puzzled. "I could do that, but why?"

"His father wanted him to have it, and I think his wife would appreciate it, too . . . enough said?"

Laurie smiled and leaned into the wind as the cutter rounded the breakwater and turned into the harbor.

RED BUTTE
SHOWDOWN

Gunthorp was walking up from the spring with two wooden buckets filled with water when he saw the boy. He was no more than thirteen, and he was running as fast as he could, his breath coming in gasps. "Hold it, son," Gunthorp called out. "What's wrong?"

The boy skidded to a halt, his eyes wide and staring, shrinking back in such fear that it chilled Gunthorp.

"They're after me!" he panted. "Kelman's men."

"What do they want?"

"They caught me and beat me—" He twisted his arm to show Gunthorp an ugly black bruise. The boy's shirt was torn and his back lacerated. Gunthorp's eyes narrowed and he felt his scalp tighten.

"Come on up to the house," he said. "We'll fix that back."

"I can't." The boy was almost beside himself with terror. "They'll catch me! Kelman's with them."

"Forget them. You come with me. No use you running off. Where would you go?" Gunthorp waved a hand at the burnt red ridges. "Nothing out there but desert. No water, nothing. You stay with me, let me handle Kelman."

He led the way to the log house and pushed open the door. A fire was burning brightly on the hearth, and the smell of coffee was in the air. "Basin's over there, son. You better get that shirt off and wash a little. I'll wash that back of yours myself, then I'll fix it up."

There was the hard pound of hoofs and the boy started as if stung. Tears of sheer terror started to his eyes, and Gunthorp looked at him with a sort of horror. He had never seen anything human so frightened.

He picked up a double-barreled shotgun and placed it beside the door. Then he opened the door and stood there, his hand on the shotgun.

The riders reined in abruptly when they saw him. The nearest was a big, powerfully built man with a clean-shaven face, and as he spoke he swung his horse broadside to the house.

"Did you see a boy running by? Just a kid?"

"He didn't run by. He's here."

"Good! You've saved us some trouble, man. We've had a time running down the little thief. Joe, you go in and bring him out."

"Joe can stay right where he is," Gunthorp said. "The kid came here, and here he stays."

Kelman's eyes were level and cold. It was not yet too dark for Gunthorp to see that expression and read it. This man was cruel. He was also a killer, and he was not used to being stopped in anything he did.

"You'd better give me that boy without trouble, my man. You're new here. When you've been around longer, you'll understand better."

"I've been around long enough. You swing your horses around and get out of here."

Kelman's temper flared. "Joe! Get that kid!"

"Joe stays where he is unless he wants a skinful of buckshot." Gunthorp lifted the shotgun with a smooth, flowing movement. "If he moves, I'll kill him with the first shot and you with the second."

Kelman's face was like a fiend's. His nostrils flared, his jaw jutted, and the anger that danced in his eyes was wicked. "You—you—fool! I'll kill you for this! I'll burn this shack over your head! I'll—"

"Get out."

Gunthorp did not raise his voice. His bleak eyes shifted from face to face. "Get out! You come around here again and I'll do my own killing. Your blood runs as free as this boy's. Maybe a good whipping is what you need."

Joe's face was white. "He means it, boss. We'd better haul our freight."

"That's good advice. You ride out, Kelman, or those men of yours can take you back lashed over a saddle. I'm not particular which. Any man who'll beat a kid like that doesn't deserve to live!"

Joe was stirred by none of Kelman's rage, and he was sure that Gunthorp would shoot. He turned his horse toward the gate, and the others moved after him. For an instant longer, Kelman stared at Gunthorp. Then, suddenly, the fury seemed to leave him.

"For you, my friend, I'll make some special plans!" he promised.

With a wicked jerk, he whipped his horse's head around and drove in the spurs. The horse literally sprang from a standing start into a dead run and charged by the other three riders at breakneck speed.

Gunthorp watched for a moment longer, then spat. Calmly, he put the gun down and closed the door. Then he looked over at the boy. "You'd better take your shirt off, son. We'll see if we can't fix that back up."

He was not a tall man, reaching just a hair over five feet nine inches, but Gunthorp was massively muscled and heavy. He walked with a rolling gait that oddly suited his build. His face was a square-jawed, mahogany-tinted combination of strength and humor atop a thick neck that descended into his powerful shoulders. As he bathed the boy's back he said, "He called you a thief. Did you steal anything, boy?"

"No, sir. Not anything of his. It was somethin' that belonged to Pop. A pocketbook."

"Money in it?"

"Only a little. I wanted some papers."

"Your father's wallet, eh?" Gunthorp dipped the cloth in the warm water again, squeezed part of the water out, and started on another cut. "Where's your father, boy?"

"He's dead—killed in a mine."

"Sorry. Was it a cave-in?"

"Yes, sir. Kelman came and said he was my guardian, and that I must do as he said. He had Pop's wallet, which he got from the drawer where Pop always left it when he went to work in the tunnel."

"Why'd he beat you?" Gunthorp looked searchingly at the boy, who was slipping into a clean shirt that belonged to Gunthorp and looked about a dozen sizes too big.

"He wanted me to tell him where Pop hid some papers he couldn't find, and he wanted me to ask the judge to have him left in charge of my father's place."

"And you wouldn't tell?"

"No, sir."

Gunthorp nodded, admiration in his eyes. "You've got grit, boy. You've a lot of grit. Don't tell anybody else about those papers for now. Do you know what's in them? What's the value?"

"I—I don't know. Only, Pop told me they were very important and I must keep them. He said that somebody might try to get them from me, but they were all he could leave to my sister and me if anything happened."

"So you have a sister? Where is she?"

"Out in California. She's going to school but I think she's coming back soon. I wrote her when Father was killed, and she said she was coming home."

"That's good." Gunthorp started putting dishes and food on the table.

While they were eating, he looked across the table at the boy. His nose was flat, and there was a scar on his upper lip. "Kelman's after something your father owned? You don't know what it could be?"

"No, sir. Unless it's the mine. It was a good mine, I think, but Pop never got much out of it. He owned a lot of land in the valley."

"That desert land? What did he want with that?"

"I don't know, sir. I think Kelman knows, though."

Gunthorp nodded. "What makes you believe so?"

"He told Pop once that he knew. I heard him say something like 'Pretty smart, aren't you, Stevens? But I've got it figured out. Are you taking me in?' It was something like that . . . pretty close, anyway."

"Hm. Interesting. It gives me a clue, boy. Stevens your name then? And the first one?"

"Lane, sir. My name is Lane Stevens."

"It's a good name. You've been well brought up, too, I can see that." Gunthorp looked up over his coffee cup. "Where's your mother, son?"

"She's dead, sir. A long time ago. I don't remember her very well."

"More credit to your father, then. Have you been to school?"

"A little, and my father taught me some, too. He taught me to read, sign, and to know the different minerals, and how to shoot a rifle and use a single jack."

"A wise man, your father." Gunthorp was listening as he spoke. "A man who knows how to teach a boy practical things. Still, they are of little account unless one knows what lies behind them. The thoughts behind things, and the reasons for them . . . that's important, too."

He got up. "Finish your supper, boy. The sheriff will be here in a few minutes for you."

Lane started up. "The sheriff?"

"Sit still. There's no reason for excitement. Let the man come. He's an unlikely man, not sure of himself, and he will come because Kelman will urge him. Tonight we can, I hope, talk him out of it. Tomorrow may be another thing."

The sound of horses on the hard-packed earth of the yard made him nod. "Of course. Now put the light out, boy, and stand away from the door. I've no trust for the look in that Kelman's eye."

"Hallo, the house!"

Gunthorp opened the door. "How are you, Sheriff Eagan. Ah, I see you've brought Kelman with you. Are you taking him under arrest then? Do want me for a witness?"

"Arrest?" Eagan was confused. "Why should I arrest him?"

"For beating the lad, for beating him until there's cuts a finger deep on his back. If you want, I'll come to town and swear out a warrant for him myself."

"Forget that and get on with it, Eagan!" Kelman snapped roughly.

Gunthorp stood in the door, his big hands on his hips, his enormous shoulders and chest seeming to fill the door. He smiled.

"Now, now, Kelman," he said mildly. "Let's not be ordering the sheriff around. Mr. Eagan knows his duties, and it isn't any citizen's place to order him about. You don't take orders from Kelman, do you, Sheriff?"

"Certainly not!" Eagan blustered. "Now enough of that. I've come for the boy. He's a thief, and I'm arresting him."

"A thief? What did he steal? A wallet, wasn't it? And the wallet belonged to his father. He is his father's heir, or one of them. You can't arrest this boy for stealing. I'm sure it wouldn't hold up."

Eagan turned toward Kelman, uneasily. "You didn't tell me the wallet belonged to Stevens," he protested.

"That's neither here nor there!" Kelman's rage was mastering him again. "Take the boy and let's go. If that blundering fool wants to try to stop us, I'll handle him!"

"Stop you?" Gunthorp smiled. "I'd never think of it, Sheriff. I've a great respect for the law and officers of the law. The boy was taken to Kelman's ranch where he was beaten to make him tell where some papers were. The boy escaped, and in escaping, took his father's wallet to which he certainly had more right than Kelman. No, Sheriff, the boy is better off here." He smiled again. "When he is needed for any court appearance, I shall gladly answer for him."

"We want him, and we want him now," Kelman flared.

Gunthorp nodded. "I'm afraid you are mistaking yourself for some sort of official, Kelman. Mr.

Eagan is his own man and he can do his own thinking. If he can't . . . well, we'll see who gets the votes in the next election."

Eagan shifted uncomfortably in his saddle. Secretly, he was afraid of Kelman, but he resented the man's arrogant manner and the ordering about he constantly took from him. The way Gunthorp was putting it, Eagan would practically prove he was crawling to Kelman's orders if he took the boy.

Gunthorp comprehended something of what was in the sheriff's mind, so he offered him an easy way out. "Anyway," he added, "Sheriff Eagan is a man who knows the law. I'm not saying the boy is here, but he can't search my house without a warrant."

Eagan clutched at the opportunity. "That's right, Kelman," he said, "I'd have to have a warrant for the boy to go into that house and search for him."

"Warrant, blazes!" Kelman exploded with rage. He flung himself toward the house. "Get away from the door!" he roared at Gunthorp.

Gunthorp did not move, but with his eyes on Kelman, he said to the sheriff, "Eagan, if he comes at me, I'll defend myself."

Before Eagan could speak, Kelman's hand swept back for a gun, and at the same instant, Gunthorp moved. His left hand shot out and gripped Kelman's wrist. His right hand dropped to Kelman's left bicep.

Kelman was a big man, and a skillful boxer, but here he had no chance. Gunthorp's big brown hands shut down hard, the right fingers digging into the muscles of Kelman's arm, the fingers of the left hand shutting down like a powerful vise on the wrist of the gun hand.

Kelman might have been stricken with paralysis. Gunthorp's hands gripped with crushing power, and Kelman's face went white. The gun had come clear of the holster, but Kelman cried out with pain, and the gun dropped from his hand. Then, still gripping him by the wrist and upper arm, Gunthorp lifted the man clear off his feet and hurled him bodily into the yard.

His face had not changed. "I'm sorry, Sheriff, but he attacked me. You saw it. I refuse to allow any search without a warrant. Go to Judge McClees and get one, if you wish."

Eagan knew just as well as Gunthorp did that Judge Jim McClees was not going to grant any warrant without making a thorough study of the case; and that would be the last thing Kelman would want.

Kelman, his right hand almost useless from the crushing grip, caught the pommel of the saddle with his left and hauled himself up. Gunthorp retrieved the gun and handed it to Eagan.

"Return this to him when you think it's appropriate," he said, smiling.

When daylight began lifting the shadows from the sun-blasted ridges, Gunthorp ate a hurried breakfast, and then he took the boy to the door.

"You see that cottonwood with the dead limb? Right opposite the end of that limb, in the wall of the cliff, is a cave. You go up there with this grub I packed and this canteen, and don't you stir out of there until I come for you . . . or till three days have gone by. If you don't hear from me in three days, somebody got me.

"In that cave there's more water. You can also see this place, but you keep still up there or somebody might see you moving."

With that, Gunthorp swung into the saddle and started for the hills. He knew where the Stevens mine was and he was taking a chance that no one would be around. He rode swiftly, and when he found himself among the piñons on the slope above the canyon where the mine lay, he ground-hitched the gelding and slid further down the hill to where he looked over the mine and a shack nearby. A half hour's careful watch showed no movement.

He went down the hill with long strides, sliding gravel around him, his weight carrying him almost at a run. When he reached the bottom of the steep slope, he surveyed the buildings once more. No movement. Swiftly, he crossed to the mine, took one quick, last look around, then disappeared into the tunnel.

As he walked along the drift, he remembered what he had seen in that quick glance. The mine was in the face of the rock at the end of a deep notch in the mountain, a notch that widened out until it opened upon the desert valley below. Stevens had purchased this canyon and considerable land in the valley, although the extent of his buying was unknown. He had told those who were curious that he did not wish to be crowded, but they had laughed and said there was no chance of anyone ever moving near him, for the land he bought was the driest and worst around.

This much Gunthorp knew, for he was a man who listened well, and there were men enough who talked freely. He carried a candle with him, and after a while he stopped to study the wall of the tunnel. There was very little mineral here, but the big vein might be further inside.

He walked swiftly, counting his paces as he went. Suddenly, he rounded a turn in the drift and was brought up short, finding himself staring at the end where the drift had collapsed. He had walked almost a quarter of a mile from the entrance.

Thoughtfully, he studied the rock around him, and particularly that in the face. Then he turned and with the same swift strides, hurried back. A quick look around showed no one in sight, so he stepped out and started for the wash.

"Hey!" The shout stopped him in his tracks, and he turned to see a man rushing toward him. "Who are you? What do you mean by going into that mine without permission?"

Gunthorp faced the unshaven, burly watchman. "Permission from who?"

"From Kelman, that's who!" The man faced Gunthorp, glaring at him. "You come back up here and wait until he comes. I ain't sure he'd like you being in there!"

Gunthorp's bleak eyes showed humor. "I'm quite sure he wouldn't, my friend. However, if I were you, I'd pick up and leave just as quickly as I could. Kelman's through in this country."

The man laughed harshly. "That's likely! He's the boss around here. You coming with me, or do I take you?"

Gunthorp chuckled. "Why, I guess you take me," he said simply. He waited, his hands down, smiling at the other man.

"Come on," the watchman blustered, "I don't want no trouble!"

"Then go on back to your shack and keep your mouth shut. If you don't tell Kelman, he'll never know I was here. Then, you won't get in trouble at all."

The watchman was disturbed. A second look told him that although this man might not be as tall as he, he was a solid mass of bone and muscle. Moving him wouldn't be easy. Staring into those bleak eyes made him doubt the advisability of trying the pistol in his holster.

A rattle of hoofs on the trail decided the man. "Get out of here, quick!" he said. "If Kelman found you here, he'd have my scalp!"

In three fast steps, Gunthorp was in among the piñons. He glanced back to see three horsemen riding up to the mine. The man in the lead was Joe, but Kelman himself was not among them.

When he reached his horse, he mounted and cut back across the mountain. There was no regular trail, but he wove in and out among the trees until he could see into a narrow canyon beyond. When he was in position, he stopped his horse and studied this new area with thoughtful eyes.

This canyon was green, deeply green, thick with cottonwoods and tamarisk and a small stream flowing along the bottom. At one point the stream disappeared into a wide area of marshy sand and reeds. Gunthorp glanced at the sun, and seeing there was yet time, turned his horse down the trail and rode down through to the cottonwoods.

The small river flowed out of the rock, described a wide half circle through a meadow, and then vanished into the sand on the same side from which it emerged. It was no more than four or five feet across, but the water was clear and cold and ran swiftly.

As his horse drank, Gunthorp turned in his saddle and surveyed the valley. Mining operations had begun here, too. Across from him he could see the mouth of a drift and the pile of waste outside it. The tunnel mouth was low down against the valley floor. Gunthorp turned his horse and started for town, his face serious.

Red Butte's residential section was composed of some forty or fifty buildings, built haphazardly down the slope from the mesa. Beyond the buildings and corrals, the land sloped away for two miles and disappeared under the unsightly waters of an alkali lake.

Gunthorp tied his horse at the hitching rail and stepped up on the boardwalk, heading for the office of Judge Jim McClees. At that moment, the door of the restaurant thrust open and Kelman stepped out, accompanied by an uncommonly pretty girl. They saw him at the same instant.

"That's the man!" Kelman pointed at him with a stiff arm. "That's him."

The girl walked right up to Gunthorp, her heels clicking on the walk. "Where is my brother?" she demanded, her eyes sparking. "I want you to take me to him at once. And you must return the papers you took from him."

She was young, and very pretty, and he liked the determined set of her chin. "Miss Stevens," he said quietly, "your brother is safe, and no thanks due to Mr. Kelman. If there are any papers, he alone knows where they are."

"Look here!" Kelman thrust himself forward. "Madge Stevens has returned to settle her father's estate, and to do that, she must have those papers. Your little scheme has failed, so you can bring the boy in and turn the papers over to me."

Gunthorp glanced at the girl. "Is that what you want?"

"It is." Her chin lifted. "You have no right to interfere in this matter, none at all. Mr. Kelman was doing all that could be done."

Gunthorp smiled. "No doubt. But is he doing what is best for your interests and the boy's, or his own?"

"That doesn't matter," she flared. "It certainly is none of your business."

"No doubt Kelman has made you an offer for the land your father owned? Was he going to take all that wasteland off your hands as a favor?"

From the puzzled look in her eyes, he knew that he was right. "What did he offer you for it?"

"That's neither here nor there." Kelman's anger was growing. "All you have to do is take us to the boy."

Gunthorp ignored Kelman. "Miss Stevens," he

said, "I don't know what he has offered you for the land, but whatever it is, I'll double it."

Her eyes widened. "For that worthless land? Why that's absurd! That would be ten dollars an acre for—"

"Ten?" Gunthorp's eyes brightened. "Miss Stevens, I'll give you more. If you say ten dollars, he must have offered you only five. I'll give you twenty dollars an acre and a twenty percent share in any profit I make."

"But I don't understand," she protested.

"The man's trying to pull the wool over your eyes," Kelman interrupted. His tone was desperate, and anger was growing in him. "Anyway, it doesn't matter now. You've sold the land to me for five dollars an acre, and you've been paid for it." He turned back to Gunthorp. "See, my friend? You are too late. Now will you turn the boy over to us and get out of here?"

Gunthorp stood flat-footed, shaken by the statement the girl did not deny. If she had sold the land . . . Suddenly, he smiled.

"Miss Stevens," he asked politely, "I know it is always wrong to ask a woman's age, but how old are you?"

"Why, I'm eighteen, almost nineteen, but how does that matter?"

Kelman's face changed. "You mean you're not of age?"

Gunthorp looked up at him. "It really wouldn't matter, Kelman," he said softly. "You see, Lane is an heir, too, and she would have no right to sign away his rights. Miss Stevens has no right to dispose of the property without authority of his legal guardian."

"But she's his older sister," Kelman protested furiously. "She's his guardian."

"Not unless the court appoints her so, and as she's underage, that isn't likely. I suggest we talk with Judge McClees."

Madge Stevens stared from one to the other, frightened and confused. In each of the three letters that had come to her from Kelman, he had assured her of his friendship for her father and herself, and had offered to dispose of the land her father had, he suggested, foolishly bought. Now this man whom Kelman had said was forcibly holding her brother was suddenly making everything seem very different.

Kelman noticed the indecision in her face. "Come over here," he said to Gunthorp. "I want to talk to you!"

Gunthorp followed him to one side, his calm eyes on Kelman's excited face. "Listen," Kelman protested when they were out of hearing. "Let's not fight over this! That land is worth a fortune! You know that as well as I do! Let's make a deal on this! If you insist, we can cut the girl in, but there's no reason why we should! You and I can handle this by ourselves! To blazes with that girl and her kid brother."

Gunthorp smiled. "Kelman," he said loudly, "I've heard a lot about you. You have already labeled yourself as a liar and a skunk, but now you hit a new low. Asking me to cheat youngsters is about as bad as a man can get!"

"You double damned—!" Kelman's hand dropped to his gun.

Gunthorp's left fist whipped up, crashing into the pit of Kelman's stomach, and then a bone-shattering wallop to the chin. Stricken, the big man toppled back off the boardwalk and fell into the street. For an instant, he lay stunned, and then he grabbed again for his pistol.

Gunthorp tried to reach him at the same instant, but Kelman had fallen a step or two away. Kelman's gun whipped up, flame stabbed from the muzzle, and Gunthorp felt his hat lift from his head. Then, Kelman's gun roared again and something struck Gunthorp solidly. His mouth widened, then closed as his body twisted under the bullet's impact.

Suddenly, things grew hazy and Gunthorp started to turn around, but seemed to trip. Hands grabbed him and eased him to the boardwalk. A man in a wide white hat with a mustache and goatee was bending over him.

"Judge—" His voice had no more focus than his eyes, and he had to fight to arrange the words properly. "Judge, you . . . care for this girl. Brother . . . her brother's in a cave . . . at my place."

Four days later Gunthorp was lying on the bed in the spare bedroom of Judge McClees's home. The door opened and Madge Stevens came in, with Lane beside her. Her eyes widened at the sight of him lying there.

"You—you're better now?"

"Sure. Doc says I'll be up and around before long. I guess I'll carry a couple of slugs, though."

"I'm so sorry . . . that I ever doubted you. Judge McClees arrested Mr. Kelman, you know. They took him away yesterday."

"That's good." He was still very weak.

"About the land?" she said. "Men have been out to look at the mine. They say it's worthless, and the land is worse."

Gunthorp smiled. "Don't you believe them. Your father knew what he was up to. That isn't a mine at all. It's a tunnel to bring water from a canyon back there. There is a great volume of water, easily enough to irrigate five hundred acres of good hay land, and the level of the land your father bought is below that of the canyon, so irrigation for growing hay will be simple."

"But hay? Is it valuable?"

"Well," he said with a grin, "last year it sold for sixty dollars a ton, and fairly good meadow land will run a ton to the acre. This land you've got, irrigated, will do a whole lot better than many mines."

"The judge said that given all that has happened he should appoint a legal guardian for my brother and me until I turn twenty-one. He thought that it should be you."

"Well, one way or another, I guess I already got started a couple of days ago," Gunthorp said.

"But Lane and I thought it should be more of a partnership. If you'll help us finish Father's tunnel, we'll split whatever we make on the hay three ways."

"With an offer as good as that there is no chance

I could turn it down . . . I always was a sucker for kids in trouble."

"Kids!" she arched one eyebrow. "I hope you are only talking about Lane." They turned and left the room, but not before she had paused to fluff his pillow and pull up the covers.

"I wonder," Gunthorp mused, "what I've gotten myself into now. . . ."

THE GHOST FIGHTER

The bell clanged. The narrow-faced man tipped his chair away from the gym wall and sat suddenly forward. Had he not known it to be impossible, he would have sworn the husky young heavyweight in the black trunks was none other than "Bat" McGowan, the champion of the world!

Tall, bronzed, lithe as a panther, the fighter glided swiftly across the ring, stabbing a sharp left to his opponent's head; then, slipping over a left hook, he whipped a steaming right to the heart.

"Salty" Burke staggered, and his hands dropped slightly. Quickly Barney Malone jabbed another left at his face, and then a terrific right cross to the jaw. The blow seemed to travel no more than six inches, yet it exploded upon the angle of Burke's chin like a six-inch shell, and the big heavyweight crashed to the canvas, out cold!

. . .

Ruby Ryan, trainer of Bat McGowan, turned as "Rack" Hendryx relaxed and leaned back in his seat. His keen blue eyes were bright with excitement.

"See? What did I tell you? The kid's got it. He can box an' he can hit. He's just what you want, Rack!"

"Yeah, that's right. But he can't take it. . . ." Hendryx mused. "Well, he's a ringer for the champ, that's for sure. Hell, if I didn't know better, I'd swear that was him in there! Why, they could as well be twins!"

"Sure," Ryan nodded wisely. "Stick the kid in an' let him box these exhibitions as the champion, an' nobody the wiser. You've heard of these 'ghost writers,' haven't you? Well, Malone can be your 'ghost fighter'! No reason why you should miss collecting just because that big lug wants to booze and raise hell. It's a cinch."

"Yeah," Hendryx agreed. "As long as nobody taps that glass jaw of his . . . Okay, we'll try it. This kid is good, an' if he's just a gym fighter, so much the better. We don't want him gettin' any ideas."

The next night three men loafed in the expensive suite at the Astor where Hendryx maintained an unofficial headquarters. Rack Hendryx did not confine himself merely to managing the heavyweight champion of the world. From behind a score of "fronts" he pulled the wires that directed a huge ring of vice and racketeering. Even Bat McGowan knew little of this, although he surmised a good deal. The three had become widely known figures: Bat McGowan, the champion; Rack Hendryx, his manager; and Tony Mada, Hendryx's quiet, thin-lipped bodyguard.

"Say, when's this punk going to show up?" McGowan growled irritably. "He hasn't taken a powder on you, has he?"

"Not a chance. Ruby's bringing' him up the back way. We can't have nobody gettin' wise to this. Why, the damned papers would howl bloody murder about the fans payin' to see the champ an' only seein' some punk gym fighter who can't take it on the chin!" Hendryx laughed harshly.

"What about the guys that already seen him?" McGowan demanded.

"He's from South Africa. An Irishman from Johannesburg. He only fought here once, and that was some little club in the sticks. Ruby Ryan also saw him in the gym."

There was a sharp rap at the door, and when Mada swung it open, Ryan stepped in with Barney Malone at his heels. For a moment, there was silence while Malone and Bat McGowan stared at each other.

"Well, I'll be—" McGowan exclaimed. "The punk sure does look like me, don't he?" Then he walked over and looked Barney Malone up and down. "Don't you wish you could fight like me, too?"

"Maybe I can," Malone snapped, his eyes narrowing coldly.

McGowan sneered. "Yeah?" Quick as a flash he snapped a left hook to Malone's head, a punch that caught the newcomer flush on the point of the chin. Without a sound the young fighter crumpled to the floor!

"Are you crazy?" Rack Hendryx grabbed McGowan by the arm and jerked him back, face livid. "What the hell d'you think you're tryin' to do, anyway? Crab the act?"

"Aw, what the hell—the punk was gettin' wise with me. I might as well put him in his place now as later."

Helped by Ruby Ryan, Malone was slowly getting to his feet, shaking his head to clear it. The old trainer's Irish face was hard, and the light in his eyes when he looked at McGowan was not good to see.

"Now lay off, you big chump!" Hendryx snapped angrily. "What d'you think this is, an alley?"

Malone looked at McGowan, his eyes strange and bleak. "So you're a champion?" he said coldly. McGowan stepped forward, his fist raised, but Hendryx and Mada intervened.

"You should know, lollypop." Bat turned and picked up his hat, then looked back at Malone and laughed.

"Just another cream puff! Well, you can double for me, but don't get any ideas, see, or I'll beat you to jelly." He turned and walked out.

"Forget that guy, Malone," Hendryx broke in, noticing the gleam in the youngster's eye. "Just let it slide. We got to talk business!"

"Nothing doing." Barney Malone looked at Hendryx and shook his head. "Not for a guy like that!"

"Come on . . . Bat won't be around much. He'll be busy with the girls. An' where can you lay your mitts on five hundred a week? Forget that guy; this is business."

"All right," Malone said. "But not for five hundred. I want five hundred, and ten percent of the take from all exhibitions I work as champion!"

"Not a chance!" Hendryx snapped angrily. "What you tryin' to do, pull a Jesse James on me?"

"Then let me out of this joint," Malone said grimly. "I'm through."

For a half hour they argued, and finally Hendryx shrugged his shoulders. "Okay, Malone, you win. I'll give it to you. But remember—one move that looks like a double cross and I give Tony the nod, see?"

Malone glanced at Tony Mada, and the little torpedo parted his lips in a nasty grin. Whatever else there was about the combination, there wasn't any foolishness about Tony Mada. He was something cold and deadly.

A month and nine exhibitions later, in the dressing room of the Adelphian Athletic Club, Barney Malone sat on the table, taping his hands. The champion's silk robe over his broad shoulders set them off nicely. He looked fit and ready.

"This Porky Dobro is tough, see?" Ryan advised. "He's tougher than we wanted right now, but we couldn't dodge him. He knows McGowan, an' has a grudge against him. You gotta be nasty with this guy, Barney. Get tough, heel your gloves, use

your elbows and shoulders, butt him, hold and
hit—everything! That's the way the champ works;
he was always dirty. This guy will expect it, so give
him the works. But, no matter what, don't let him
near that jaw of yours . . . you can outbox him, so
don't try anything else."

"That's right, kid," Hendryx agreed. "You been
doin' fine. But this Dobro isn't like the others, he's
bad medicine—an' he ain't going to be scared!"

Hendryx walked out, with Mada at his heels. Malone
watched them go, and then looked back at Ruby
Ryan. The old Irishman was tightening a shoelace.

"How'd you happen to get mixed up with an
outfit like that, Ruby?"

Ryan shrugged. "Same way you did, kid. A guy's
got to live. Rack knew I was a good trainer, an' he
hired me. I made McGowan champ. Now they both
treat me like the dirt under their feet."

They hurried down the aisle to the ring, where
Porky Dobro was already waiting for them. He was
a heavy-shouldered fighter with a square jaw and
heavy brows. A typical slugger, and a tough one.

"All right, champ, box him now!" Ryan mur-
mured as the bell sounded.

Dobro broke from his corner with a rush. He
was a huge favorite locally, and it was the real thing
for the hometown fans to see a local heavyweight in
a grudge battle with the world's champion.

Dobro rushed to close quarters but was stopped
abruptly by a stiff left jab that set him back on his
heels. Before he could regain his balance, Malone

crossed a solid right to the head, and hooked two lefts to the body, in close. Dobro bored in, taking more blows. Bobbing and weaving, he tried to go under Malone's left, but it followed him, cutting, stabbing, holding him off.

Then Barney's left swung out a little, and Dobro managed to drive in close, where he clinched desperately, cursing. Malone tied him up calmly and pounded his body with a free hand. Ryan was signaling from his corner and, remembering, Malone jerked his shoulder up hard under Dobro's chin. As the crowd booed, he calmly pushed Dobro away and peeled the hide from a cheekbone with the vicious heel of his glove.

The crowd booed again, and Dobro rushed, but brought up sharply on the end of a left that split his lips and started a stream of blood. Before he could set himself, Malone fired a volley of blows to his body. The bell sounded, and the crowd mingled cheers with the booing.

"Nice goin', kid," Ryan assured him. "You should be in the movies. You look so much like McGowan, I hate you myself! But keep up the rough stuff, that's what we want."

The clang of the bell had scarcely died when Dobro was across the ring, but again he met that snapping left. He plunged in again, and again the left swung a little wide, letting him in. Then Malone promptly tied him up.

As they broke, Dobro took a terrific swing at Malone's jaw, slipped on some spilled water, and plunged forward, arms flailing. Stumbling, he tried to regain his balance, then plunged headfirst into a steel corner-post! He slumped, a dead weight, upon the canvas, suddenly still.

Quickly, Malone bent over him, helping him to his feet, face white and worried. The referee and the man's seconds crowded around, working madly over the fighter, who had struck with force enough to kill. Malone was suddenly conscious of a tugging at his arm, and looked up to find Ruby Ryan motioning him to the corner.

"He's all right, kid," Ryan assured him. "But if he came to and found you bent over him, worried like that, the shock would probably kill him! Remember, you're supposed to hate him and everything about him."

Finally, Dobro came around, but insisted on going on with the fight after a brief rest.

When the bell sounded again, Dobro came out fast, seemingly none the worse for his bump, but Malone stepped away, sparring carefully. Dobro plunged in close and slammed a couple of stiff punches to the body, then hooked a hard left to the head without a return. Malone stepped away, boxing carefully. He could still see Dobro's white face and queer eyes as he lay on the canvas, and was afraid that a stiff punch might—

A jolting right suddenly caught him on the ear, knocking him across the ring into the ropes. He caught himself just in time to see Dobro plunging in, his eyes wild with killer's fire. Malone ducked and clinched. As Dobro's ear came close, he whispered:

"Take it easy, you clown, an' I'll let you ride awhile!"

Then the referee broke them, and Malone saw Dobro's brow wrinkle with puzzlement. He realized instantly that he had overplayed his hand. Hesitant to batter Dobro after his fall, he had acted as Bat McGowan would never have acted. Dobro bored in, and Malone put a light left to his mouth, but passed up a good shot for his right. Suddenly, in close, his eye caught Dobro's; Dobro went under a left and clinched.

"Say, what is this?" he growled. "You're—"

Panic-stricken, Malone shoved him off with a left and hooked a terrific right to the chin that slammed Dobro to the canvas. But he was up at nine, boring in, still puzzled, conscious that something was wrong. Malone put two rapid lefts to the face, and then stepped back, feinting a left and then letting it swing wide again. But this time, as Dobro lunged to get in close, Malone caught him coming in with a short, vicious right cross to the chin that stopped him dead in his tracks. Dobro weaved and started to drop, already out cold, but before he could fall, Malone whipped in a steaming left hook that stretched him on the canvas, dead to the world.

The next morning, Ruby Ryan walked into the room where Barney Malone was playing solitaire and handed him a paper.

"Take a gander at that, son. Looks like they're eating it up; but just the same, I'm worried. Porky is dumb enough, but even a dumb guy can stumble into a smart play."

On one side of the sport sheet, black headlines broadcast the fight of the previous evening:

McGOWAN STOPS DOBRO IN SECOND
Champ Looks Great in Grudge Battle
with Slugging Foe

But across the page, and in a column of comment, Malone read further:

How does he do it? In the past thirty days, Bat McGowan has flattened ten opponents in as clean-cut fashion as ever a champion did. But in the same space of time, he has been seen drunk and carousing no less than seven times. Even Harry Greb in his palmy days never displayed such form as the champion has of late, while at the same time burning the candle at both ends.

We have never cared for McGowan; the champion has been as consistently dirty, and as unnecessarily foul as any fighter we have ever seen. But last night with Porky Dobro, he intentionally coasted after the man had been injured by a fall. It was the act of a champion—but somehow, it wasn't like McGowan as we have known him.

"Well, what do you think, kid?" Ryan looked at him curiously. "You're making the champion a reputation as a good guy."

"It's all the same to me, Ruby. Champion or no champion, I've been giving the fans a run for their money. I'm going to keep it up, even if McGowan does get the credit."

"You know, son, you've changed some lately, do you realize that?"

"How d'you mean?"

"You stopped Porky Dobro in the second round last night. The last time they fought, McGowan needed seven rounds to get him, and had quite a brawl. And Dobro stayed the distance with him twice before, once in Reno, and again in Pittsburgh. You've improved a lot."

There was a sharp rap at the door, and Ryan looked up, surprised. When he opened the door it was to admit Bat McGowan, Tony Mada, and a very excited Rack Hendryx.

"All right, Ryan, you were smart enough to tip me off to this ghost fighter business. Now give me an out!"

"What's up?"

"Almost everything. Major Kenworthy called me this morning and told me to come to the Commission offices, and right away. I went, and they want to know why McGowan is gallivanting around the country, knocking off setups and not defending his title. They say the six months are up, and they want him to defend his title at once. They had Dickerson, the promoter, up there, and had papers all ready to sign, and wanted to know if I had any objections to letting the champ defend his title against Hamp Morgan—and in just six weeks! McGowan here can't get in shape to fight in that time!"

"Hamp Morgan, eh?" Ryan frowned. "He's a

tough egg, and been comin' up fast the past few months. Can't you stall a little?"

"Stall? What d'you think I've been tryin' to do? They say the champ's in great shape, they saw him beat Dobro and a couple of other guys. There's a lot of talk now, and they say it will draw like a million bucks. And when we got the fight for the title, we posted ten thousand bucks in agreeing to defend the title in six months!"

"Why not let Barney fight?" Ryan asked softly.

"Malone? Say, what are we talkin' about? Hamp Morgan is no setup!" McGowan snarled angrily. "Think I want that punk to lose my title for me? You're nuts!"

"Yeah? What about Porky Dobro? How long did it take you to stop him last time? And did he or did he not bust you around plenty?" Ryan demanded. "Maybe Barney can't take it—but how many of these bums been touchin' him? Well, I'll tell you— none of them have! He was hurt on the ship workin' his way over from South Africa and hasn't been able to take 'em around the head since. But he can box, an' he can hit."

"Maybe we don't have a choice, Ruby," Hendryx said thoughtfully. "Bat is hog-fat. He'd be twenty pounds over Malone's weight easy."

"Hey!" the champ scowled at Hendryx.

"You are! You'd be in a hell of a spot if the Commission put you on a scale. I ain't made much money with this title, an' I can't afford to gamble. It looks to me like Barney has to fight Morgan."

Bat turned suddenly, facing Malone. "Well, what d'you say about it? Are you game? Or are you yella?"

Barney Malone got up slowly. For a minute he stared coldly at Bat McGowan. Then he turned to face Hendryx. "You're the one that has it to lose. Sure, I'll fight Morgan. I've been playin' champ a month now, an' I like it!"

"Kind of cocky, ain't you?" McGowan said suddenly, his eyes hard. "It seems to me you're gettin' pretty smart for a guy with a glass chin! Why, I just brushed you with a left and flattened you the first time I ever laid eyes on you!"

"Fight him yourself!" Barney snapped back.

"Forget it," Hendryx barked. "Sit down, Bat, an' shut up. What're you always gettin' hard around Barney for? He's been doin' your dirty work, and makin' money for all of us."

"Why? Because he's yella, because he's too pretty to suit me! Because he thinks he's a nice boy! Why, I'd—"

"You'd nothing!" hissed Hendryx. "If you were just another pug I'd have your knees broken—I'd have you whacked! You're the pretty face around here, and you're lettin' someone else do all the work. Now everybody listen close; Malone you win this fight or I'll make you sorry . . . and Bat, you stop drinkin' and get yourself in shape! If you don't make me some money I'm gonna let you swing, understand?"

For a long time after they'd left, Malone stared out the window into the gathering darkness. Ryan walked up finally and stood by his chair.

After a moment—"Well, kid," he began, "we've

come a long way together. When I first spotted you in that gym, I knew you had it. If you don't get careless, none of these punks are goin' to hit you. But just remember, Barney—the champ knows, see? An' if you ever let McGowan start a fight with you, he'll try to kill you!"

"I know. Hell, Ruby, everything looked good when I left Capetown. I'd had seventeen fights, and won them all by knockouts. Then I had that fall, and the doc told me I could never fight again. But I have to fight. It's all I know. I was stopped twice in the gym, and then practically knocked out that day by McGowan."

"Ain't there anything a doctor can do?" Ryan asked.

"Doesn't seem so. But this doc told me I might get over it, in time. An' Ruby, do you remember the Dobro battle? He hit me twice on the head, an' though one of them hurt, I didn't go down."

Sixty thousand people crowded the vast open-air arena to see Bat McGowan defend his heavyweight title against Hamp Morgan, the Butte, Montana, miner. For only six weeks the publicity barrage had been turned on the title fight, but it had been enough. Morgan's steady string of victories and the champion's ten quick knockouts in as many exhibitions had furnished the heat for the sportswriters. They all agreed that it should be a great battle. Morgan had lost but two decisions, and these almost three years before. The champion looked great in training, and everyone marveled at his recent record even during a long period of dissipation. The betting was three-to-one on the champ.

In Hamp Morgan's dressing room "Dandy Jim" Kirby was giving his fighter a few last-minute tips. Salty Burke, Morgan's sparring partner and second, whom Barney Malone had knocked out on the day Ryan spotted him, stood nearby. Porky Dobro had dropped in to wish Morgan the best of luck and a better "break" than he himself had got. Though they had all been competitors at one time or another, there was one thing they could all agree on: No one liked the champ.

"You know, Hamp," Dobro mused, "it's funny, but Bat eased up on me in the last scrap we had. He was boxing like a million, had me right on the spot after I got hurt, and then offered to let me ride. If I hadn't known him so well, I'd have sworn there was something crooked about the deal. McGowan has a trick of cussing a guy in the clinches, an' a funny way of biting his lip, an' that night he didn't do either!"

Burke looked up and grinned. "Maybe Hendryx stumbled on that punk I fought a few months ago."

Kirby looked queerly at Burke, his eyes narrowing slightly. "What d'you mean, the guy you fought?"

"Why, several months ago I boxed a guy who looked enough like McGowan to be his twin. A fella named Barney Malone, from Johannesburg, South Africa. He stopped me quick. Hit like a mule, he did, but I'd seen him get stopped in the gym a couple of times by small boys, and figured I could take him."

"And you say he looked like the champ?" Kirby said thoughtfully.

"Yeah," Burke agreed. "An' say, I hadn't remembered it before, but I seen him talkin' to Ryan one time. . . ."

"Did he sound like he was from South Africa, you know, did he have an accent?" Kirby asked Dobro.

"Had the mouthpiece in—he sounded like a guy talkin' past the world's biggest chaw."

"You say he was stopped by somebody?"

"Yeah, hit on the head, both times. Back around the ear. I thought I could cop him myself, but he was in better shape, an' he never give me no chance."

Nearly ring time. "Dandy Jim" Kirby walked slowly down the aisle toward his ringside seat, a very thoughtful man. Kirby was nobody's fool. He had been around the fight racket as a kid, and he'd heard the smart fight managers talk, guys who'd been in the business since the days of Gans and Wolgast. He knew Rack Hendryx well enough to know he was no more honest than he had to be. Somehow—He paused momentarily, running his long fingers through his slightly graying hair.

Now, let's see: McGowan, nasty as they make 'em, wins the title by a kayo. He is a slugger with a chunk of dynamite in each mitt, and plenty tough. He starts drinking and chasing women. Then, about two months later, he suddenly starts a campaign of exhibition fights.

McGowan carouses, and yet is always in perfect shape. Tonight his face is puffy and eyes hollow— tomorrow he is lean, hard, and clear-eyed. There is another heavyweight who looks like McGowan, and Ruby Ryan knows them both. . . .

Kirby dropped his cigarette and rubbed it out with his toe. Then he turned and walked back toward the dressing room. His eyes were bright. He met Hamp Morgan coming toward the ring.

"Listen, Hamp," he said quickly. "When you go out there tonight, I want you to hit this guy on the ear, see? Hit him, an' hit him hard, get me?"

For years, fans were to remember that fight. It was one for the books. For four rounds, it was one of the most terrific slugging matches ever seen, with both boys moving fast and slamming away with a will. It was a bitter, desperate fight, and when the bell rang for the fifth, the crowd was on the edge of their seats, every man hoarse from yelling.

The "champion" stopped Morgan's first rush with a lancing left jab. A hard right to the body followed, and Morgan backed up, taking two lefts as he was going away. Then he lunged in, whipped both hands for the body, and then missed a long overhand right to the head. The "champion" backed away and Morgan followed. Suddenly Barney Malone stopped, feinted a left, and shook Morgan to his heels with a driving right to the jaw. Hamp Morgan dropped swiftly to a crouch, and suddenly, so quickly that the eye could not follow, he whipped over a terrific right to the head that crashed against Malone's ear! With a sound, the "champion" pitched forward on his face and lay still.

Amid the roar of the crowd, the referee's hand began to rise and fall, slowing tolling off the seconds. In the ringside seat, Rack Hendryx sat tensely, swearing under his breath in a low, vicious monotone. Ryan leaned over the edge of the ring, fists clenched, almost breathless.

Kirby, the championship almost in his hands, was watching Hendryx, and then his eyes slid over to Tony Mada.

The crowd was in a frenzy, but Mada was cold and silent. He was not looking at the ring; his gaze was fastened upon "Dandy Jim" Kirby. Kirby felt his mouth go dry with fear. Then, amid the roaring of the crowd, the bell sounded. Probably not more than a dozen people heard it, but it sounded at the count of nine.

The first thing Barney Malone understood was the dull roar in his ears and the bright lights over the ring. He felt someone anxiously shaking his head, and a whiff of smelling salts nearly tore his skull off.

Then—"Come on, son, you got to snap out of it!" Ryan was pleading. "Come on!" As Malone's eyes opened, Ryan leaned forward, whispering, "Now's your chance! Go out there like you were gone, see? Stagger out, act like you don't know where you are.

Then let him have it, just as hard as you can throw it, get me?"

The sound of the bell was lost in the howl of the crowd, and Hamp Morgan was crossing the ring, tearing in, punching like a madman, throwing a volley of hooks, swings, and uppercuts that had Barney Malone reeling like a drunken man; reeling, but just enough to keep most of Morgan's blows pounding the air. And then, like a shot from the blue, his right streaked out and crashed against Morgan's chin with the force of a thunderbolt. Hamp Morgan spun halfway around and dropped at full length on the canvas!

Malone crawled stiffly out of bed and sat staring across the room. One eye was swollen, and he felt gingerly of his ear. Thoughtfully, but cautiously, he worked his jaw around to find the sore spots. There were plenty.

He was shaving when suddenly the sound of the key in the lock made him look up. It was Ruby Ryan.

"Look, kid," he said excitedly, "we got to scram. Somebody is stirrin' up a lot of heat! Look at this!"

He pointed at the same daily column of sports comment that had been giving so much space to the activities of the champion, both in and out of the ring.

Where is Barney Malone? That question may or may not mean anything, but this A.M., as we recovered from last night's fistic brawl in which

Bat McGowan (or somebody) hung a kayo on Hamp Morgan's chin, we received an anonymous note asking this very question: Where is Barney Malone?

Now, it is true that we are not too well aware of who this Malone party is, but an enclosed clipping from a Capetown, South Africa, paper shows us a picture entitled BARNEY MALONE, a picture of a fighter whose resemblance to Bat McGowan is striking, to say the least. The accompanying story assures the interested reader that Mr. Malone is headed for pugilistic fame in the more or less Land of the Free.

Can it be possible that this accounts for the startling alterations in the appearance and actions of Bat McGowan? And if so, who knocked out Hamp Morgan? Was it indeed our beloved champion, or was it some guy named Jones, from Peoria, or perhaps Malone, from Capetown?

I wonder, Major Kenworthy, if Bat McGowan has a large ear this morning?

There was a light step behind them as Malone finished reading, and they whirled about to confront Tony Mada. He smiled.

"Hello, kid, the boss wants to see you."

"Hendryx? Why don't he come over here like he always does?" Ryan demanded. "He knows it's dangerous to have Barney on the streets."

"We got a car, Barney, a closed car. Come on, he's waiting for you."

Ryan was standing by the window, and he turned his head slightly, glancing at the car across the street.

Suddenly his face went deathly white. Behind the wheel was "Shiv" McCloskey, another of Hendryx's muscle men. He had the feeling that Barney Malone was about to disappear, forever.

Malone picked up his hat, straightened his tie. In the mirror he caught a glimpse of Ryan's face, white and strained. A jerk of the head indicated the car, with McCloskey at the wheel. Mada was lighting a cigarette.

Without a word, Barney Malone spun on his heel, and as Mada looked up, his fist caught the torpedo on the angle of the jaw. Something crunched, and the gunman toppled to the floor. Quickly, Ryan grabbed the automatic from Mada's shoulder holster.

"Come on, kid, we got to scram—"

Suddenly in the door of the room stood Major Kenworthy, Rack Hendryx, Bat McGowan, and two reporters. Kenworthy stepped over to Mada, and then glanced out the window. He turned slowly to Hendryx.

"I don't know quite what this is all about yet, Hendryx," he said dryly, "but I'd advise you to call off your dog out there. He might become conspicuous. It seems"—he smiled at Ryan and Malone—"that your other shadow has met with an accident."

"Are you Malone?" asked one of the reporters.

"Of course he's Malone," Kenworthy interrupted. "Just what else he is, we'll soon find out. But before asking any questions or listening to any alibis, I'm going to speak my piece. Apparently, Malone"—he eyed Barney's bruised ear—"fighting as the champion, defeated Hamp Morgan. This means"—he looked at Hendryx—"that your ten thousand dollars is forfeit. Apparently, Malone, you scored ten knockouts while posing as champion. This is all going to be public knowledge, but you and McGowan are going to get a chance to make it right with the fans. A chance I'd not be giving either of you but for the good of the game. You can fight each other for the world's title, the proceeds, above training expenses, to go to charity . . . that, or you can both be barred for life. And if you can also be prosecuted, I'll see that it's done. What do you men say?"

"I'll fight," Barney Malone said. "I'll fight him, and only too willing to do it."

Hendryx agreed, sullenly, for the scowling McGowan.

"Don't miss any guesses, Barney," Ruby Ryan whispered. "Watch him all the time. Remember, he won the title, and he can hit. He's dangerous, experienced, and a killer. He's out for blood and to keep his title. Both of you got everything to fight for. Now, go get him!"

The bell clanged, and Malone stepped from his corner, stabbing a lightninglike jab to McGowan's face. McGowan slid under another left and slammed both hands into Malone's ribs with jolting force, then whipped up a torrid right uppercut that missed by a hairsbreadth. Malone spun away, jabbing another left to the chin, and hooking a hard right to the temple that shook McGowan to his heels.

But Bat McGowan looked fit. For two months, he had trained like a demon. Ryan had not been joking when he said that McGowan was out for blood. He crowded in close, Malone clinched, and McGowan tried to butt him, but took a solid punch to the midsection before the break.

McGowan crowded in again, slugging viciously, but Malone was too fast, slipping over a left hook and slamming him on the chin with a short right cross. Bat McGowan slipped under another left, crowded in close to bury his right in Malone's solar plexus.

Malone staggered, tried to cover up, but McGowan was on him like a tiger, pulling his arms down, driving a terrific right to the side of his head that slammed him back into the ropes. Before he could recover, McGowan was throwing a volley of hooks, swings, and uppercuts, and Malone was battered into a corner, where he caught a stiff left and crashed to the canvas!

He was up at nine, but McGowan came in fast, measured Malone with a left, and dropped him again. Slowly, his head buzzing, the onetime ghost fighter struggled to his knees, and caught a strand of rope to pull himself erect. McGowan rushed in, but was a little too anxious, and Malone fell into a clinch and hung on for dear life.

At the break, McGowan missed a hard right, and the crowd booed. Malone circled warily, boxing. Bat McGowan crowded in close, but Malone met him with a fast left that cut his eyebrow. Then just before the bell, another hard right to the head put

Malone on the canvas again. The gong rang at seven.

"Say, you sap," Ruby Ryan growled in his ear, "who said you couldn't take it? Whatever has been wrong with you is all right. You've taken all he can dish out now. Keep that left busy, and keep this guy at long range and off balance, got me?"

The second round opened fast. Malone was boxing now, using all the cleverness he had. McGowan bored in, then hooked both hands to the head. But Malone took them going away. A short right dropped Bat McGowan to his knees for no count, and then the champion was in close battering away at Malone's ribs with both hands. Just before the bell, Malone staggered the champion with a hard left hook, and then took a jarring right to the body that drove him into the ropes.

Through the third, fourth, fifth, and sixth rounds the two fought like madmen. Toe to toe, they battered away, first one having a narrow lead, then the other. It was nobody's fight. Bloody, battered, and weary, the two came up for the seventh berserk and fighting for blood. McGowan's left eye was a bloody mess, his lips were in shreds; Malone's body was red from the terrific pounding he had taken, his lip was split, and one eye was almost closed. It had been a fierce, grueling struggle with no likelihood of quarter.

McGowan came out slowly and missed a hard right hook, which gave Malone a chance to step in with a sizzling uppercut that nearly tore the champion's head off! Quickly Malone feinted a left, tried another uppercut, but it fell short as McGowan rolled away, then stepped in, slamming both hands to the body, and then landed a jarring left hook to the head. Slipping away, Malone jabbed a left four times to the face without a return, danced away. McGowan put a fist to Barney's sore mouth, but took a fearful right and left to the stomach in return that made him back up hurriedly, plainly in distress. McGowan swung wildly with a left and right, Malone ducked with ease, and came up with a torrid right uppercut that stretched the champion flat on his shoulder blades!

McGowan came up at seven and, desperate, swung a wicked left that sank into Malone's body, inches below the belt!

There was an angry bellow from the crowd and a rush for the ring amidst a shrilling of police whistles! But Malone caught himself on the top rope, and as McGowan rushed to finish him, the younger fighter smashed over a driving right to the chin that knocked the champion clear across the ring. Staying on his feet with sheer nerve, Barney Malone lunged across the canvas and met McGowan with a stiff left as he bounded off the ropes, then a terrific right to the jaw and McGowan went down and out, stretched on the canvas like a study in still life!

Ruby Ryan threw Malone's robe across his shoulders, grinning happily. "Well, son, you made it! What are you going to do now?"

Barney Malone carefully raised his head. "A couple more fights. Then I'm goin' back home . . . buy a farm up north near Windhoek . . . find a wife. I need to be in a place where a man can just be himself without having to be someone else first!"

In the press benches, a radio columnist was speaking into the mike: "Well folks, it's all over! Barney Malone is heavyweight champion of the world, after the first major ring battle in recent years in which neither fighter was paid a dime! And"—he glanced over at McGowan's corner, where Hendryx was slowly reviving his fighter—"if Major Kenworthy is asked tomorrow morning whether Bat McGowan has a large ear, he will have to say 'Yes,' and very emphatically!"

WINGS
OVER BRAZIL

CHAPTER 1

Ponga Jim Mayo walked out on the terrace and stood looking down the winding road that led across the miles to Fortaleza and the Brazilian coast. Behind him the orchestra was rolling out a conga. Under the music he could hear the clink of glasses and the laughter of women.

His broad, powerful shoulders filled the immaculate white dinner coat, and as he walked to the edge of the terrace, he thrust his big, salt-hardened hands into his coat pockets, bunching them into fists.

"It doesn't make sense," he muttered, "something smells."

"What is it, Captain Mayo? What's troubling you?" He knew, even as he turned, that only one woman could have such a voice. Señorita Carisa Montoya had been introduced to him earlier, but he knew well enough who she was. She was visiting from São Paulo, and he had met her ships in a score of ports, knew of her mines and ranches. He had been surprised only that she was so young and beautiful.

He shrugged. "Troubling me? I'm curious why the skipper of a tramp freighter is invited here, with this crowd."

He glanced out over the spacious, parklike grounds. All about him was evidence of wealth and power. A little too much power, he was thinking. And the people dancing and talking, they were smooth, efficient, powerful people. They represented the wealth and ambition of all Latin America.

She smiled as he lit her cigarette. "You seem perfectly at home, Captain," she said, "and certainly, there isn't a more attractive man here."

"At home?" He studied her thoughtfully. "Maybe, but being invited here doesn't make sense. I had never met Don Pedro Norden before."

"Possibly he has a shipping contract for you," Carisa suggested. "With his holdings, shipping is a problem during a war."

"Might be." Ponga Jim was skeptical. "But with your ships and those of Valdes, he wouldn't need mine."

"You're too suspicious," she told him, smiling. She took him by the arm. "Why don't you ask me to dance?"

They started toward the floor. "Suspicious? Of course I am, this is wartime."

She glanced at him quickly. "But aren't you a freelancer? A sailor of fortune? I hear you take cargo wherever you choose to go, regardless of the war."

"That's right. But I'm still an American," he said

simply. "Even sailors of fortune have their loyalties."

Three men stepped out of a door. One was Don Ricardo Valdes, a shipping magnate from the Argentine. The other two were strangers. One tall, slightly stooped, middle-aged. His gray face was vulpine, his eyes intent and cruel.

The other man was slightly over six feet, but so broad as to seem short. His blond hair was trimmed close in a stiff pompadour, and he had a wide, flat face with a broken nose. He looked like a wrestler, and had actually been a top-notch heavyweight boxer.

"Captain Mayo?" Valdes held out a hand. "I'd like to present Dr. Felix Von Hardt and Hugh Busch."

Von Hardt's hand was what Mayo expected, careful, dry, and without warmth. Busch had a grip to match his shoulders, and when Ponga Jim met the challenge, strength for strength, the German's face flushed angrily.

"If the señorita will excuse us?" Von Hardt's voice was smooth.

"Of course." Carisa looked at Ponga Jim. "But I'll be expecting you later, Captain. We must have our dance."

When she was gone, Valdes lit a cigarette. "Captain, we've heard you have an aircraft—an eight-passenger ship? We'll give you fifty thousand dollars for it."

The plane was stowed away on the *Semiramis* at Fortaleza. No one had been aboard but the crew and government officials, so how did these men know of the plane?

"Sorry." Mayo's voice was regretful. "It's not for sale."

Did they know where he got the plane, he wondered? He had taken it, as one of the fortunes of war, from Count Franz Kull, a German espionage agent and saboteur, in New Guinea. It was specially built, an amphibian with a few hidden surprises that the agent had paid dearly for.

"I'll double the price," Valdes said. "One hundred thousand."

"Sorry, gentlemen," Mayo repeated. "That plane is one of my most prized possessions."

"You'd better take what you can get," Busch said harshly, "when you can get it."

Ponga Jim measured the German. "I don't like threats, friend. Now, if you'll excuse me—"

Valdes halted him. "Think it over, Captain," he suggested. "We can turn a lot of business your way. Especially," he added meaningfully, "after the war."

Ponga Jim's fists balled in his coat pocket. "I'll take my chances, Valdes," he said coldly. "I don't like the odor of your friends."

Señorita Montoya was dancing. For once Mayo would have liked to cut in. But it was a practice he had never cared for, and everywhere, but in the United States, was considered grossly impolite.

He had taken but a few steps when she was beside him. "Have you forgotten our dance, Captain?"

Ponga Jim looked at her and caught his breath. She was radiantly beautiful. Too beautiful, he thought, to believe. He remembered that again, a moment later.

"I hope you made the deal, Captain," she said, "it would be wise."

"Why?" Over his shoulder he saw Von Hardt talking to Don Pedro. The big Spanish-German was a powerful man physically with a domineering manner thinly veiled by a recent layer of polish.

"Because I like you, Captain," she said simply, "and these are dangerous times."

His eyes narrowed. Another threat? Or a warning? "Think nothing of it," he said, smiling again. "All times are dangerous in my business. I play my cards as they fall, the way I want to play them. I'll make my own rules and abide by the consequences."

He knew Busch, at least, was a full-fledged Nazi. Von Hardt probably was. Scanning the room, Mayo noticed at least a dozen others with a pronounced military bearing.

Don Ricardo, he knew, was hand in glove with the Falange. Just before the war, on a visit to Spain, the man had spent much time with Suner, the pro-Nazi foreign minister. If ever a room was filled with Nazi sympathizers, this was it.

He was startled from his meditations by a sudden stiffening of Carisa's body under his hand. Her eyes were over his shoulder, and turning, he glanced toward the French doors.

A slender, broad-shouldered man stood there alone. He was undeniably handsome, but was only a trifle over five feet tall. One hand touched the neatly waxed mustache, and the other was in his coat pocket. He surveyed the room with all the sang-froid of a ringmaster watching a group of trained horses perform.

A subtle change had come over the guests. Men had stopped talking. Faces had stiffened. Mayo glanced at Norden and saw the multimillionaire's face slowly change from rage to a cold, ugly triumph. All evening he had felt the charged atmosphere of danger at Castillo Norden. Now for the first time, it had centered on one object. However, the small man in the door was undisturbed.

Then Mayo saw something else. A dark form flitted past the French doors behind the man and faded into the shadows beside the window. Then another. Two more men, hard-looking customers in evening clothes, were walking toward the window, talking quietly. Another man left his partner and lit a cigarette.

They were coming, closing in. Slowly, casually, as in a well-rehearsed play. And the little man kept watching the room with an air of blasé indifference.

Carisa's face was deathly pale. "Please!" she whispered. "Let's go to the conservatory. I feel faint."

He was fed up with wondering who was on what side and pretending that he had an open, cosmopolitan attitude about such things. He had been invited here so that he could be conned into selling his aircraft by a bunch of Nazis and he was expected to politely not notice.

"Sorry," he said. "You go. I want to talk to that man." He was startled by the fear in her eyes.

"No!" she whispered. "You mustn't. There's going to be trouble."

He laughed at her. "Of course," he said, "that's why I'm going."

Casually, he walked over to the man standing by the windows. The musicians were playing another piece now, a louder one.

"Hi, buddy," Mayo said softly. "I don't know who you are, but you're right behind the eight ball. There are four or five men on the terrace and more here in the room."

The smile revealed amazingly white teeth. "Of course." The little man bowed slightly. "They do not like me here. I am Juan Peligro. Your name?"

"Mayo. Jim Mayo."

Peligro's eyebrows lifted. "So?" He looked at Ponga Jim thoughtfully. "I have heard of you, Captain. Have they made an offer for your amphibian yet?"

Ponga Jim glanced at Peligro quickly. "How did you know?"

"One learns much. They need planes, these men."

A burly man with a square, brutal face suddenly stood beside Mayo. "Captain Mayo? Don Ricardo wishes to speak with you."

"Why not let him come here?" Ponga Jim said. "I like it in this room."

The man's face darkened. "You'd better go," he insisted. "This man does not belong here. He is going to be dealt with."

Ponga Jim grinned suddenly. He felt amazingly good. "I like him," he said. "I like this guy. You deal with him, you deal with me."

The man hesitated. Obviously, they wanted no outward disturbance. "We don't want any trouble," the man said, "you—"

His right hand dropped to his pocket too slowly. Ponga Jim's left hand closed on his wrist, and his right moved also, in the form of a fist. That punch struck the man in the solar plexus and knocked every bit of wind out of him.

As he started to fall, Ponga Jim caught him by the shoulders and spun him around. Using the man as a shield, he started for the door. "Let's go," he said over his shoulder.

Don Pedro Norden and Dr. Von Hardt were standing at the door. Von Hardt's expression was stiff. Norden was purple with rage. "You fool," he snarled angrily. "I'll have you bullwhipped."

"Try it," Ponga Jim said, smiling.

At the outer door, the man Mayo was holding made a sudden lunge. Instantly, Mayo pushed him hard between the shoulders. As the man fell down the steps, the two made a dash into the shrubbery beyond the drive.

Running swiftly across the grass, Peligro spoke to Ponga Jim. "Gracias, amigo. But you make trouble for yourself."

"What would I do? That gang was tough."

Behind them Mayo heard running feet. Somewhere a motor roared into life, then all was still. But he was under no illusions. The pursuit would be swift, efficient, and relentless. Worst of all, it was more than ten miles to Fortaleza.

They had started across another curve of the drive when a car rounded a bend and they were caught dead in the headlights. Before they could get off the drive, the car swept alongside.

"Quickly!" It was Carisa Montoya at the wheel, and Ponga Jim did not hesitate. Peligro was in beside them and the car rolling almost as soon as she had spoken.

Miraculously, the gate was unguarded. The broad highway to the port lay open before them. Yet before they had been driving more than two minutes, Carisa slowed and sent the big car into a side road that led off down a steep grade through clumps of trees.

She slowed down. The car purred along almost silently. Huge boulders loomed up and were passed. Trees cast weird shadows over the road. Then they turned again and swung in a narrow semicircle back toward the hacienda.

"The highway is a trap," Carisa explained swiftly. "Don Pedro has five guards between the Castillo Norden and Fortaleza. No one can approach his place without permission."

"You'd better drop us and get back," Mayo warned. "This is all right for us, but for you it might be bad."

"Yes, please," Peligro said suddenly. "Let us out. The stable road will take you back without their knowledge. Then instantly to bed. We can go on from here."

The car slid soundlessly away. Ponga Jim Mayo looked after her. "That woman's got nerve," he said. "But not the best of friends."

Peligro was already moving, and before they had gone a hundred yards, Mayo knew that he was not walking blind. The little man knew where he was going.

"They will scour the country," Peligro said. "Don Pedro will be angry that I came here tonight."

"Will the señorita be able to get back all right?" Mayo asked.

Peligro shrugged. "She? But of course. The stable road, it is most safe. The peóns are there, but then, they see what they wish to see."

"Would Norden kill a woman?"

Peligro chuckled without humor. "He would kill anyone. He lives for power, that man."

"Is he a Nazi? Busch looked it."

"*Si*, Busch was a storm trooper. Von Hardt is also a Nazi. But Don Pedro Norden? He is a Nordenista, amigo, and that is all. He uses the Nazis as they use him."

"What about you?"

"I?" Peligro chuckled. "Let us say I love what Don Pedro hates. Perhaps that is sufficient. But then, I am a Colombian."

"The fifth column is strong in Colombia." Mayo studied the figure ahead of him.

"*Naturalmente*. Everywhere. But my country could never be a Nazi domain. There are more book shops in Bogotá than cafés. Think of that, amigo. Men who read are not Nazis."

Peligro stopped suddenly, then deliberately pushed through a thick wall of brush beside the path. After a few minutes, they stood in a small clearing. Under the arching branches was an autogyro, the outline of its rotating wing lost in the shadows.

Ponga Jim looked at the Colombian with respect. "Well, I'm stumped," he said. "You think of everything, don't you?"

Juan Peligro winked. "One does or one dies, my friend."

CHAPTER 2

It was still dark when Ponga Jim Mayo came alongside the ship. Only a dim anchor light forward, and the faint glow over the accommodation ladder. He paid the boatman and watched him start for the Custom House Pier. For some reason, he felt uneasy.

He glanced forward at the bulking stern of the freighter that lay a ship's length beyond the *Semiramis*. She was a Norwegian ship, the *Nissengate*.

Mayo had mounted the ladder and was just stepping to—the deck when a dark figure hurled itself from the blackness beyond the light. A shoulder struck him a terrific blow in the chest, and he was knocked off balance into the hand-line.

It caught him just at the hips, and overbalanced, he fell headfirst into the sea. He hit the water unhurt and went down, deep, deeper. He caught himself and struck out for the surface.

A dark body swirled by him, and a knife slashed. Avoiding it, he shot through the surface, and an instant later his attacker broke water not six feet away. Ponga Jim dived and grabbed the man's wrist, wrenching the knife from his grasp. Then closing with him, Mayo began to smash powerful blows into his body.

The man sagged suddenly. All the breath had been knocked from his body. The platform of the accommodation ladder seemed only a few feet away. Ponga Jim struck out, reached it, and crawled up. He dragged his prisoner with him.

He lay still, getting his wind. Then he got up and pushed the stumbling man ahead of him up the ladder.

"What iss?" A big man with a childlike pink face stepped out of the dark.

Instantly, Ponga Jim knew his mistake. Fighting and swimming, they had worked their way forward until alongside the Norwegian ship, boarding it by mistake. Glancing back toward the other ship, he could see they had swung nearer on the tide.

"Sorry," Mayo said. "This fellow jumped me as I came aboard my ship. I'll call a boat and we'll go back."

The seaman stared at him warily. He was carrying a short club and a gun. He looked like a tough customer. "How I know dat's true?"

The man who had attacked Ponga Jim came to life. "It's a lie," he burst out. "He attacked me."

"Aboard my own ship?" Mayo laughed. "Hardly." He swung the man into the light. He was short and thick, almost black. There was an ugly scar over one eye, another on his cheek. He glared sullenly at Mayo, then with a jerk, broke free.

Ponga Jim grabbed at him, but the watchman

stepped between. "How do I know yet which iss lyin'?" he demanded.

"Ask the men aboard my ship." Ponga Jim gestured aft. "The *Semiramis*."

The man peered at him. "Dot iss not der *Semiramis*. I neffer see no ship by dot name. Dot iss der *Chittagong*, of Calcutta."

"What?" Mayo stared aft. The dark loom of the ship was unfamiliar. Her bridge was too high, and there were three lifeboats along the port side of her boat deck, not two as on the *Semiramis*.

"You come aboard der wrong ship, mister," the seaman told him. "I t'ink you better go ashore now."

The man with the scarred face leered at him, his yellowish eyes triumphant. Ponga Jim looked from one to the other, but their expressions did not change. Dripping with water, he turned and went down the gangway.

When he had hailed a harbor boat, he had himself sculled aft. The other ship was a flush-decker at least a thousand tons heavier than the *Semiramis*. There were four other ships in the harbor, all unknown to him.

Ponga Jim Mayo scowled and let his memory travel back for a moment. Shortly after eight-thirty that morning, he had walked down the accommodation ladder and been taken ashore. Slug Brophy and Gunner Millan, his first and second mates, had leaned on the rail as he went. Beyond, several of the crew had been working about the deck.

Back on the Custom House Pier, Mayo took stock of the situation. He had been through too much with his crew to doubt their loyalty. He knew Brophy would never consent to move without ample reason, for Brophy was not a man to be bluffed or imposed upon.

Somewhere in the background would be Norden and his Nazi friends. Fourteen hours earlier, Mayo had left the ship with a full crew. Now she was gone.

In the meantime, he had received an offer for his amphibian plane. Upon refusing the offer, he had been threatened. The affair of Juan Peligro had brought about an open break with his host.

The Spanish-German might have had the ship removed from the harbor. If so, he would have laid deliberate plans to conceal his action. He would be ruthlessly efficient. No doubt the officials in port were all in his pay.

Coolly, Ponga Jim went to a hotel, obtained a room, and went to bed. In the morning after a good breakfast, he sought out the port captain. "What happened to the *Semiramis*?" Ponga Jim asked. "When I went ashore yesterday she lay aft of the *Nissengate*. When I returned she was gone."

The Brazilian looked at him thoughtfully. "The *Semiramis*, you say? I never heard of it."

"The pilot who brought me in was Du Silva," Mayo said.

Captain Duro studied Ponga Jim curiously, then shrugged. "I don't think so. Señor Du Silva has not come to work all week . . . I believe he is sick."

"Now that's a bunch of . . ." Then he stopped. "I see," he said warily.

"If I were you," the man told him lazily, leaning toward him, "I'd go home and get some sleep."

Ponga Jim's hand shot out and took the port officer by the throat. "And if I were you," he said coldly, "I'd figure out another story before the American consul and President Vargas begin to ask questions."

Duro's face paled, but he merely stared at Mayo, his eyes ugly.

"What could you tell them? That your ship, armed with a full crew, had been stolen from the harbor? It could be very amusing, señor."

Ponga Jim slammed the port captain back into his chair. "No," he said flatly, "I'd tell them Don Pedro Norden was a traitor, and that you were his tool."

He strode from the office. After all, Duro was right. It would be an utterly preposterous story. Ships of several thousand tons displacement do not vanish into thin air. As for witnesses, no doubt fifty people had noticed the *Semiramis*, but how many could see her name at that distance? The *Chittagong*, moored in the same place, would be considered the same ship. The few who knew better could be bribed or frightened.

Then, he was aware of the fact that his own reputation did not appeal to many government officials. He had been in action against the Japanese and Germans in the East Indies before the war began. That his aid had been invaluable to the Dutch and British was data burned deep into reports of their intelligence services. The fact that he had usually profited from those services would be enough to blacken his reputation with some people.

A man of Norden's strength could build a sub-stantial case against a lone captain of a tramp freighter with a mixed crew. Even if he won in the end and proved his point, it would require months of red tape and argument. In the meantime, what of his ship and his men?

Just why Norden wanted planes Mayo did not know, but the presence of Nazis on the hump of Brazil boded no good for the Allies. It was too near the source of bauxite for American planes. It was a place of great wealth and poverty, two elements that were often unstable when combined.

What Ponga Jim Mayo wanted done he must do himself. No doubt the communications were con-trolled by Norden, and it was to be doubted if any message he might send would be allowed to leave Fortaleza.

No doubt the freighter had been moved to some nearby river mouth or minor port where the plane would be removed. Possible anchorages were few, but there was nothing he could do to search. For the moment, the *Semiramis* and her crew must get along on their own. Don Pedro would expect him to protest to the government. He would expect ex-cited demands, protests, much noise. In that case, it would be very simple for Don Pedro to have him sent to an insane asylum. Certainly, a man claiming someone had stolen an unknown ship and its crew would be insane enough for most people.

Long ago, Ponga Jim Mayo had discovered that attack was the best defense. He had discovered that plotters like to take their own time. He knew that one man with energy and courage could do much. So he wasn't going to protest or demand, he wasn't going to argue. He was going to carry the fight to the enemy.

Jim bought a suit of khakis, and returning to the hotel, changed from the bedraggled suit. Castillo Norden was on a spur of Mount Jua, approximately ten miles from town. In the side street not far from the hotel was a disreputable Model A. Nearby a Brazilian loitered. He was a plump, sullen man with a mustache and round cheeks.

"How much to rent the car all day?" Mayo asked.

The Brazilian looked at him, bored. "You go to Castillo Norden, my friend," he replied, "you go to trouble."

Ponga Jim grinned. "Maybe I'm looking for trouble. Do we go?"

The Brazilian tossed his limp cigarette into the gutter.

"Why not?" he said with a shrug.

They rattled out of town and drove in silence for several miles. The man paid no attention to the main road, but took side roads toward Mount Jua. "I am Armando Fontes," he said, "always in troubles." He looked at Ponga Jim, his eyes sullen. "You have a gun?"

At Mayo's nod, he drew back his own coat and showed an enormous pistol stuffed in his waistband. "I, too!" he spat. "These men are bad. You better watch out. They got plenty stuff."

Leaving Fontes with the car, Ponga Jim walked up the stable road. He saw no one. It was easy to understand why Carisa and Peligro had been sure the road was safe.

It led through two rows of trees that would have allowed quick concealment in case of need.

Then he passed the stables and went on through the garden. He glanced back and saw a workman at the stables had straightened and was watching him, but when the *obrero* saw himself observed, he hastily bent over his work.

It was late afternoon when Ponga Jim slipped behind the boll of a palm, then behind a clump of hibiscus at the edge of the terrace where he had stood the night before.

He was waiting there when the French doors opened suddenly and Don Pedro Norden came out, walking with Don Ricardo. "You will see," Norden was saying, "the planes will be here. The fields have been ready for months. As you know, there has been no passport control at Fortaleza and we've been importing technicians, army officers, engineers, all sorts of men, most of them Germans."

"What about the Japanese?" Valdes suggested.

"Ready. The colonies around Cananea and Registro will act simultaneously with those here in Ceará and those on the Amazon. Our men have been posted in key spots for weeks now, ready for the day. The transport planes will move them where they are needed."

Valdez smiled grimly and nodded.

"You will give the word?"

"Soon. There are approximately three million Germans, Japanese, and Italians in this country. Most, of course, want no trouble but our men will hide in those communities and when the time comes they will make sure that the right kind of incidents occur. I think we can count on a good many joining us once they are threatened by the government.

"First, seventy key men will be assassinated. To allow for mistakes, each man is covered by two groups. Vargas and Aranha are among the first, of course. Both are strong, capable men, and without them the army will have to step in.

"São Paulo will be seized—it is practically in our hands now. Also Manáos. The Amazon will be closed to traffic, all available shipping will be impounded. Our airfields here and at Teresina will be receiving and refueling planes. We will have Brazil before Vargas realizes we are moving."

Valdes nodded. "A good plan, and a careful one."

Norden snorted. "How did I make my money, Don Ricardo? By taking chances? I made it by planning. At all my properties in South America there are bases. Fuel is stored, the two ships in Fortaleza harbor are full of munitions for our cause, we are ready. This amphibian we picked up today—it will be priceless in getting about. We need many planes now, and they are hard to get."

"What of the United States?" Valdes asked. "Will they interfere?"

"The Germans believe so. I doubt it. The Axis backs this move because they want a diversion, something to divide the strength of the North Americans. The Yankees will send some forces here, but we can handle what they send. The Americans are soft—their own correspondents say so."

Valdes nodded. "Perhaps, but this Mayo, he took that situation over last night too fast to suit me."

"Him?" Norden sneered. "I'll have him in an asylum before the week is out. He will be telling people his wild story of a stolen ship. It is too preposterous!"

"Perhaps." Don Ricardo was uneasy. "You have been successful but perhaps you are too sure." Valdes hesitated, biting his lip. "Don Pedro," he said slowly, "I have been hearing stories. When the amphibian landed here one of the men recognized it. The plane is special, made to order for Count Kull, one of Germany's most dangerous secret agents. It was taken from him by an adventurer in the East Indies."

"You mean—Mayo?" Don Pedro was scowling.

"Just that. What I'm saying, Don Pedro," Valdes insisted, "is that Ponga Jim Mayo may be a very dangerous man."

Norden paused. "Perhaps. All right. You have convinced me. I'll give the order that he be killed on sight. Now let us go in. I could use a drink."

CHAPTER 3

Killed on sight. Ponga Jim watched them go. At least it was all in the clear now. The amphibian was here. If he only knew where the *Semiramis* was!

He stood still, staring out across the spacious grounds that surrounded the Castillo Norden. What a fool he was to believe he could cope with all this alone. Don Pedro Norden had stood upon the terrace like a king, a man who knew great power, yet thirsted for more. He was no petty criminal, no agent of a foreign power. He was playing the Axis off against the United States to win more power for himself.

Even to hope seemed foolish. Yet, instinctively, he knew that to plan was to play Norden's game. The man was shrewd, he had power and held all the strings. Ponga Jim stood behind the hibiscus and knew that there was only one way out—right through the middle. Don Pedro had built well, but could the structure stand attack?

He glanced around. There was no one in sight. He caught the rack on which the wisteria grew and went up, hand over hand, to the balcony above.

He flattened against the building. He had been unobserved so far as he could see. He stepped to the window and pushed it inward. Carisa Montoya sat before a mirror in her robe, polishing her nails.

"Hello," he said cheerfully. "Did I come at the wrong time?"

She stiffened and swallowed a scream. "You? But, Jim, are you mad? If they find you here, they'll kill you. You've got to get away!" She caught him by the arm. "You must—now!"

"After all my trouble getting here? Anyway, why are you worried? And whose team are you on, anyway?"

"Not on theirs," she said. "But I have to be careful. And I'm worried because you're too good a dancer to die so young."

He grinned. "Shucks, and I thought it was my

boyish smile. All right, tell me one thing and I'll go. Where is Don Ricardo's room?"

Her face paled. "You mustn't. That would be insane."

"Tell me," he insisted. "The longer you stall the greater the danger."

"Across the hall and the third door on your left."

He walked to the door, and turning the key, glanced out. The hall was empty. He stepped out and pulled the door shut softly. Then he walked quietly across the hall to the third door. He touched the knob, and it turned gently under his hand.

Ponga Jim Mayo opened the door and stepped in—and found himself looking into the business end of a Luger in the hands of Hugo Busch.

"So," the German said. "We meet again."

Jim said nothing. The German's left hand was holding the telephone handset which had evidently just been replaced on the cradle. Carisa! Could she—

The door opened behind him, and then he heard Valdes's crisp voice. "May I ask what this means?" he demanded.

"The American came in, I followed," Busch said, shrugging. "How he got here, I don't know."

"Don Ricardo," Ponga Jim said coolly, "do you think if he followed me in that I would be standing near the door? I came in and found him."

"He lies," Busch snapped. "What would I be doing in your rooms?"

Valdes looked at the German thoughtfully. "What, indeed? Nevertheless, Herr Busch, it will bear thought. Now, if you like, take him away. I must dress for dinner."

Without a word Busch marched Ponga Jim to a square building near the stables. The windows were heavily barred. A man working nearby glanced up and saw Jim, then went on repairing a wagon, uninterested.

Hugo Busch, keeping carefully out of reach, swung open a cell door and pushed Jim inside. Then, suddenly, and before Mayo could turn, Busch struck him over the head with the gun barrel.

Jim staggered and almost went to his knees, then Busch hit him again. Ponga Jim tottered against the wall, blood running into his eyes from a cut scalp, blinded by pain and the ruthlessness of the sudden attack. Calling a guard, Busch handed the soldier the gun. Then he turned around and walked up to Jim.

"So? You come to cause trouble, eh? We'll see about that. Maybe I'll give you all the trouble you want."

His left smashed Jim on the jaw, knocking him across the cell. Ponga Jim pawed blindly at his face to get the blood out of his eyes.

On the second jab, Jim went under it and smashed Busch under the heart with his right. Before Busch could clinch, Jim hooked a left to the jaw and jarred the German to his heels.

Bursting with rage, Hugo Busch rushed back. Using all the power and skill that had once carried him to the Olympics he went to work. Blinded by blood and pain from the two brutal blows with the gun, Jim could get no power into his blows. Busch came up with a sweeping hook that lifted Mayo bodily and knocked him against the wall. He hit hard, slipped to the floor, and his head banged against the steel cot.

In a bloody haze, he tried to get up, and slipped back. He felt a heavy kick in the ribs, then another, but consciousness slipped from him, and he lay still.

It was dark when he opened his eyes, pitch dark. He rolled over, his body one endless wave of pain. Struggling, he got his knees under him and straightened. His head felt heavy and rolled on his neck. Fumbling, he felt of his face. It was cut and swollen, and his head had two long gashes from the gun barrel, and a big lump from the blow against the cot.

How long he stayed on his knees he did not know, but suddenly, he came to himself and got up. Then he was suddenly sick, and going to the corner, retched violently. Feeling around, he found a bucket of water, took a long drink, then poured some in the basin and splashed it over his face and head.

Then he lay down on the cot and after a while, he fell asleep. It was morning when he awakened.

A fumbling of a key in the lock awakened him, and he staggered to his feet to see Hugo Busch come in, stripped to the waist. The man was muscled powerfully, and he grinned at Mayo. There was a welt on his jaw, and a bit of a blue lump over one eye.

"Ready for a workout?" Busch grinned.

Unbelieving, Jim saw the man meant to beat him again. Busch walked up and swung his open hand at Jim's face. Bleary from the frightful beating of the night before, Mayo could barely roll his head out of the way, but Busch missed his careless slap, and it made him angry.

He jabbed a left at Jim's cut eye, and Jim started to go under it, but Busch was ready and dropped the left. The punch took Mayo between the eyes, and grabbing suddenly, he got Busch by the arm and jerked him into a right to the body. The punch lacked force, but had enough to hurt.

Busch tried to get loose, but Ponga Jim clinched and hung on.

Then the fighter broke free and went to work like a butcher at a chopping block. When the German left, he was covered with blood—Jim Mayo's blood. He laughed harshly.

"I'll be back," he said. "I'll be back tomorrow. We're going to put you in a ring to see how you Americans take it."

Ponga Jim backed up and sat down. After he had bathed his face again, he lay down and stared up at the ceiling through his swollen eyes. He had to get out. In time these beatings would kill him. If he had a chance to recover, and could start from scratch, it might be different. Now, there was no chance. Or was there?

For a long time he thought, and out of the thinking came a dim memory of a fight he had seen ten years before, of a fellow who used a Kid McCoy type of stunt. Out of that memory came a plan.

But it was a plan that covered only one phase. It did not cover escape. He had to get away, had to get out and let the authorities know what was being planned here.

It was then he heard the plane. Only a few minutes later, another, then several at once. He sat up abruptly. The transports were coming. That meant the day was soon to come.

In the morning he was still stiff and sore. He was battered, and he knew his cuts would open easily. A glance into a mirror showed he was hardly to be recognized. But he shadow-boxed a little to loosen up, and rubbed his muscles. He was, he knew, in no shape for such a battle as he would now have. But he was in better shape than Hugo Busch believed.

Valdes was with them when they came to get him. He frowned when he saw Ponga Jim's face.

"Been giving it to you, has he? Well, I don't like it."

Jim said nothing, and he was led to a ring that had been pitched in the open under some trees. Seats had been placed around, and there were at least thirty German officers there. One of them, an elderly man, scowled when he saw Mayo's face. He put a monocle in his eye and studied Jim briefly. Then he removed the monocle and started away. He took three steps but then walked back briskly.

"Good luck," he said briefly. "For myself, I don't care for this sort of thing."

Ponga Jim was stripped to the waist, and they were tying on the gloves when he looked up to see Carisa coming down the lane with Don Pedro and

Von Hardt. She involuntarily put a hand to her mouth when she saw Jim's face.

Busch got into the ring, and Jim barely had time to take the piece of tissue paper from under his arm and put it a little higher, so it would not be noticed. The action passed unseen.

Someone struck a bell, and Busch walked out. Jim came to meet him, then lifted his left arm. From the armpit the thin sheet of tissue paper floated toward the floor.

For an instant, Busch stared. Involuntarily, his hands dropped. An instant only, but it was enough. Ponga Jim threw his right high and hard.

There was a sodden smack, then Hugo Busch crumpled to the canvas without so much as a sound.

For a moment, there was dead silence. Then, from the crowd there arose a roar of anger, mingled with a few cries of approbation, and one definite hand clap. It was from the elderly officer with the monocle.

Lifted from the floor, Busch was showered with water. For an instant he stared, wondering. Then with a cry of rage, he shook off his handlers and rushed.

"Enough."

The voice did not seem loud, but suddenly everyone froze. Even Hugo Busch stopped his rush in midstride.

Not a dozen feet away, standing alone at the edge of the crowd, was Armando Fontes.

In his right fist he held his huge pistol. It was aimed at Don Pedro Norden!

CHAPTER 4

Armando Fontes was holding a large sweet potato in his left hand, and was gnawing at it contentedly. He was still wearing his soiled whites. His belt barely retained his bulging stomach.

"If you move," Fontes said, "I will kill Don Pedro. Señor Mayo, get out of the ring and walk to me."

For just a moment there was startled silence.

Ponga Jim, holding his breath, crawled through the ropes. Only then did anyone move. A German officer, at the opposite end of the line from Don Pedro, reached for his gun.

Fontes scarcely seemed to move, but the gun roared, and the German fell facedown, blood spattering the ground.

"Next time, Don Pedro," Fontes said, undisturbed, "it is you. If you no want to die, tell these men to stand still."

"Don't move," Norden said. "The fool really will shoot."

Fontes shrugged and backed slowly away after Jim Mayo. Around the corner of the stable, the Brazilian wheeled about and darted between two sheds. Almost at once a heavy cart laden with hay moved into the space, and a silent, unspeaking *obrero* began to work over the wheel.

Fontes knew his way. Quickly, and with devious turns, he led Mayo into the rocks along the side of Mount Jua. Behind them, men were scattering out. The cart in the opening between the sheds would delay pursuit. It would save a minute, perhaps two, for the line of stables and sheds was unbroken for some distance in either direction. And every second counted.

Armando, for all his weight, moved with surprising agility. He stopped once to hand Jim his gun.

"I take it from the guard," he said, "the carabinero was angry—but no matter."

Only a few paths led across the face of Mount Jua at this point. Don Pedro had obviously planned to have the mountain protect his rear, and certainly, only one who knew the paths could have traveled where Fontes was going.

Surprisingly, at the foot of the mountain trail the battered Model A was standing in the shade. They got in, and the motor coughed into life. Over a rocky, broken road, Fontes guided the car, seemingly more by instinct than sight.

"You saved me a beating," Ponga Jim Mayo said.

The Brazilian shrugged. "I don't like those men. They make troubles."

Ponga Jim went into the side entrance of the hotel and reached his room unnoticed. Armando sat down on the bed and took off his torn fedora, wiping his forehead.

"Is hot," he said. He looked solemn. "I wished to shoot him, that Don Pedro."

There was a light tap on the door, then even as Ponga Jim's gun slid into his hand, the door opened and Juan Peligro stepped in. He glanced quickly at Fontes.

"Who is this?" he demanded.

Mayo introduced them. Quickly, Peligro turned to Jim. "I have located your ship. It is in the Acaraú River. There are twenty men aboard, men other than your crew."

Ponga Jim explained quickly what he had overheard at the Castillo Norden, and what had happened there. When his story ended, Peligro looked at Fontes with respect.

"You could work for me, my friend," he said.

Armando shrugged. "It is no good work for other man," he said. "I work for myself. When I want to rest—I rest—want to work, I work. I like it this way."

Suddenly, a car rolled up to the front of the hotel. They all heard it. They also heard the sharp commands as men unloaded. Ponga Jim rushed for the door just in time to see a file of Norden's thugs come up the steps. He ducked back into the room. It was empty.

He stared about, unbelieving. But Peligro and Fontes were gone. Then he noticed the open window, its curtain blowing in the light breeze. A fist pounded on the door, and there was a sharp command to open.

Ponga Jim went out the window to the ledge, then dropped to the roof of the shed below it, and then into the street. A German rushed at him. They grappled for an instant, then Jim broke free and punched him solidly in the jaw.

Even as the man dropped, Jim jerked open a doorway and walked into a cantina. Mayo walked through to the street, went outside, dodged through the light traffic, and stepped into the car in front of his own hotel. It was a large, powerful car from the Castillo Norden.

The man on guard at the door of the hotel wheeled as the motor roared into life. Then as the guard realized what was happening, he raised his gun and took careful aim. Ponga Jim was dead in his sights, and for an instant, Mayo looked death in the face.

From across the street there was a great coughing gunshot. The soldier folded, his rifle going off harmlessly into the air. Even as Ponga Jim let the clutch out, he saw Armando Fontes, his huge pistol dangling in his fingers, leaning against the corner of the building across from the hotel.

The big car swung into a curve, and Jim stepped down on the accelerator and opened her up. Whatever else she had, the car had power. He headed out the road toward Castillo Norden, and when the car hit the highway it was doing ninety.

Norden's road was guarded. That was all right with Mayo. He roared past the first guard station with the motor wide open, and saw two men waving wildly as he went through.

Peligro had told him just where the amphibian was. It was gassed up and kept ready for instant flight. If he could get to it, and away, things would start to look up.

The big car whirled down the private road to the landing field. Dust clouds billowed out behind. Yet even as he swung onto the field, he saw Don Pedro, Von Hardt, Valdes, and Busch starting for the amphibian, whose propeller was turning lazily.

Crouching behind the wheel, Ponga Jim headed straight for them. They took one look and dived for shelter. He let the car shoot past the flying boat, then spun the wheel and turned it on a dime. For a split second he thought the big car would roll over, but it righted itself and he pointed it at the nearest transport in the row.

Jamming down the accelerator then shifting into neutral, Ponga Jim leaped from the running board. He landed hard, and scrambled to his feet, spitting dust. Beyond the amphibian he heard a tremendous crash as the speeding car smashed into the plane. Then there was an explosion, and both were in flames.

Mayo ran to the amphibian and crawled inside. The German pilot looked up. Mayo pulled his .45 and stuck it in the man's face. He herded the German out the hatch. An instant later he had it rolling down the runway. He eased back on the stick and the ship took off. It cleared the low hedge easily and mounted into the sky.

He climbed, cleared his guns with a burst, then swung the ship around. She was specially built, faster and more maneuverable than the basic model. He went back over the field, the four wing guns blazing. He saw men lift their rifles, then tumble into the dust. One man rushed for a .50-caliber machine gun on a hangar roof, but a burst of fire caught him and threw him bodily to the ground below. Ponga Jim drew the stick back and climbed steadily away from the Castillo Norden. One glance back showed the flames still roaring. Then he headed for the Acaraú River, and the *Semiramis*.

. . .

His head was aching fearfully. His swollen face still throbbed. In his dive from the car he had injured one leg, not badly, but enough for it to be painful. He flew steadily toward the river, remembering its position on the chart. It was, he remembered now, one of the few rivers along this section of the coast that could be entered by a ship of any size.

What would happen now, he could not guess. Juan Peligro and Armando Fontes were free, so far as he knew. If they could remain free they would be fortunate. What had been done was enough to force Don Pedro to move. The shooting in Fortaleza and the burning of the planes would be sure to excite comment in regions beyond Norden's control. Peligro, too, would be in touch with his government, and possibly with Vargas.

If Don Pedro hoped to win he must act at once. There was no chance for delay, no time for hesitation. His power had been flouted. The people of Fortaleza would know that there was opposition. Such petty officials as Duro would begin to shake in their boots. Such men always followed the winning side, and now there could be doubt.

Below he saw the winding thread of the Acaraú, and he circled the plane above the *Semiramis*. Then he made a shallow dive and waggled his wings. It was his old signal to his crew all was well. If any were on deck, they would be expecting him.

Ponga Jim had lost his own cap, so now he picked up a beautiful Panama that had been left in the cabin of his plane. From his pocket he took his gun and reloaded it. Then he took another from a locker in the plane, slipping it into his waistband.

Finally, he glided down to a landing, let the amphibian fishtail into the wind, and lay just a few yards from the *Semiramis*'s beam. After anchoring the plane, he stood up and straightened his clothes. A boat was coming toward him. Mayo now planned to try a colossal bluff, counting on the fact that no one aboard would know him but his own men.

As the boat drew alongside, he stepped in. Holding out his arm, hand open, he snapped a greeting.

"Heil Hitler!" he said.

The man in the launch returned the salute clumsily.

"To the *Semiramis*!" Mayo barked. "A message from Don Pedro."

Expecting nothing else, the man turned the launch and ran over to the accommodation ladder. Ponga Jim got up, pulled down the brim of his Panama, and eased his automatic in its shoulder holster. Then he went up the ladder.

Norden's captain, a wide-faced *mestizo*, was at the gangway with another man. Beyond them, working over some running gear, was Big London. The surprised Negro turned abruptly away from Jim, then stepped around the corner of the hatch where he could watch without seeming to notice. But Mayo had no time to waste.

As the captain opened his mouth to speak, Ponga Jim thrust the automatic into his stomach.

"*Manos arriba!*" he snapped.

The man gulped and lifted his hands, as did the man beside him. Ponga Jim spoke no Portuguese, but Spanish was close enough. Jim drew their guns and tossed them to London.

"Get the crew out," he said.

In a matter of minutes, the crew was on deck . . . the ship taken back before the guards realized just what was happening. The surprise was complete.

Ponga Jim grabbed Brophy. "Get under way," he said quickly. "I want you to run up to Fortaleza. There are two ships there, the *Nissengate* and the *Chittagong*. Both are loaded with munitions. Sink them."

Slug Brophy jerked a thumb at the armed freighter nearby. "What about him?"

"Leave him to me," Mayo said grimly. "Get four bombs aboard the amphibian. They won't notice because this ship lies between."

Brophy snapped into action, and Jim noticed the guns being cleared for trouble. Within twenty minutes after he landed, he was taking off. He climbed to a thousand feet, swung around, and started back for the armed freighter.

Even as he swung back he could see the *Semiramis* pulling up to her anchor. The captain of the armed freighter was shouting something at the *Semiramis* when Ponga Jim released his first bomb.

Ponga Jim had come in slowly, taking his time, and the crew of the ship were expecting nothing. The bomb hit the starboard bridge, glanced off, and struck the deck. It exploded with a terrific concussion.

Jim swung back over again, ignoring the men

trying to man an AA gun, and let go with another. That bomb hit the water within a foot of the ship and the explosion blazed a fountain of water high into the air. The freighter heeled over violently, and Ponga Jim could see flames roaring in the 'tween decks through the gaping hole torn in her deck and hull by the first explosion.

He banked steeply and soared off over the hills, heading to Natal. As he left he saw the *Semiramis* open fire on the crippled freighter with her 5.9-inch guns.

Quartered at Natal there were American troops. Also, there would be, he hoped, some Vargas officials who were loyal. Despite himself, he was worried. Don Pedro Norden was no fool. He was an utterly unscrupulous and ruthless man who knew how and when to act. That Ponga Jim had won this last move was due largely to the daring of his performance and the fact that Don Pedro underrated him.

CHAPTER 5

It was dark when he flew back to Fortaleza. Earlier, he had located a small lake in an uninhabited region. It was set among some wooded sand dunes, and as he glided in he could see no signs of life. He paddled ashore in his rubber boat, and concealed it in some thick brush, then he started walking toward the city.

Flying up, he had seen no sign of the *Semiramis*, and he was worried. He had swung wide to get a glimpse of the field at Norden's estate; it was empty. The planes had gone. Even the signs of the fire had been eradicated. All that had him worried, too; it would have been more to his liking for there to have been government officials circulating, asking difficult questions . . . forcing Don Pedro to spend time and energy in a cover-up.

The streets of Fortaleza were quiet, too quiet. A few men walked here and there about their business. A few straggled into the theaters. A group of hard-faced men stood on a corner, talking in low voices. As he passed, Ponga Jim saw them turn to look. The Panama was pulled low, and his face showed but little in the vague light.

He walked on. There were other clusters of men. These groups stood in strategic positions, and he saw the city was dominated by them. Several planes flew over the town, headed inland. A woman passed him, her face stiff with fear, and hurried down a side street.

"You must get off the streets, amigo," a low voice whispered. "They mean to kill you on sight."

Mayo turned to find Peligro at his elbow.

"What of you, *chiquito*?" he said grinning. "From what I heard you aren't exactly welcomed around here yourself."

Juan Peligro shrugged. "I fear you are right, señor. They do not appreciate my talents. Don Pedro has practically occupied Fortaleza. The planes are flown inland."

"To Teresina and his mines and plantations, I'll bet. He has bases there for them." Jim looked around. "What will happen now?"

"I don't know," Peligro shrugged. "At midnight the word is to go out. The killings will start, there will be risings all over Brazil. In Colombia, too. There is to be peace with the Axis and war with the Allies."

Ponga Jim looked at him. "From where will they send the message? Here? Or from Castillo Norden?"

"From the Castillo. I heard—only now—that Norden is soon to leave. That is to be the signal. He himself, you see, plans to be unaware of the murdering until it is completed. If it is successful then he will make a speech, and later will give medals and jobs to the murderers."

Up the street there was a crash of glass and a shout of fury. The bunch nearest Jim started for a store, and one man put his shoulder against the door. It burst open, and the thugs from the street corner dragged a shouting shopkeeper into the street. One struck him, another kicked him.

"We might as well start here," Ponga Jim said grimly. He turned on his heel and walked up behind the nearest troublemaker. Mayo grabbed him by the collar and hurled him into the street. From a brown shirt nearby came a shout of rage. The other men whirled about. Ponga Jim's first punch knocked a man rolling. Grabbing a stick from another, he laid about him furiously. Another man tumbled, and then someone fired. Instantly, Jim went for his gun. Standing in the middle of the sidewalk, he fired coolly and steadily. Two men dropped, and another staggered, then ran off.

Suddenly at the corner, a heavy gun boomed. Glancing over, Mayo saw Armando Fontes standing in the street with his big pistol. Juan Peligro had gone into action, too, and cheered by their support, shopkeepers and other Vargas sympathizers rushed into the streets with weapons.

Then something happened that stopped them all, both sides, dead in their tracks.

A dull boom sounded from the east. Next the scream of a shell. As one man, the people stopped fighting and stared toward the harbor. The *Semiramis* steamed in, swung broadside, and then her 5.9's began to fire.

For the first time in the three years he had owned her, and in all the actions she had come through, Ponga Jim Mayo could stand on the sidelines and watch his ship in action. Only a dark shadow on the water now, lighted by constant blasts of gunfire, but he knew every line of her, every spot of rust, every patch of red lead.

Shells screamed overhead, blasting the hangars of the airfield into flaming ruins and turning level runways into pitted, pockmarked uselessness. Then the fire ceased, and when it opened again, the guns were fired on the *Nissengate*.

It was point-blank range. Jim could almost hear Gunner Millan's crisp orders, could see the powerful muscles of Big London and Lyssy, passing shells to the crew.

A shell exploded amidships. Another blasted the stack into a canted, swaying menace, hanging only by its stays. The after wheelhouse vanished in the crimson blare of an explosion, and then a shot pierced the hull and exploded.

All sound was lost in a tremendous blast as

though someone had suddenly exploded a balloon that was miles in diameter. The burst of air and the concussion left them deaf and silent amid crashing glass of broken windows in the town. They stared at each other, mouths open, and eyes goggled at the tremendous pillar of flame that shot suddenly skyward.

People began to run. Nordenistas, Falangists, and the supporters of Vargas all in one mass, they ran.

Peligro grabbed Ponga Jim's arm, but Jim was waiting, his eyes bright. The *Semiramis* swung a little, and the 5.9's covered the *Chittagong*. The latter vessel was armed, and her own guns began to roar, but the crews kept overshooting badly.

A shell from the *Semiramis* landed on the poop of the *Chittagong* and exploded. Then more guns began to hammer, and Jim could see, even at that distance, the black figures of men as they dove overboard from the *Chittagong*. Three were fighting desperately to launch a boat. Then the ship caught fire.

Jim wheeled, and with Juan Peligro beside him, started on a run for the edge of town. Only a couple of hundred yards, and then Armando Fontes came alongside in his panting Model A. They scrambled in, and following Jim's directions they started over the sand hills toward the amphibian.

They left the car in the brush and walked down to the water, and Jim got the rubber boat from the brush. They had reached the plane and Mayo was getting in when he saw a flicker of movement.

A boat had appeared at the tail of the ship, and

he saw himself staring into three submachine guns. He thought, for one breathless instant, of risking a dive into the lake, then gave up. Even if he succeeded, Fontes and Peligro would be shot down like sheep.

"Get in." It was Hugo Busch. "Get in the plane."

Mayo reluctantly stepped aboard. Von Hardt was sitting there, gun in hand.

When the plane was in the air, Busch came back to where they were sitting. He grinned widely as he sat down nearby.

"You've been putting on a show, Mayo," he said, "and Norden is quite unhappy. What I'd have done to you would be nothing to what you'll get now."

Busch turned his head to stare at Fontes. "Where did you pick this up?" he said. "He looks like somebody you found in a Hollywood comedy."

Fontes said nothing. But he stared at Busch, his eyes sullen. Then coolly, he rolled his quid and spat. The tobacco juice splashed on the German's chin and shirt collar, and Busch went white with fury.

With a lunge, the German grabbed Fontes by the throat, but bound as he was, the Brazilian was powerless to defend himself.

"Hugo!" Von Hardt's voice cracked like a bull-whip. "None of that."

Busch subsided, his face livid. Armando Fontes rolled himself into a sitting position and stared at Busch, still sullen and unperturbed.

Twenty minutes later, still bound, the three were taken from the plane to the library of Castillo Norden. Don

Pedro and Carisa Montoya sat waiting for them, Don Pedro staring with cruel eyes. Nearby, Carisa sat, more beautiful than ever.

Norden studied the three, then looked up.

"Leave them, Herr Busch," he said sharply. "Tell Enrico to get the radio warmed up. It is almost time."

Don Pedro got up. Despite himself, he was alive with anticipation and could not refrain from showing it. He looked at Mayo.

"So? You thought to interfere? Well, you have courage, even if you have no brains. You have changed my plans, Captain Mayo. But for the better. I have decided not to wait. The zero hour was to have been three days from now. But this interference has decided me. The time is now." Don Pedro Norden shoved his hands down his coat pockets, and his hard eyes gleamed with triumph. "In just fifteen minutes the word goes out. The hour to strike has come."

Fifteen minutes!

Then it was too late! All he had planned, his trip to Natal, everything was in vain. They could do nothing to warn the officials now. Brazil would be caught flat-footed. There was, nowhere, any knowledge of such a power as Norden had welded together. Nowhere but in Berlin and Tokyo.

Shoved down into chairs, Mayo and his two companions were bound hand and foot. Don Pedro seemed to have forgotten them. He pressed a button and several men came in. To each he handed a brief, typewritten sheet. His orders rapped out thick and fast.

Norden had planned well, the plan was set to function, and each man was dropping into his position to await the final order.

Ponga Jim glanced at Peligro. The Colombian was perspiring, his face a deathly pallor. Armando Fontes, his eyes narrow, was staring at Norden.

Carisa Montoya, her face stiff, watched what was happening. At Natal, Major Palmer was ready with his bombers and fighters, but he would be too late, and once the plan was under way his force would be too small.

The plan was simple, concise, beautifully organized. The risings in Cananea, Registro, and other Japanese-inhabited localities would make each a central headquarters for a series of forces striking out into loyal territory. Rio Grande do Sul, with its large German population, would fall into the conspirators' hands like a ripe plum. With submarines to halt naval interferences, rapid moves could in a few hours have much of Brazil in the hands of Don Pedro; the entire South American situation would be changed, forever.

The new government of the Argentine would do nothing. Chile would be uneasy, but would sit quiet. Paraguay was ready, Uruguay might fight, although surrounded by enemies.

With the fall of Brazil, Don Pedro would set up a dictatorship, refuse to allow the passage of bombers to Africa, and the southern supply route to Egypt would be forced into the North Atlantic, where German submarines hunted like packs of wolves. Axis sub and plane bases in Brazil would give them complete control of the Caribbean and passage around the Cape of Good Hope. Tunisia, Egypt, India, Iraq, Iran, and Russia would be denied help except what could reach them through the blockade of the Pacific.

The United States military would be too late. The move within the country, carefully supplemented by just a little outside help, would be successful and the situation of the Allies would suddenly become infinitely more hazardous—even desperate.

Ponga Jim glanced at the clock. Five minutes. Suddenly, he looked at Carisa. The intensity was gone from her expression. It was suddenly calm and resolute. For an instant, their eyes met, then they flickered away and stopped.

Slowly Mayo's eyes followed. Don Pedro's automatic lay forgotten on his smoking stand beside his desk, not six feet from Carisa's hand. Their eyes met, and almost imperceptibly, he nodded.

Abruptly he spoke.

"You can't get away with this, Norden," he protested. "Take a tip from me and get out from under while you can."

Norden turned a little in his chair, as Jim had hoped he would do. The man was superbly confident.

"Get out from under? Don't be absurd, Captain. I have a foolproof plan. You have seen enough here today to tell how perfectly it will function. I'll admit, however, that your ship has caused me no end of inconvenience.

"Right now, though"—he glanced down at an order at hand—"we know where she is; the *Semiramis* is in a small harbor not far from Natal. We will have her attacked at daybreak by three dive-bombers. She cannot escape.

"News of her action never left this province. That was carefully arranged. By the time that information reaches Rio, I will be in command there."

"You've overlooked something," Jim said. Carisa had edged a trifle closer to the gun. "That I made a trip to Natal while in the amphibian."

Don Pedro's eyes flickered. "To Natal?" He studied Mayo thoughtfully. "What difference could that make?"

"This difference," Jim told him flatly, "that our officer there immediately sent word to the United States. Ships and planes in force will arrive here in a matter of hours. They may even be coming in now."

Even as he spoke, Ponga Jim knew the folly of what he said. Palmer and Wagnalls had done no such thing. Palmer had said his hands were tied, that there was nothing he could do but inform President Vargas of the plot.

CHAPTER 6

But Jim Mayo could see the possibility disturbed Norden. The plan was too perfect to risk making any changes. It all must work, or the parts each became insecure. Ponga Jim's suggestion, simple as it was, left him uncertain. He did not believe the story, yet it could be.

"So?" He studied Jim, and Jim smiled slowly. "I just wanted, Don Pedro, to let you stick your neck way, way out. I wanted you in so deep you couldn't pull back. When you give that order in just one minute, you'll seal your own doom."

"Don't take me for a fool!" Norden snapped. "You're bluffing!"

He started to get up, and in that instant, Carisa reached out and grasped the gun. Even as the butt slipped into her hand, Don Pedro, sensing something wrong, whirled about.

With a snarl of fury, he grabbed Carisa's hand. Instantly, Jim hurled all his weight forward and his chair tipped over under Norden's feet. The big man fell over him with a crash, the gun breaking loose from his hand and flying across the room.

Norden struggled to get up, and Carisa tripped him again. Ponga Jim, remembering an old trick he had used before, rolled atop the fallen man. Fontes and Peligro were struggling madly to escape, and Carisa scrambled to her feet and ran across the room after the gun. In that instant, the door opened, and Von Hardt stepped in.

His mouth opened in a cry for help when Armando Fontes suddenly heaved from his chair and lunged across the room. He hit Von Hardt with what resembled a flying tackle, knocking the man clear out into the spacious hall.

Von Hardt shouted wildly. Fontes leaped up from the fallen man, then wheeled and darted back into the room, kicking shut the door. Carisa had struck Norden over the head and was fighting desperately to get Jim untied. Peligro was still bound.

In a few seconds both men were free. Norden was struggling to get up, and Ponga Jim walked across and slugged him, knocking the financier into a heap. Peligro rescued their guns and tossed Jim's to him.

Shouts were ringing through the house now, and they could hear running feet. Mayo grabbed Carisa.

"Quick," he shouted. "Which way to the radio room?"

Leading the way, Carisa opened a small door in the corner and ran down a hall. Behind them, fists were thundering on the library door.

They found the radio room empty, and Peligro dropped into place at the controls. The typewritten orders lay beside the radio, stacked neatly on the left-hand side of the mike.

Ponga Jim grabbed the microphone as Fontes and Carisa began moving a filing cabinet against the door. "Mayday . . . Mayday . . . Calling S.S. *Semiramis* . . . calling *Semiramis* . . . calling—"

The reply was distinct and clear. "*Semiramis* ready . . . what is it? . . . *Semiramis* answering Mayday . . . *Semiramis*—"

"Mayo speaking. Get out of that harbor now. Bombers to attack at daylight."

A machine gun rattled and the door was riddled with bullets. Ponga Jim turned, watching the door, and talking coolly and calmly. As he continued to broadcast, sending a warning to Rio describing the day's events and the plot, he grabbed up the pile of typewritten orders and shoved them into his pocket.

Fontes had drawn back to one side and had his gun ready. Carisa, her face deathly pale, was holding the small automatic she had taken from Don Pedro. Mayo signed off as the door began to splinter.

Fontes's gun exploded, and there was a shrill

scream of pain outside the door. Peligro began methodically smashing the radio.

Seeing a window, Ponga Jim darted across. Four feet below and two feet to one side was the parapet of a lower section of roof. While Fontes kept up occasional blasts at the door, Jim opened the window and lowered Carisa, then Peligro, to the parapet.

"All right," Jim said, "you're next."

Fontes shrugged. "You, señor. I will stay."

"Nuts," Jim said. "Beat it."

Fontes swung to the wall, and Peligro caught his feet and held them until he was balanced. Ponga Jim leaped to the sill and with his gun in hand, dropped one leg outside, then the other.

The door came in with a splintering crash, and Jim's automatic bucked in his hand. The first man plunged over on his face, and then a bullet smashed the wall near Jim, stinging his face with tiny fragments of mortar and stone. He fired back, edging along the parapet. The gun locked open, out of ammunition.

Mayo turned, balancing on the edge of the parapet, then dropped to the roof.

Peligro was waiting for him.

"Quick. The others are below."

Dropping to the ground, the two men darted through the thick shrubbery and headed for the amphibian.

But the search was closing in. Behind them there was shouting, and off to the left they heard the crashing of men in the brush. Everywhere, their enemies were searching. Leading the way now, Ponga

Jim took them into a low place on the edge of the airfield.

"Stay here and keep out of sight. I'll get that ship, bring her down here to take off; you come running."

Without waiting for a reply, he pushed his way into the brush. He took his time, working his way carefully, to make no noise. Norden would kill now. He would kill without hesitation.

The amphibian was in plain sight, and the motors were turning slowly. Beside the ship a mechanic was loafing, and Jim could see the glow of his cigarette. There were three other planes on the ground nearby.

Walking swiftly, Ponga Jim started across the field. He was within a few feet of the mechanic when the man saw him—too late. Jim lunged and swung, knocking the man into a heap under the wing. He had no more than regained his balance when a cold voice cut across his consciousness. "You again, is it?"

Mayo turned, slowly. Hugo Busch was standing there looking at him.

"I knew you'd come here," Busch said, "so I waited. They are hunting you back there in the trees. . . . We will have a little time together so I could finish what I started."

Ponga Jim's mouth felt dry. The lights from the hangars showed the ground smooth and clear of obstacles. He could see the German's broad, powerful shoulders, and he remembered the driving power of his punches.

They were the same height, but Busch was at least twenty pounds heavier than Jim's own two hundred.

"All right," Jim said quietly, "if that's the way you want it."

The German walked in, smiling, superbly confident. Then his left shot out, but Jim went under the punch with a smashing right to the heart. In a split second the two men were standing toe-to-toe slugging it out. Blood flew, furiously, desperately, each suddenly conscious that the end might mean death, each aware of so much at stake, and each filled with a killing fury.

The German hit Jim with a wicked right hook that knocked his head back on his shoulders, and then slammed a left into his body. That punch turned Jim sick at the stomach. He clinched, and hurled the German to the ground. Busch came back up like a cat. Hugo rushed, and Jim took two driving blows to the body, then his head rocked with a wicked right that had him hanging on while Busch ripped into him with short, driving blows.

Ponga Jim broke loose. He smashed the German's nose with a short right. Then he hooked a left to the head, took a smashing right, and landed with both hands to the body.

The German seemed to have limitless strength. He kept coming, boxing skillfully at times, then dropping his skill to fight like a demon.

Yet Ponga Jim was learning. He was surer of himself now. He began to push the fight more and more. He caught the hardest blows on his shoulders and pushed his way ahead. Years of rugged living, of fresh sea air, hard work, and clean living had left him hard as nails. He drove on in now, slugging in a kind of bloody haze, confident of only one thing, that he was going to win. Busch set himself and feinting, threw a hard right.

This was the chance Jim had been waiting for. He put everything he had in his own right. It landed with a thud like an ax striking a log, and Hugo packed ground. Drunkenly, Mayo almost collided with the plane.

Ponga Jim started the plane forward in a groggy haze. Guiding it by instinct, he paused at the end of the field. Juan Peligro, Armando Fontes, and Carisa came running. Jim took off, circled, then headed back over the flying field. His mind was clearing, and though his body was hurt, felt better than he had expected. He had taken all the big German had been able to give, and he had won.

The amphibian, he noticed, had been loaded with bombs. It was carrying six. He let one go as he swung in toward the field, another over the sheds, then he swung around, and in a rattle of machine-gun fire, let go two more over Castillo Norden. As the plane circled away, they could look back and see flames leaping high.

Peligro was at the plane's radio, and now his eyes brightened.

"They are coming!" he said excitedly. "Your Navy is coming!"

They landed once more on the small lake near Fortaleza and started back toward the city.

Ponga Jim Mayo's face was cut and swollen. Peligro looked tired, and Carisa Montoya walked almost in a dream. Only Armando Fontes looked the same; his round, fat face was sullen, his eyes somber when they passed the light of a window.

The streets were empty. Two bodies lay in the gutter where they had fallen earlier, and the sidewalks were littered with broken glass. A heavy smell of smoke from the explosion and fire tainted the air, and the waters of the bay were littered with wreckage. It was almost day, but the moon was still bright.

In the vague light the streets looked like those of a long-deserted city. Yet as they rounded a corner, a file of soldiers in Brazilian uniforms turned into the street from the opposite direction. They marched past, stepping briskly along, a cool, efficient, soldierly body of men. "That means that Vargas acted," Ponga Jim said. "Everything will be over soon enough."

They reached the steps of the hotel and started in when two men came out. One was Major Wagnalls from Natal. The other was Slug Brophy, Jim's chief mate.

The major smiled and held out a hand. "So you made it! One of our boys just radioed word that Castillo Norden was in flames, the hangars destroyed, and three planes burning on the field.

"A transport landed there a few minutes ago

from Rio. Von Hardt has been arrested by Major Palmer, and they found Hugo Busch beaten unconscious. A mechanic said you did it." Wagnalls looked at Jim. "I didn't think anybody could do that."

"Neither did I," Mayo said simply. "I guess I was lucky."

"What about Don Pedro?" Peligro interrupted. "He is the one we want."

Wagnalls's brow creased. "That's the missing item. He escaped. It doesn't matter, for the government will confiscate his holdings here, so his power is broken. But I dislike to see him free.

"Especially," he added, "since Señorita Montoya will soon be known as a government agent. . . . President Vargas was suspicious, and Miss Montoya knowing Don Pedro, volunteered to investigate."

"What I want to know," Mayo demanded, "is how they captured my ship?"

Brophy grinned sheepishly. "Duro, the port captain, Du Silva, and an army officer came out. They had three girls along, so we didn't expect trouble.

"They came aboard, and Duro said he had to search my cabin for dope. We started for the cabin. No sooner had we left the deck than men came up the ladder and deployed about the deck."

"There's still some fighting going on but all the principal plotters are taken care of but Don Pedro," Wagnalls said. "But we'll have him soon."

"I don't think so."

Ponga Jim Mayo felt himself turn cold. His back was to the speaker, but he needed no more than those few words to tell him who it was. The voice had been low, but heavy with menace. He turned.

Thirty feet away, Don Pedro Norden stood in the street near the mouth of a narrow alleyway. In his hands he held a submachine gun. His brilliantly conceived plot had fallen to pieces, the men he hated had won. Yet he had a gun, and the little group before the hotel were covered, helpless.

Norden's clothing was torn and bloody, his face looked thinner, harder, more brutal. If ever a man was seething with hate, it was this one. Never in his life, Jim knew, had he been so close to death. The man was fairly trembling with triumph and killing fury. The architects of his defeat—Juan Peligro, Major Wagnalls, Brophy, Carisa, and Ponga Jim— were all in range. He could in one burst of fire wipe the slate clean of his enemies.

Norden's teeth bared in a grimace of hate, and when he spoke his voice was choked with emotion. "Perhaps I will be captured, but not yet. . . ."

The submachine gun lifted, and Jim thought that even at that distance he could see the man's finger tighten.

A gun roared, and the submachine gun began to chatter, but the muzzle had fallen, and the bullets merely bit against the stones of the street and ripped the dust into little fountains of fury.

Don Pedro Norden, a great black hole between his eyes, the back of his head blown away, fell slowly on his face.

Turning, they saw Armando Fontes, the big pistol clutched in his right hand, leaning nonchalantly against a corner. With a match in his cupped left hand, he was lighting a cigarette.

For a long moment, they stared, relief soaking through them. Ponga Jim looked at the disreputable little man.

"All right, Armando," he asked. "Tell us. Who are you agent for? What's your part in this?"

Fontes shrugged, his eyes lidded. He drew on his cigarette and took the occasion to slip the big gun back into his waistband.

"I, señor? I am but a little man. A little man who likes his government."

He turned, and with a deprecating wave of his hand, walked down the street, and away.

THE VANISHED BLONDE

Only one light showed in the ramshackle old house, a dim light from a front window. Neil Shannon hunched his shoulders inside the trench coat and looked up and down the street. There was only darkness and the slanting rain. He stepped out of the doorway of the empty building and crossed the street.

There was a short walk up to the unpainted house, and he went along the walkway and up the steps. Through the pocket of the trench coat, he could easily reach his .38 Colt automatic, and it felt good.

He touched the doorbell with his left forefinger and waited. Twice more he pressed it before he heard footsteps along the hall, and then the door opened a crack and Shannon put his shoulder against it. The slatternly woman stepped back and he went in. Down the hall, a man in undershirt and suspenders stared at him. He was a big man, bigger than Neil Shannon, and he looked mean.

"I've some questions I want to ask," Shannon said to the man. "I'm a detective."

The woman caught her breath, and the man walked slowly forward. "Private or Headquarters?" the man asked.

"Private."

"Then we're not answering. Beat it."

"Look, friend," Shannon said quietly, "you can talk to me or the DA. Personally, I'm not expecting to create a lot of publicity unless you force my hand. Now you tell me what I want to know, or you're in trouble."

"What d'you mean, trouble?" The man stopped in front of Shannon. He was big, all right, and he was both dirty and unshaven. "You don't look tough to me."

Shannon could see the man was not heeled, so he let go of the gun and took his hand from his pocket.

"Get out!" The big man's hand shot out.

Shannon brushed it aside and clipped him. It was a jarring punch and caught the big fellow with his mouth open. His teeth clicked like a steel trap and he staggered. Then Shannon hit him in the wind and the big fellow went down, his hoarse gasps making great, empty sounds in the dank hallway.

"Where do we talk?" Shannon asked the woman.

She gestured toward a door, then opened it and walked ahead of him into a lighted room beyond. Shannon grabbed the big man by his collar and dragged him into the room.

"I want to ask about a woman," he said, his eyes sharp. "A very good-looking blonde."

The woman's face did not change. "Nobody like

that around here," she said sullenly. "Nobody around here very much at all."

"This wasn't yesterday," Shannon replied. "It was a couple of years ago. Maybe more."

He saw her fingers tighten on the chair's back and she looked up. He thought there was fear in her eyes. "Don't recall any such girl," she insisted.

"I think you're wrong." He sat down. "I'm going to wait until you do." He was on uncertain ground, for he had no idea when the girl had arrived, nor how, nor when she had left. He was feeling his way in the dark.

The man pulled himself to a sitting position and stared at Shannon, his eyes ugly.

"I'll kill you for that!" he said, his voice shaking with passion.

"Forget it," Shannon said. "You tried already." His eyes lifted to the woman. "Look, you can be rid of me right away. Tell me the whole story from beginning to end, every detail of it. I'll leave then, and if you tell me the truth, I won't be back."

"Don't recall no such girl." The woman pushed a strand of mouse-colored hair from her face. Her cheeks were sallow and her skin was oily. The dress she wore was not ragged from poverty, merely dirty, and she herself was unclean.

Disgusted, Shannon stared around the room. How could a girl, such as he knew Darcy Lane to be, have come to such a place? What could have happened to her?

· · ·

He had looked at her picture until the amused expression of her eyes seemed only for him, and although he told himself no man could fall in love with a picture, and that of a girl who was probably dead, he knew he was doing a fair job of it.

Right now he knew more about her than any woman he had ever known. He knew what she liked to eat and drink, the clothes she wore and the perfume she preferred. He had read, with wry humor, her diary and its comments on men, women, and life. He had studied the books she read, and was amazed at their range and quantity.

He had sat in the same booth where she had formerly come to eat breakfast and drink coffee, and in the same bar where she had drunk Burgundy and eaten Roquefort cheese and crackers. Yet despite all the reality she had once been, she had vanished like a puff of smoke.

Alive, beautiful, talented, intelligent, filled with laughter and friendship, liked by both men and women, Darcy Lane had dropped from sight at the age of twenty-four as mysteriously as though she had never been, leaving behind her an apartment with the rent paid up, a closet full of beautiful clothes, and even groceries and liquor.

"Find her," Attorney Watt Braith had said. "You've three months to do it, and she has a half million dollars coming. You will get twenty-five dollars a day and expenses, with a five-hundred-dollar bonus if you succeed."

Whatever happened to Darcy Lane had happened suddenly and without preliminaries. Nothing in all her effects gave any hint as to what such a girl would be doing in a place like this. Yet it was his only lead, flimsy, strange, yet a lead nonetheless.

The police had failed to find her. Then their attention had been distracted by more immediate crimes; the disappearance of one girl who, it was hinted, had probably run off with a lover, was forgotten. Now, he had a tip, just a casual mention by a man he met in Tilford's Coffee Shop, to the effect that he had once seen the beautiful blonde, who used to eat there, living in a ramshackle dump in the worst part of town. The description fit Darcy Lane.

Six months after she disappeared, prospector Jim Buckle was killed in a rockslide that overturned his jeep and partially buried him, and Darcy Lane sprang into the news once more when it turned out that Buckle had two million dollars' worth of mineral holdings and that he had left it to four people, of whom Miss Lane was one.

"Talk," Neil Shannon said now to the disreputable-looking pair before him, "and you might get something out of it. Keep your mouths shut and you're in trouble. You see," he smiled, "I've a witness. He places the girl in your place, and you both were seen with her. You"—he pointed a finger at the man—"forced her back into a room when she wanted to come out."

The man glared balefully at him. "She was sick," he said, "she wasn't right in the head."

Neil Shannon tightened, but his face did not change. Now he had something. At all costs, he must not betray how little it was, how the connection was based on one man's memory, a memory almost three years old. "Tell me about it."

He reached in his pocket and drew out a ten-dollar bill, smoothing it on his knee. The woman stared at it with eager, acquisitive eyes.

"He found her," she said. "She was on the beach, half naked, and her head cut. He brought her here."

"Shut up, you old fool!" The man was furious. "You want to get us into trouble?"

"Talk, and maybe you can get out of it. You're already in trouble," Shannon assured them. "If the girl was injured, why didn't you take her to a hospital? Or report it to the police?"

"He wanted her," the slattern said malevolently. "That's why he did it. She didn't know who she was nor nothin'. He brung her here. He figured she'd do like he said. Well, she wouldn't! She fought him off, an' made so much fuss he had to quit."

"What about you?" the man sneered. "You and your plans to make money with her?"

Sickened, Shannon stared at them. What hands for an injured girl to fall into! "What happened?" he demanded. "Where is she now?"

"Don't know," the man said. "Don't know nothin' about that."

Neil got up. "Well, this is a police matter, then."

"What about the ten?" the woman protested. "I talked."

"Not enough," Shannon said. "If you've more to say, get started."

"She'd been bumped or hit on the head," the

woman said. "First off, I thought he done it, but I don't think he did from what she said after. She was mighty bad off, with splittin' headaches like, an' a few times she was off her head, talkin' about a boat, then about paintin', an' finally some name, sounded like Brett."

"Where did you find her?" Shannon asked the man.

He looked up. "On the beach past Malibu," he said. "I was drivin' along when I thought I saw somebody swimmin', so I slowed down. Then she splashed in an' fell on the sand. No swimmin' suit, nor any dress, either, nor shoes." He wiped his mouth with the back of his hand. "She was some looker, but that gash on her head was bad. I loaded her up an' brung her on home."

"What happened to her?" Shannon watched them keenly. Had they murdered the girl?

"She run off!" The man was vindictive. "She run off, stole a dress an' a coat, then took out of here one night."

"You ever seen her again?"

"No." Shannon felt sure the man was lying, and he saw the woman's lips tighten a little. "Never seen nor heard of her after."

When he was back in the street, he walked a block, then crossed the street and came back a little ways, easing up until he could slip close to the house, the dripping rain covering his approach. Listening, he could hear through a partly opened window, but at first nothing but the vilest language and bickering.

Finally, they calmed down. "Must be money in it," the man said. "Mage, we should've got more out of that feller. Private detective. They ain't had for nothin'."

"How could we ever git any of it?" the woman protested.

"How do I know? But if there's money, we should try."

"I told you that lingerie of hers was expensive!" Mage proclaimed triumphantly. "Anyway, she ain't writ this month. She ain't sent us our due."

"This time," the man said thoughtfully, "I think I'll go see her. I think I will."

"You better watch out," Mage declared querulously. "That detective will have an eye on us now. We could git into trouble."

There was no more said, and he saw them move into a bedroom where the man started to undress. Neil Shannon eased away from the window and walked down the street. He was in a quandary now. Obviously, the two had been getting mail from the girl, and from the sound of it, money. But for what?

They had found her with a cut on her head. That part would fit in all right, but what would she be doing in the sea? And who had hit her? If she had been struck, she might have amnesia, and that would explain her not returning to her apartment. That she was an excellent swimmer, he knew. She had several clippings for distance swimming, and others telling of diving contests she had won.

She must have come from a boat. Yet whose boat, and what had she been doing on it? One thing he resolved. These two must never learn that she was Darcy Lane, and heiress to a half million—if they did not already know it.

Before daylight, he was parked up the street, and he saw the man come from the house and start in his direction. From where he sat, he saw the man draw nearer and, without noticing him, drop a letter in a mailbox. As soon as the man was out of sight, Shannon slid from his car and, hurrying across the street, he shoved a dozen blank sheets of paper from his notepad after it.

They would, he knew, provide an effectual marker for the letter he wanted to see. It was almost two hours later that the mail truck came by, and he got out of his car and crossed the street again. He flashed his badge.

"All I want to see is the top envelope under those blank pages I dropped in."

"Well"—the man shrugged his shoulders—"I guess I can let you see the envelope, all right, but only the outside."

From their position, there were three letters that it could have been. He eliminated two of them at once. Both were typewritten. The third letter was written in pencil, judging by the envelope, and it was addressed to Miss Julie McLean, General Delivery, Kingman, Arizona. The return address was the house down the street, and the name was Sam Wachler.

"Thanks," Shannon said and, noting the address, he climbed into his car and started back for his office.

• • •

When he opened the door, a tall, slender man with sharp features and a white face rose. "Mr. Shannon? I am Hugh Potifer, one of the Buckle heirs."

Shannon was not impressed. "What can I do for you?" he asked, leading the way into his private office.

"Why, nothing, probably. I was wondering how you were getting along with your search for Darcy Lane?"

"Oh, that?" Shannon shrugged. "Nothing so far, why?"

"There isn't much time left, Mr. Shannon, and she has been gone a long time. Do you really think it worthwhile to look?"

Shannon sat down at his desk and took out some papers. His mind was working swiftly, trying to grasp what was in the wind.

"I get paid for looking," he replied coolly, "it's my business."

"Suppose"—Potifer's dry voice was cautious—"you were given a new job? Something that would keep you here in town? Say, at one hundred dollars a day?"

Neil Shannon looked up slowly. His eyes were darker and he felt his gorge rising. "Just what are you implying? That I occupy myself here, and stop looking for Darcy Lane?"

"At one hundred dollars a day—that would be seven . . . no . . . six hundred dollars." Potifer drew out his wallet. "How about it?"

Shannon started to tell him to get lost, then hesitated. A sudden thought came to him. Why should

Potifer call on him at this time? What was the sudden worry? It was easy to understand that he might not want Darcy to show up now and lay claim to her share, which otherwise would be divided among the remaining three heirs. But why come right now? There was little time left and no indication that the girl would ever be found. So what did Hugh Potifer know?

Shannon shrugged. "Six hundred is a nice sum of money," he admitted, stalling. "On the other hand, you'd stand to make well over a hundred thousand more if she doesn't appear. That's a nicer sum, believe me!"

Potifer pursed his thin lips. "I'll make it a thousand, Mr. Shannon. An even thousand."

"Why," Shannon asked suddenly, "did you specify that I stay in town? Do you have reason to believe she is alive, but out of town?"

From Potifer's expression, Shannon knew he had hit it. Certainly, Potifer knew something, but what? And how had he found out? Suppose he had been the one who—but no. None of these three admitted to knowing each other or Darcy before becoming heirs to the Buckle estate. Further, Darcy had vanished six months before Buckle died, and none of them had known about the will. Or had they?

"You forget," Shannon said quietly, "there's a five-hundred-dollar bonus if I find her—and one would suspect that she might be quite grateful herself. Why, she might give a man four or five thousand dollars for finding her in time!"

"Well?" Potifer got to his feet. "You're trying

to boost the ante. No, Mr. Shannon. You have my offer."

Neil Shannon tipped back in his chair. "So you know something about Darcy Lane's whereabouts? If I were you, I'd do some tall talking, right now and fast!"

"You can't frighten me, Shannon," Potifer said coldly. "Good day!"

When the door had closed behind Potifer, Shannon rose. Thrusting all the papers into a briefcase, he raced around to his apartment and hurriedly packed a bag with the barest necessities for a two-day trip. Then he went down to his car.

He was afraid to take the time, but he drove by Braith's office to check in. He met the attorney coming toward the street. Braith was a tall, handsome man with a quick smile.

"Any luck, Shannon?" he asked. "Only a week left, you know."

"That's what I was coming to see you about," he said. "I got a lead."

"What?" Watt Braith was excited. "You don't mean it!"

"Yes, I'm going to investigate now. I'm driving over to Kingman."

"Arizona?" Braith stared at him. "What would a model be doing over there?"

"Well, she was a secretary before she was a model, you know. A year of it, from the records. Anyway, I've a good lead in that direction. I think," he added, "that Potifer knows something, too. He dropped around today and tried to bribe me to lay off."

"I'm not surprised. He stands to make more money if she's not found; however, I doubt if he had anything to do with her disappearance. What information do you have?"

"Not enough to be definite. But, from what I know, I'm fairly certain that we have our girl."

"Kingman, eh? Any idea what name she's using?"

Shannon hesitated, then he said, "If I did, I'd be a lot better off. But there will be lots of ways of finding out, and she's a girl who is apt to be remembered."

Watt Braith studied him sharply. "You know anything you're not telling, Shannon? I hired you, and I want whatever information you have."

Shannon just looked at him.

Braith didn't like it. "Have it your own way. It's probably a wild-goose chase, anyway. If she had been able to, she would have communicated with us long since."

"She may not have known anything about this Buckle will. Even if she has returned to her right senses and normal attitude, she may have decided to stay on."

Braith shook his head. "I doubt it. This trip to Kingman seems a wild-goose chase. Probably the girl drowned or something, and her body simply wasn't recovered."

"Drowned?" Shannon laughed. "That's the last thing I'd believe."

"Why, what do you mean?" Braith stared at him.

"She was a champion swimmer. It was an old gag of hers to tell new boyfriends that she couldn't swim, and seven or eight of them gave her lessons, and Darcy Lane started winning medals for swimming when she was twelve!"

Watt Braith shrugged. "Well, a lot of other things could have happened. Only, I hope none of them did. Let me know how you come out."

After the attorney had left, Neil Shannon stood there in the street, scowling. Braith acted funny; that part about the swimming had seemed to affect him strangely.

He was imagining things. Only three people stood to gain from an accident to Darcy Lane, and they were Amy Bernard, Stukie Tomlin, and Hugh Potifer. There was no use considering Braith, for that highly successful young lawyer stood to profit in no way at all. And, anyway, Darcy Lane had been missing for six months before the death of Jim Buckle brought the matter to a head.

Neil Shannon stood there scowling, some sixth sense irritating him with a feeling of something left undone. It was high time that he started for Kingman, yet walking down the street he debated the whole question again, and then he got on the telephone.

When he hung up, he sat in the booth, turning the matter over in his mind, and then he dialed another number and still another. He placed a call to the Mojave County sheriff's office, in Kingman. Another to a real estate agent, and a third to a lawyer that he sometimes worked for. Details began to click together in his mind, and as he worked, he paused from time to time to mop the sweat from his face and curse telephone booths for being so hot.

His last call convinced him, and when he left the booth, he was almost running. He made one stop, and that a quick one at his own apartment. There he picked up the diary of Darcy Lane and hurriedly leafed through it. At a page near the end, he stopped, skimming rapidly over the opening lines of the entry. Then he came to what he was seeking.

. . . At the Del Mar today, met a tall, and very handsome young man whose name was Brule. One of those accidental meetings, but we had a drink together and talked of yachting, boating and swimming. He noticed my paints and commented on them, expressing an interest. Yet, when I mentioned Turner, he was vague, and he was equally uncertain about Renoir and Winslow Homer. Why do people who know nothing about a subject seem to want to discuss it as an expert with someone who is well educated?

Shannon closed the diary with a snap and locked it away, and then ran for his car. He took the road to Kingman and drove steadily, holding his speed within reason until he was in the desert and then opening the convertible up.

He glanced at his watch. It was not so late as he had believed. He had got the address from the letter Sam Wachler had mailed at some time around eight in the morning. Potifer had been in his office when he arrived there, which was nearly an hour later. Potifer had been with him awhile, and then he had gone to his own apartment. Having been up much of the night, and at his post so early in the morning, the day had seemed much advanced to him when actually it was quite early. And that meant that Braith had been leaving his office early, too. Or for a late lunch.

The check of the diary had taken a little time, but now he was rolling. He drove fast, turning the problem around in his mind. It was lucky that he knew something of Kingman, and knew a few people there. It would make his search much easier.

As the pavement unwound beneath the wheels, he studied the problem again and was sure that he had arrived at the correct conclusion. Yet, knowing what he did, he realized that every second counted, for Darcy Lane . . . if alive as he believed, was again in danger.

He was alone on the road now, and the setting sun was turning the mountains into ridges of pink and gold, shading to deeper red and then to purple. A plane moaned overhead, and suddenly realizing that one of those involved might travel by air, he felt sick to the stomach and speeded up, pushing the convertible faster.

Hugh Potifer was a mystery. How much did the man know? He seemed to know that Darcy was alive, and even to have some hint as to her whereabouts, yet how could he have found her? It could, of course, have been an accident. Potifer was an assayer and, though based in Las Vegas, was in touch with many miners and prospectors in the Kingman area.

Old Jim Buckle had been a lonely man, without relatives, and interested solely in the finding of gold. Potifer had accommodated him a number of times. Amy Bernard had done some typing for him and had forwarded things to him at various places in Arizona and Nevada. Stukie Tomlin had been a mechanic who kept his jeep in repair, and Darcy Lane had merely been a girl who talked to him over coffee, then took him out to show him the Los Angeles nightlife and had secretly hoped that he might meet a woman and settle down.

Shannon recalled that part of the diary very well. How Darcy had found herself seated beside the old man. He had seemed very lonely, and they had talked. He had shamefacedly confessed it had always been his wish to go to the Mocambo or Ciro's—places he had read about in the papers. Touched, Darcy had agreed to go with him, so the kindly old man and the girl who had just become a model had made the rounds. From the diary and from Watt Braith, Shannon had a very clear picture of Buckle. He had been a little man, shy and white-haired, happy in the desert, but lost away from it. Darcy's thoughtfulness had touched him, and none of the four had known of the will—except maybe Potifer. He might have.

Kingman's lights were coming on when he swung the car into a U-turn and parked against the curb in front of the Beale Hotel. For a moment he sat there thinking. It was well into the evening. The chances were that Darcy would be at home, wherever that might be. He got out of his car and went in, trying the phone book first.

No luck. He called the operator, asking for Alice, whom he had known years before. She was no longer with the phone company, moved east with her husband, and he could get no information about Julie McLean. And then he remembered someone else. Johnny had been a deputy sheriff here in Mojave County. His father had been one of the last stage drivers in the West. Time and again he had regaled Shannon with stories of his father's days on the Prescott and Ash Fork run. He was the kind of man who knew what was going on around town, even in retirement.

Hualapi Johnny Anson sat on his porch watching the last blue fade from the western sky. He greeted Shannon with a wave and offered him a White Rock soda from a dented cooler sitting on a chair beside him.

"Haven't seen you in a while," he said.

"Haven't been here in a while." Shannon went on to tell Anson what he was up to. In ten minutes he was back in his car and headed back up the road and Hualapi Johnny was dialing the sheriff's office in Kingman.

Johnny had reminded him of a box canyon they had once visited many years ago. There was a gravel road that led to it and a bottleneck entrance. It was a cozy corner where people went for picnics when he had last seen it. There was a house there now, and it was rented to a young lady.

Strangely, his mouth felt dry and there were butterflies in his stomach. He knew it was not all due to the fact that he was in a race with a murderer. It was because, finally, he was about to find Darcy Lane.

He slowed down and dimmed his lights, having no idea what he was heading into. And then, almost at the entrance to the small canyon, he glimpsed a car parked off the road in the darkness. It had a California license, and it was empty. He was late—perhaps too late!

He drove the car into the canyon, saw the lights of the house, then swung from the car and ran up the steps. The door stood open and on the floor lay a dark, still figure.

Lunging through, he dropped to his knees, then grunted his surprise. It was a man who lay there, and he lay in a pool of blood.

Shannon turned him over, and the man's eyes flickered. It was Stukie Tomlin.

"Shannon!" The wounded man's voice was a hoarse whisper. "He's—he's after her. Up—up on the cliffs. I tried to—help. Hurry!"

"Listen," Shannon said sharply, bringing the wounded man back to consciousness. "Help is on the way. Where is she? Did she go up on the cliffs tonight?"

"No"—the head shook feebly—"this—afternoon. To paint. I warned her. I came myself, tried to stop him. He shot me, went up cliffs—sundown."

Sundown! Hours ago! Feebly, Tomlin gasped out directions and, vaguely, Shannon recalled the path up the cliffs. To go up there at night? With someone waiting with a gun? Shannon felt coldness go all over him, and his stomach was sick and empty.

He left the house, moving fast, stumbled on the end of the path more through luck than design, and then started up.

When he was halfway up, the path narrowed into an eyebrow that hung over the box canyon, with a sheer drop of seventy feet or so even here, and increasing as the path mounted. Probably, he reflected, there was some vantage point from the cliff top where she could paint. Yet by this time, whatever the killer had come to do was probably done, and the man gone, long since.

Cool wind touched his face, and then he heard a voice speaking. He stopped, holding his breath, listening intently. He could make out no words, only that somewhere ahead, someone was talking.

On careful feet, he moved to the top of the cliff, holding himself low to present no silhouette. Before him were many ledges of rock, broken off to present a rugged shoulder some fifteen feet high, all of ten feet back from the promontory. He crouched, for the voices were clearer now.

"You'd better come out, Julie. Just come out and talk to me. It will be all right."

That voice!

Choking anger mounted within Neil Shannon, and he shifted his feet, listening.

"Go away." Her voice was low and strained. "I'm not coming out, and when morning comes, people will see us."

The man laughed. "No, they won't, Julie. It's hours until morning, and you can't hang there that long. Besides, if you don't come out, I'm going up higher where I can throw rocks down. People will just think you got too near the edge, and fell."

There was no reply at all. Trying to reconstruct the situation, Shannon decided that Darcy had seen the man before he got to her. She must have got around the cliff on some tiny ledge where he could not follow or reach her.

There had to be an end now. He rose to his feet and took two quick steps, then stopped.

"All right!" His voice rang sharply. "This is the end of the line! Come away from there, your hands up!"

The dark figure whirled, and Shannon saw the stab of flame and heard the gun bellow. But the man fired too fast, missing his shot. Involuntarily, Shannon stepped back. A rock rolled under his foot and he lost balance. Instantly, the gun roared again, and then the man charged toward him. Shannon lunged up, swinging his own gun, but the man leaped at him feet first.

Rolling dangerously near the cliff edge, Shannon scrambled as the man dove for him. Shannon slashed out with the pistol barrel, but caught a staggering blow and lost his grip on his gun. He swung a left and it sank into the man's stomach. He heard the breath go out of him, and then Shannon lunged forward, knocking the other man back into an upthrust ledge of rock.

They struggled there, fighting desperately, for the other man was powerful, and had the added urgency of fear to drive him. All he had gambled for was lost if he could not win now, and he was fighting not only for money, but for life.

A blow staggered Shannon, but he felt his right crash home, took a wicked left without backing, and threw two hard hooks to the head. He could taste blood now, and with a grunt of eagerness, he shifted his feet and went in closer, his shoulders weaving. His punches were landing now, and the fellow didn't like them, not even a little. This was a rougher game than the other man was used to, but Shannon, who had always loved a rough-and-tumble fight, went into him, smashing punches—until the man collapsed.

It was pitch dark even atop the mountain, and Shannon was taking no chances that the man was playing possum. When he felt the man go slack under his punches, he thrust out his left hand making a crotch of his thumb and fingers and jammed it under the fellow's chin, jerking him erect. Then he hooked his right into his midsection again and again. This time when he let go, he wasn't worried.

Swiftly, in a move natural to every policeman, he rolled the fellow on his face and handcuffed his hands behind his back. Then, at last, his breath coming in painful gasps, sweat streaming from him, he straightened.

"It's all right, ma'am," he said quietly. "You can come back out."

Her voice was strained. "I—I can't. I'm afraid to let go. I—"

Quickly, he went to the cliff edge, then worked his way around. Only the balls of her feet were on a narrow ledge, and her fingers clutched precariously at another. Obviously, she had clung so long that her fingers were stiffened. He moved closer, put his left arm around her waist, and drew her to him.

Carefully, then, he eased himself back until they stood on the flat rocks, and suddenly she seemed to let go and he felt her body loosen against him, all the tension going out of her. He held her until she stopped crying.

"Better sit down right here," he said quietly then. "We won't try the path for a little while, not until you feel better. I've got to take him down, too."

"But who—who are you?" she protested. "I don't know you, do I?"

"No, Miss Lane." He heard her gasp at the name. "You don't. But I know all about you. I'm a private detective."

He told her, slowly and carefully, about Jim Buckle and his will, about the search for her, about Hugh Potifer, Stukie Tomlin, and Amy Bernard. From a long way off a siren approached, red lights flashed against the rocks. He'd worry about the sheriffs in good time. . . .

"Now," he said, "you tell me, and then we'll get this straight, once and for all."

"I can't!" There was panic in her voice. "I—I don't know . . ."

"Take it easy," he said sympathetically, "and let's go back to the day you met that chap Brule. It was him, wasn't it?"

He saw her nod. The moon was coming up now, and the valley off to the right and the canyon below them would soon be bathed in the pale gold beauty of a desert night. The great shoulders of rock became blacker, and the face of the man, who lay on the rocks, whiter.

"After I met him, only a few days after, I was painting. I was on an old oil dock—where there was one of those offshore wells, you know? He came along in a motorboat and wanted me to come for a ride, offered to drop me back at Santa Monica. I had come up on the bus, so I agreed.

"We started back, but he kept going farther and farther out. I—I was a little worried, but he said there were some sandbars closer. Then he stopped the boat and said something about a lunch. He told me it was under a seat. I stooped to get it, and something struck me. That was the last I remembered. The last, except—well, I felt the water around me. I remember then that when he struck me I fell over the side and went down."

"Nothing more—until when?"

"It was"—she hesitated—"days later. I was on a bus, and—"

"Wait a minute," he said quietly. "Before that. You remember Sam Wachler?"

Her gasp was sheer agony, and he took her hand. She tried to draw it away, but he held it firmly.

"Let's straighten this all out at once, shall we?" he insisted. "There's a bunch of people down below who are going to want to know what's been going on. So, no secrets anymore. And let me promise you. You have nothing to be worried about, frightened of, or ashamed of."

"You—you're sure?" she pleaded.

"Uh-huh," he said carefully, "I've followed your

every footstep for the last year; I would know. But I've an idea that Wachler told you something, didn't he?"

She nodded. "Both of them. It was—that second day. I was beginning to remember, but was all—all sort of hazy about it. I saw the calendar, and it didn't make sense to me until later. They told me that I'd killed a man, that they were my friends, and they had brought me away to safety, and that if I did as they told me to, they would keep my secret."

"You didn't believe them?"

"Not really, but they showed me blood on my clothes. Afterwards, I thought it was from my cut head, but I couldn't be sure. So I ran away. I stole a dress, and they had taken my watch off, but I stole it back. I pawned that and bought a ticket out of the state.

"I didn't know where to go, but this place was in Arizona, and Jim Buckle had owned it, so I came here. They traced me somehow, and I had to— I sent them money. It was all very hazy. They sent me some clippings about a man found dead, and I didn't know what the truth was, and couldn't imagine why that Brett Brule had struck me like that, so I was really scared they were right."

An ambulance arrived, adding to the flashing lights in the canyon. Questioning voices drifted up to them.

He stood up. "Let's go down below. Better to go to them before they come to us." Catching the bound man by the coat collar, he dragged him after them. At the bottom, he said, "There's another thing. What about Stukie Tomlin?"

"Oh." She turned sharply around. "I'd forgotten him. He came here a few days ago and said I was in danger. He told me that I was to inherit a lot of money, but that somebody was asking a lot of odd questions and that I should be careful. I didn't know what to believe. But, you see, I'd met Stukie before—when I was with Mr. Buckle."

Tomlin was awake when they came in; a medic was working on him, and he grinned weakly when he saw Darcy. Shannon dropped his burden on the floor, then looked down into the face of Watt Braith.

"I thought so," Shannon said. He turned to Darcy. "This is Brule, isn't it?"

She nodded. "Yes . . ."

"Hey, mister!" A deputy sheriff stepped forward. "You going to explain all this?"

"Give him a minute and I expect he will, Hank." Hualapi Johnny spoke up from the doorway.

Shannon turned back to Darcy Lane, but he spoke for the others, too. "His real name is Braith. He was Buckle's lawyer. If anything happened to one of the heirs, that estate would be in his hands for five years. With five years and two million dollars to work with, a man can do plenty. So he decided to kill you, Miss Lane. He probably figured on sinking your body, but his blow knocked you over the side. You'd told him you couldn't swim, so he figured he was pretty safe."

"But Buckle was alive!" she protested.

"Sure. He was alive for six months. You hadn't showed up, so Braith went ahead and killed Buckle."

"You'll have a time proving that," Braith growled.

"I can already prove it," Shannon said quietly. "Within twenty minutes after I left you yesterday, I knew it."

"That's like I figured," Tomlin interrupted. "I'd lent the old man some tools, stuff I needed. I drove over here to get them back, and saw where he died. I prowled around and found that slide might have been caused by somebody with a crowbar. I told the sheriff about it and we both looked around, but there was nobody around then who seemed to have a motive, so we dropped it."

"And then the will came out in the open?"

"Yeah," Hank said, "and the boss still couldn't figure it. We all liked that old man. He was mighty nice. Potifer knew about the will. Buckle had told him, but he didn't fit the other facts."

They picked Stukie Tomlin up and were carrying him out. He caught Darcy's sleeve. "I saw him in town. I didn't know what was up but I never trusted him so I thought I'd warn you."

Darcy touched his shoulder. "Thank you."

Shannon sat down and lit a cigarette. "I made some calls and checked into the guy. I found he had made a lot of money with real estate he had handled, and his success began with the death of Buckle. Then, I got in touch with the Mojave County sheriff, and he told me somebody else had been suspicious, also, and that he had checked all strangers in and out of the county at that time. One of them answered the description of Braith, here. He said if I could produce the man, he had the men to identify him. We know one of them is Tomlin."

"We'll meet with the sheriff in the morning," said Hank. "But it doesn't sound like we'll have to spend much time explaining what happened. You-all need to be here for that meeting, though." He shoved the cuffed Braith ahead of him out the door.

Darcy Lane sat, her legs still trembling from her ordeal on the cliffs.

"You must have done a lot of work on this to locate me," she said.

"Uh-huh." He grinned at her. "I even read your diary."

She blushed. "Well," she protested defensively, "there was nothing in it to be ashamed of."

"I agree. In fact," he added seriously, "there was a lot to be proud of. So much that I often found myself wanting to meet you . . . even if I couldn't find you."

She smiled at him and laughed, and after a moment, he did too.

AFTERWORD

By Beau L'Amour

This collection contains a couple of our earliest short stories and a couple of the latest. "The Ghost Fighter" and "Fighter's Fiasco" were the second and third stories that Louis sold and the first two that he sold to editor Leo Margulies. "The Hand of Kuan-yin" was written in 1956 and was sold with the intention of its being the pilot episode for a CBS television show called *Hart of Honolulu*. I have no idea if this show was actually shot or, if it was, if it ever aired. Louis wrote the story in the weeks after he and my mother acquired an ivory Kuan-yin, the first piece of valuable art that they ever bought (not as valuable as the one in the story by a long shot). "May There Be a Road" was written in 1960 and attempted to alert people to the Red Chinese invasion of the Tibetan plateau. Though submitted to *The Saturday Evening Post*, it was never published.

"Wings over Brazil" is one of the last two short

stories in the Ponga Jim Mayo series. It is interesting to note the scene where Mayo fights the German boxer while trying to steal a plane. Both this and the scene in "South of Suez" (published in *West from Singapore*) where Ponga Jim escapes from the Egyptian tomb filled with snakes seem to have ended up (in a slightly different form) in the movie *Raiders of the Lost Ark*. Dad and I went to see that movie together (we had both loved the trailers for it), and during the scene with the snakes he leaned over and whispered "I think I wrote this part." If those scenes were actually inspired by his material I'm here to tell you he was very flattered.

We have one more book of short stories, which will be published in the spring of 2002. It will include the last of the Jim Mayo stories, "Voyage to Tobali," a few more boxing yarns, a couple of thrillers, and one last western. There will be more of Louis L'Amour's material available, however, on our website, **louislamour.com.** We will be expanding the site to include an area containing a selection of Louis's articles, journals, reading lists, and, most importantly, fragments of many stories that Louis did not complete in his lifetime.

When Dad was hard at work on a story he would often get ideas for other tales that he was inspired to tell. Usually, he would take a few hours out to write what he believed the first chapter would be like. Many times Louis would begin a story and then run out of inspiration or be drawn away by another project that was more ready to be completed. In the coming months we will be posting many of these fragments and beginnings for your enjoyment. I will be doing whatever I can to draw the bigger picture that these various pieces of work fit into. Many other interesting items, photographs, and information will appear in this section of the website . . . please come and visit us.

The biography project is slowly changing shape; research is slowing down and the focus of our work is changing to organizing the materials that we have on hand. Still, as always, there are loose ends to be dealt with. Below are the names of the people whom I would like to contact. Although it may seem the same year after year, there have been some additions and deletions. Please, if you are interested at all, read it carefully. If you find your name on the list, I would be very grateful if you would write to me. Some of these people may have known Louis as "Duke" La-Moore or Michael "Micky" Moore, as Louis occasionally used those names. Many of the people on this list may be dead. If you are a family member (or were a very good friend) of anyone on the list who has passed away, I would like to hear from you, too. Some of the names I have marked with an asterisk (*); if there is anyone out there who knows *anything at all* about these people I would like to hear it. The address to write to is:

Louis L'Amour Biography Project
P.O. Box 41183
Pasadena, CA 91114-9183

Because of the many demands on our time we will no longer be responding to fan mail sent to this address . . . it is for correspondence regarding the biography only!

J. E. Sparks—A special education teacher at Beverly Hills High School in the 1960s and '70s. Any information on recordings of Louis L'Amour that he made for his classes would be greatly appreciated.

Ted Nelson—Took a trip to Wyoming with Louis back in the 1940s or 1950s.

Bill and Nadine Hamon—Louis used to know them in Oklahoma City and at one time they used to work the Fine Arts Institute in Omaha, NE.

Irving Kahn and Ben Lyon—Worked in Hollywood during the late 1940s.

Kathy Greenlaw—A friend of Louis's in the late 1940s.

Truman—Of "Truman's," a restaurant in Westwood in the 1940s.

Tully Brown—Who had a position with the Wilshire Bank of America in 1949.

Jack Berges—Had a store in Hollywood in the late 1940s.

Ed Roth—Who lived in Hollywood in the late 1940s and was often seen with a woman named Maxene.

Alphonso Bedoya—Actor. Best known for his role as "Goldhat" in *The Treasure of Sierra Madre*. I'm looking for someone who knew him personally in the '40s or '50s or if anyone knows if there has ever been a biography done on him that details the same period.

Bob and Gail "Boots" Davis—Wasn't she in a western TV series? Louis knew them in 1949.

Frank Godsoe—An Amarillo sportswriter.

Harry Gilstrap—Who flew to Tascosa with Louis in 1946.

Maggie Savage, Cully Richards, Orry Kelly, Joe Frisco, Cyril Smith, Sam Roberts, Nicky Conners—I am looking for any of these people or anyone who personally knew them.

Al Holdcraft—A friend whom Louis occasionally met in Hollywood in the 1940s.

Scotty—Who worked for the *Citizen News*.

Joe Zdana—Whom Louis knew in the late 1940s.

Becker—A friend of Louis and Joe's.

Welch—Who took a trip with Louis in 1947.

Ray Gray—A policeman in LA as of 1949.

Bodil Mueller—A Danish actress Louis met in 1949.

Ed Jacobs—Who was in the 670th Tank Destroyers with Louis and was friends with him in LA after the war.

Marcel Clower—Who introduced Louis to Mauri Grashin.

Jim Hendryx, Charles N. Heckelmann, Mike Tilden, Jim O'Connell—Editors from New York City.

Adolphe DeCastro—A friend of Louis's who wrote him some letters of recommendation to various people in Mexico.

Marian Payne—Married a guy named Duane. Louis knew her in Oklahoma in the mid- to late 1930s. She moved to New York for a while; she may have lived in Wichita at some point.

Chaplain Phillips—Louis first met him at Fort Sill, then again in Paris at the Place de Saint Augustine

Officer's Mess. The first meeting was in 1942, the second in 1945.

Anne Mary Bentley—Friend of Louis's from Oklahoma in the 1930s. Possibly a musician of some sort. Lived in Denver for a time.

*Pete Boering**—Born in the late 1890s. Came from Amsterdam, Holland. His father may have been a ship's captain. Louis and Pete sailed from Galveston together in the mid-1920s.

Betty Brown—Woman whom Louis corresponded with extensively while in Choctaw in the late 1930s. Later she moved to New York.

*Jacques Chambrun**—Louis's agent from the late 1930s through the late 1950s.

Des—His first name. Chambrun's assistant in the late 1940s or early 1950s.

*Joe Friscia**—One of two guys who joined Hagenbeck & Wallace circus in Phoenix with Louis in the mid-1920s. They rode freights across Texas and spent a couple of nights in the Star of Hope mission in Houston. May have been from Boston.

*Harry "Shorty" Warren**—Shipmate of Louis's in the mid-1920s. They sailed from Galveston to England and back. Harry may have been an Australian.

*Joe Hollinger**—Louis met him while with Hagenbeck & Wallace circus where he ran the "privilege car." A couple of months later he shipped out with Louis. This was in the mid-1920s.

*Joe Hildebrand**—Louis met him on the docks in New Orleans in the mid-1920s. Then ran into him later in Indonesia. Joe may have been the first mate and Louis second mate on a schooner operated by Captain Douglas. This would have been in the East Indies in the later 1920s or early 1930s. Joe may have been an aircraft pilot and flown for Pan-Am in the early 1930s.

*Turk Madden**—Louis knew him in Indonesia in the late 1920s or early 1930s. They may have spent some time around the "old" Straits Hotel and the Maypole Bar in Singapore. Later on, in the States, Louis traveled around with him putting on boxing exhibitions. Madden worked at an airfield near Denver as a mechanic in the early 1930s. Louis eventually used his name for a fictional character.

*"Cockney" Joe Hagen**—Louis knew him in Indonesia in the late 1920s or early 1930s. He may have been part of the Straits Hotel, Maypole Bar crowd in Singapore.

*Richard LaForte**—A merchant seaman from the Bay Area. Shipped out with Louis in the mid-1920s.

*Mason or Milton**—Don't know which was his real name. He was a munitions dealer in Shanghai in the late 1920s or 1930s. He was killed while Louis was there. His head was stuck on a pipe in front of his house as a warning not to double-cross a particular warlord.

*Singapore Charlie**—Louis knew him in Singapore and served with him on Douglas's schooner in the East Indies. Louis was second mate and Charlie was bo'sun. He was a stocky man of indeterminate race and if I remember correctly Dad told me he had quite a few tattoos. In the early 1930s Louis helped get him a job on a ship in San Pedro, CA, that was owned by a movie studio.

Renee Semich—She was born in Vienna (I think) and was going to a New York art school when Louis met her. This was just before WWII. Her father's family was from Yugoslavia or Italy, her mother from Austria. They lived in New York; her aunt had an apartment overlooking Central Park. For a while she worked for a company in Waterbury, CT.

Aola Seery—Friend of Louis's from Oklahoma City in the late 1930s. She was a member of the "Writer's Club" and I think she had both a brother and a sister.

Enoch Lusk—Owner of Lusk Publishing Company in 1939, original publisher of Louis's *Smoke from This Altar*. Also associated with the National Printing Company, Oklahoma City.

Helen Turner*—Louis knew her in late 1920s Los Angeles. Once a showgirl with Jack Fine's Follies.

James "Jimmy" Eades—Louis knew him in San Pedro in the mid-1920s.

Frank Moran—Louis met him in Ventura when Louis was a "club second" for fighters in the late 1920s. They also may have known each other in Los Angeles or Kingman in the mid-1920s. Louis ran into him again on Hollywood Boulevard late in 1946.

Jud and Red Rasco*—Brothers, cowboys, Louis met them in Tucumcari, NM. Also saw them in

Santa Rosa, NM. This was in the early to mid-1920s.

Olga Santiago or Scarpone—Friend of Louis's from late 1940s Los Angeles. Last saw her at a book signing in Thousand Oaks, CA. She married a guy named Ray Scarpone in the early '50s.

Jose Craig Berry—A writer friend of Louis's from Oklahoma City in the late 1930s. She worked for a paper called the *Black Dispatch*.

Evelyn Smith Colt—She knew him in Kingman at one point, probably the late 1920s. Louis saw her again much later at a Paso Robles book signing.

Kathlyn Beucler Hays—Friend from Choctaw, taught school there in the 1930s. Louis saw her much later at a book signing in San Diego.

Floyd Bolton*—A man from Hollywood who came out to Oklahoma to talk to Louis about a possible trip to Java to make a movie in 1938.

Lisa Cohn—Reference librarian in Portland; family owned Cohn Bros. furniture store. Louis knew her in the late 1920s or early 1930s.

Mary Claire Collingsworth—Friend and correspondent from Oklahoma in the 1930s.

C. A. Donnell—Guy in Oklahoma City in the early 1930s who rented Louis a typewriter.

Captain Douglas*—Captain of a ship in Indonesia that Louis served on. A three-masted auxiliary schooner.

L. Duks*—I think that this was probably a shortened version of the original family name. A first mate in the mid-1920s. I think that he was a U.S. citizen, but he was originally a Russian.

Maudee Harris—My aunt Chynne's sister.

*Parker LaMoore and Chynne Harris LaMoore**— Louis's eldest brother. Parker was secretary to the governor of Oklahoma for a while, then he worked for the Scripps-Howard newspaper chain. He also worked with Ambassador Pat Hurley. He died in the early 1950s. Chynne was his wife and she lived longer than he did, but I don't know where she lived after his death.

Mrs. Brown—Who worked for Parker LaMoore in the 1930s through the 1950s.

*Haig**—His last name. Louis described him as a Scotsman, once an officer in the British-India army. Louis says he was "an officer in one of the Scottish Regiments." Louis knew him in Shanghai in the 1930s and we don't know how old he would have been at the time. He may have been involved in some kind of intelligence work. He and Louis shared an apartment for a while, which seems to have been located just off Avenue King Edward VII.

Lola LaCorne—Who along with her sister and mother were friends of Louis's in Paris during World War II. She later taught literature at the Sorbonne, had (hopefully still has) a husband named Christopher.

Dean Kirby—Pal from Oklahoma City in the late 1930s who seems to have been a copywriter or something of the sort. Might have worked for Lusk Publishing.

Bunny Yeager—Girlfriend of Dean Kirby's from Oklahoma City. Not the famous photographer for *Playboy*.

Virginia McElroy—Girl with whom Louis went to school in Jamestown.

Guardsman Penwill—A British boxer in the period between the mid-1920s and the mid-1930s.

Arleen Weston Sherman—Friend of Louis's from Jamestown, when he was thirteen or fourteen. I think her family visited the LaMoores in Choctaw in the 1930's. Her older sister's name is Mary; parents' names are Ralph and Lil.

Harry Bigelow—Louis knew him in Ventura. He had a picture taken with Louis's mother, Emily LaMoore, at a place named Berkeley Springs around 1929. Louis may have known him at the Katherine Mine, near Kingman, AZ, or in Oregon.

Tommy Pinto—Boxer from Portland; got Louis a job at Portland Manufacturing.

Nancy Carroll—An actress as of 1933. Louis knew her from the chorus of a show at the Winter Garden in New York and a cabaret in New Jersey where she and her sister danced occasionally, probably during the mid- to late 1920s.

Judith Wood—Actress. Louis knew her in Hollywood in the late 1920s.

Stanley George—The George family relocated from Kingman, AZ, to Ventura, CA, possibly in the late 1920s.

*Francis Lederer**—Actor that Louis knew in late 1920s Los Angeles. I'm looking for anyone who knew him in Hollywood between 1926 and 1931.

Lt. Rix—Who served in the 3622 Quartermaster Truck Co. in Europe in 1944–45.

Pablo De Gantes*—Ex-soldier of fortune who occasionally wrote magazine articles for *Lands of Romance* in the 1930s. This man used several names and I believe he was actually a Belgian. He lived in Mexico at one time.

Lt. King—Who traveled all the way from Camp Beale, California, through Camp Reynolds, Pennsylvania, and on to England with Louis when he was shipped overseas in early 1944.

K. C. Gibson or his two nephews—Louis met them when they picked him up hitchhiking in October of 1924. They were crossing New Mexico and Arizona bound for Brawly, CA.

Wilma Anderson—A friend of Louis's from Oklahoma who worked in the Key campaign headquarters in 1938.

Johnny Annette—A boxer Louis fought a bout with in Woodward, Oklahoma (or Kansas) in the 1930s.

Harry Bell—A boxing promoter Louis worked with in Oklahoma City in the 1930s.

Joe Bickerstaff*—Also an occasional boxing promoter who knew Louis in Klamath Falls in the late 1920s.

Pat Chaney—Friend of Louis's from Choctaw, OK, in the late 1930s.

Mr. Lettsinger*—An older man Louis knew in Klamath Falls, OR, in the late 1920s. I think that he was from the Midwest or South.

Tommy Danforth*—A boxing promoter from Prescott, AZ, in the mid-1920s. Was using the VA hospital at Fort Whipple.

Ned DeWitt*—Knew Louis in Oklahoma in the 1930s, also a friend of Jim Thompson.

Austin Fullerton—Who sold tickets for athletic events in Oklahoma City in the late 1930s.

Martha Nell Hitchcock—A friend from Edmond, OK, in the 1930s.

Tommy Tucker*—Boss Stoker on British Blue Funnel ships in the mid-1920s to mid-1930s period.

Dynamite Jackson*—An African-American fighter Louis helped promote in Oklahoma in the 1930s.

Orry Kelly—Designer in Hollywood; Louis knew him in the late 1940s.

Dorothy Kilgallen—A newspaper columnist who worked in LA in the 1950s. We have several good accounts of her death and so are looking for someone who actually knew her.

Henry Li—Whom Louis knew from 1943 when he was at Camp Robinson, AR.

Savoie Lottinville*—Of the University of Oklahoma.

Julio Lopez—Whom Louis worked for very briefly in Phoenix in the mid-1920s.

Joe May—A rancher Louis boxed with in Fort Sumner, NM, in the 1920s.

Ann Mehaffey—Friend of Louis's from the time he spent at Camp Robinson, AR.

Sam Merwin or Sam Mines*—Who once worked with Leo Margulies at Standard Magazines/Better Publications.

Jack Natteford—Screenwriter who worked with Louis in the 1950s.

Joe Paskvan—Once of the Oklahoma Writer's Project, whom Louis knew in the late 1930s.

Billy Prince—Who went to sea in the late 1930s on the *Wallace E. Pratt,* a Standard tanker.

Countess Dulong de Rosney (Toni Morgan)*— Whom Louis knew from France in the mid-1940s.

Dot and Truitt Ross—Brother and sister Louis knew in Oklahoma in the 1930s.

Mary Jane Stevenson—A friend of Louis's from LA in the late 1940s.

Orchid Tatu—Who lived in Sparta, Wisconsin, in the mid-1940s.

Florence Wagner—Wife of Rob Wagner of Rob Wagner's Script.

Doris Weil—A roomer in the flat where Louis lived in the late 1940s.

Anyone who served on *S.S. Steel Worker* between 1925 and 1930. In particular Captain *C. C. Boase,* 2nd Mate *Ralph Jones,* 3d Mate *Raymond Cousins,* Radio Operator *Stanley Turbervil,* Carpenter *George Mearly,* Bo'sun *H. Allendorf,* Chief Engineer *C. B. Dahlberg,* 1st Asst Eng. *O. E. Morgan,* 2nd Asst Eng. *W. Haynes,* 3d Asst Engineers *George G. Folberth & William Stewart,* Oilers *A. Chagnon & A. Kratochbil,* Firemen *William Hohroien, J. Perez, Manfrido Gonzales, John Fennelly, & E. G. Burnay,* Wipers *A. Sanchez, J. J. Dalmasse, & F. Clifford,* Steward *J. Shiel,* Messmen *Dean Bender, William Harvey, & J. H. Blomstedt,* Able-bodied Seamen *Ernest Martin, Chris Moore, Karl Erickson, Steve Schmotzer, Michael Llorca, Louis Armand, Joseph Morris, Herbert Lieflander, William Reichart, & H. F. Waite.*

Anyone familiar with *Singapore in the late 1920s,* the old Straits Hotel, and the Maypole Bar.

Anyone who is very knowledgeable in the *military history and/or politics in western (Shansi, Kansu, and Sinkiang provinces) China* in 1928–36.

I am also looking for seamen who served on the following ships: the *Catherine G. Sudden* between 1925 and 1936. The *Yellowstone* between 1925 and 1936. The S.S. *Steadfast* between 1924 and 1930. The *Annandale,* a four-masted bark, between 1920 and 1926. The *Randsberg,* a German freighter, between 1925 and 1937.

Anyone who knows anything about an old square-rigged sailing vessel called the *Indiana* that was used in movies in the 1920s and '30s. This ship was docked at San Pedro.

Anyone who knows anything about the following boxers: *Jonny "Kid" Stopper, Jack Horan, "Kid" Yates, Butch Vierthaler (Bill Thaler), Ira O'Neil, Jimmy Roberts, Jimmy Russo, Jack McGraf, or Jackie Jones*—Guys Louis met in Phoenix in October of 1924. None of these men was born after 1909.

Anyone who knows anything about *a fight (I assume with small arms) between two trading schooners* that was stopped by a British warship near Pinaki in the South Pacific. This would have been between 1926 and 1932.

Anyone from *the family or group that Louis guided around Egypt* sometime between 1926 and 1937. Although he very much looked the part, Louis finally admitted that he wasn't a real guide and that he'd been using a tour book from a library to learn about where he was taking them. They may have been staying at Shepherd's. Some or all of the party were Americans, and there may have been as many as twelve of them.

Anyone who might know about a *flight that Louis took across Africa* with a French officer with stops at Taudeni and Timbuktu. This would have been between the mid-1920s and late 1930s.

Anyone familiar with *an island in the Spratly group called Itu Aba.*

Anyone who knows anything about a very short-lived magazine published in Oklahoma City in 1936 called *Uptown Magazine.*

Anyone who knows if *Norman Foster and Rex Bell (George Francis Beldam)* ever went to sea during the 1920s or early 1930s.

Anyone who knows where the personal and business papers of *B. P. Schulberg (not Budd) and Sam Katz* are archived. Both of these men worked at Paramount Publix Pictures. The period that I am interested in is the late 1920s to the early 1930s.

Anyone familiar with the *Royal Government Experimental Hospital in Calcutta, India.*

I would like to hear from men who served in the following military units: the *3622 Quartermaster Truck Company* between June of 1944 and December of 1945. The *3595 Quartermaster Truck Company* after October 1945 and before January 1946. The *670th Tank Destroyer Battalion* in 1943 at Camp Hood, Texas. The *808th Tank Destroyer Battalion* at Camp Phillips, Kansas, in 1943.

Soldiers or Officers who: took *basic training at Camp Robinson, Arkansas,* between September 1942 and January 1943. Took *winter training at Camp McCoy, Wisconsin,* and near Land o' Lakes and Watersmeet in the Northern Michigan peninsula between October 1943 and February 1944. Remembers Louis in early 1944 when he was staying at the *St. Francis Hotel and the Belleview in San Francisco.* During this time he worked at the *Oakland Air Base and Fort Mason, CA.* Later he was at *Camp Beale, CA.*

Anyone who worked with the *Oklahoma WPA Writer's Project.*

Any recordings that anyone knows about of any of Louis's speeches.

ABOUT LOUIS L'AMOUR

"I think of myself in the oral tradition—as a troubadour, a village tale-teller, the man in the shadows of the campfire. That's the way I'd like to be remembered—as a storyteller. A good storyteller."

It is doubtful that any author could be as at home in the world re-created in his novels as Louis Dearborn L'Amour. Not only could he physically fill the boots of the rugged characters he wrote about, but he literally "walked the land my characters walk." His personal experiences as well as his lifelong devotion to historical research combined to give Mr. L'Amour the unique knowledge and understanding of people, events, and the challenge of the American frontier that became the hallmarks of his popularity.

Of French-Irish descent, Mr. L'Amour could trace his own family in North America back to the early 1600s and follow their steady progression westward, "always on the frontier." As a boy growing up in Jamestown, North Dakota, he absorbed all he could about his family's frontier heritage, including the story of his great-grandfather who was scalped by Sioux warriors.

Spurred by an eager curiosity and desire to broaden his horizons, Mr. L'Amour left home at the age of fifteen and enjoyed a wide variety of jobs including seaman, lumberjack, elephant handler, skinner of dead cattle, miner, and was an officer in the transportation corps during World War II. During his "yondering" days he also circled the world on a freighter, sailed a dhow on the Red Sea, was shipwrecked in the West Indies and stranded in the Mojave Desert. He won fifty-one of fifty-nine fights as a professional boxer and worked as a journalist and lecturer. He was a voracious reader and collector of rare books. His personal library contained 17,000 volumes.

Mr. L'Amour "wanted to write almost from the time I could talk." After developing a widespread following for his many frontier and adventure stories written for fiction magazines, Mr. L'Amour published his first full-length novel, *Hondo,* in the United States in 1953. Every one of his more than 100 books is in print; there are more than 260 million copies of his books in print worldwide, making him one of the bestselling authors in modern literary history. His books have been translated into twenty languages, and more than forty-five of his novels and stories have been made into feature films and television movies.

His hardcover bestsellers include *The Lonesome Gods, The Walking Drum* (his twelfth-century historical novel), *Jubal Sackett, Last of the Breed,* and *The Haunted Mesa.* His memoir, *Education of a Wandering Man,* was a leading bestseller in 1989. Audio dramatizations and adaptations of many

L'Amour stories are available on cassette tapes from Bantam Audio Publishing.

The recipient of many great honors and awards, in 1983 Mr. L'Amour became the first novelist ever to be awarded the Congressional Gold Medal by the United States Congress in honor of his life's work. In 1984 he was also awarded the Medal of Freedom by President Reagan.

Louis L'Amour died on June 10, 1988. His wife, Kathy, and their two children, Beau and Angelique, carry the L'Amour tradition forward with new books written by the author during his lifetime to be published by Bantam.

LOUIS L'AMOUR

AMERICA'S FAVORITE FRONTIER WRITER

Be sure to read all of the titles in the Sackett series: follow them
from the Tennessee mountains as they head west to ride the trails,
pan the gold, work the ranches, and make the laws.

Ask for these titles wherever books are sold,
or visit us online at *www.bantamdell.com*
for ordering information.

LL3 5/02